PRAISE FOR
KATIE MacALISTER

Memoirs of a Dragon Hunter
"Bursting with the author's trademark zany humor and spicy romance . . . this quick tale will delight paranormal romance fans."—*Publishers Weekly*

Sparks Fly
"Balanced by a well-organized plot and MacAlister's trademark humor."—*Publishers Weekly*

It's All Greek to Me
"A fun and sexy read."—The Season for Romance
"A wonderful lighthearted romantic romp as a kick-butt American Amazon and a hunky Greek find love. Filled with humor, fans will laugh with the zaniness of Harry meets Yacky."—*Midwest Book Review*

Much Ado About Vampires
"A humorous take on the dark and demonic."—*USA Today*
"Once again this author has done a wonderful job. I was sucked into the world of Dark Ones right from the start and was taken on a fantastic ride. This book is full of witty dialogue and great romance, making it one that should not be missed."—Fresh Fiction

The Unbearable Lightness of Dragons
"Had me laughing out loud. . . . This book is full of humor and romance, keeping the reader entertained all the way through . . . a wondrous story full of magic. . . . I cannot wait to see what happens next in the lives of the dragons."—Fresh Fiction

ALSO BY KATIE MACALISTER

Dark Ones Series
A Girl's Guide to Vampires
Sex and the Single Vampire
Sex, Lies, and Vampires
Even Vampires Get the Blues
Bring Out Your Dead (Novella)
The Last of the Red-Hot Vampires
Crouching Vampire, Hidden Fang
Unleashed (Novella)
In the Company of Vampires
Confessions of a Vampire's Girlfriend
Much Ado About Vampires
A Tale of Two Vampires
The Undead in My Bed (Novella)
The Vampire Always Rises

Dragon Sept Series
You Slay Me
Fire Me Up
Light My Fire
Holy Smokes
Death's Excellent Vacation (short story)
Playing WIth Fire
Up In Smoke
Me and My Shadow
Love in the Time of Dragons
The Unbearable Lightness of Dragons
Sparks Fly
Dragon Fall
Dragon Storm
Dragon Soul
Dragon Unbound

Dragon Hunter Series
Memoirs of a Dragon Hunter

Time Thief Series
Time Thief
Time Crossed (short story)
The Art of Stealing Time

Matchmaker in Wonderland Series
The Importance of Being Alice
A Midsummer Night's Romp
Daring in a Blue Dress
Perils of Paulie

Papaioannou Series
It's All Greek to Me
Ever Fallen in Love

Contemporary Single Titles
Improper English
Bird of Paradise (Novella)
Men in Kilts
The Corset Diaries
A Hard Day's Knight
Blow Me Down
You Auto-Complete Me

Noble Historical Series
Noble Intentions
Noble Destiny
The Trouble With Harry
The Truth About Leo

Paranormal Single Titles
Ain't Myth-Behaving

Mysteries
Ghost of a Chance

Steampunk Romance
Steamed

EVER FALLEN IN LOVE
A PAPAIOANNOU NOVEL

KATIE MACALISTER

FAT CAT BOOKS

Cover by Croco Designs
Formatting by Racing Pigeon Productions

This book is dedicated to you. Yes, you. I know, no one ever dedicates a book to you, and that's so wrong, isn't it? Think of all you do for people! All the work you slog through every single day just to make life nice for everyone, and what thanks do you get? You work, you slave, you spend time doing things that you don't particularly want to do, but you do it because you know it will make others happy.

You so deserve a book dedicated to you, and now you have it. Feel free to show this book to everyone, and offer to sign this page for them. It is, after all, dedicated to you.

ONE

I never did figure out if it was the man or the baby that drove me into action and changed the course of my life in the blink of an eye. Thinking about it later, I was inclined to believe it was the child, but somewhere deep in my heart, I had a suspicion that if the man hadn't been the one holding the baby, I might have passed them by.

I noticed them first just as I was in the middle of coping with a crippling panic attack. For one dazzlingly terrifying second, I thought I recognized the set of shoulders on a blond man standing a little way down the train station platform, and I froze, fear cramping my belly.

"No," I whispered in horror, both hands clutching my bag, too terrified to move. "Oranges. Apples. Bowling balls. Those little metal balls on strings that sit on executives' desks."

"Pardon?" the woman next to me asked, giving me a look that marked me as someone who should be bouncing off padded walls.

"Sorry," I choked out an answer, my body slumping with relief when the man turned and I saw that it wasn't Mikhail, just a terrifying facsimile of him. I felt weak with both the terror that had gripped me and, two seconds later, the knowledge that I was safe—he hadn't somehow followed me to Auckland. I gathered my wits and turned with a slight smile at the middle-aged woman who had stopped next to me to toss away a paper latte cup. "Swami Betelbaum says that when you're stressed, you should focus on round things. That calms your chakras. Or is it enlightens your ka? It was one of those two."

"Round things," the woman said, and after giving me a wary once-over, she moved off, her briefcase held tightly, as if she thought she might have to use it as a shield against sudden attack.

"As if," I murmured to myself. "Snowballs. Crystal balls. Christmas ornaments."

The station was packed with early-afternoon commuters, all of whom were pursuing their routine with steadfast determination. I was buffeted by men and women in business suits, busily carrying on with their lives and careers. For a moment, I stood marooned in the sea of humanity, alone, isolated, untouched even though I was surrounded by others, but self-preservation drove me to hurry over to a small oasis of quiet next to a bench littered with discarded newspapers.

Slowly, my heart began to calm, and my hands stopped shaking. "Those little chocolate candies with the yummy filling. Snow globes. Gumballs. Babies' heads."

Now, that was odd—I'd never really thought of babies' heads as being round, but not ten feet from me, a couple stood arguing in low voices, a baby in his stroller next to them apparently forgotten. The baby had a very round head, and a pair of lungs on him that hinted at a future in opera or one of those reality shows where people yelled at one another all the time.

I frowned at the couple, distracted from my own troubles by the scene in front of me. How could they not be aware that their child was screaming his lungs out? What sort of parents were they that they were too caught up in their own argument to take care of their obviously upset child?

The woman, I decided, looked like trouble. She was tall and elegant, her long black hair as glossy as a bird's wing swinging down to brush her hot pink miniskirt. A matching bodice showed off just about everything she had, and she had a lot.

"Breasts," I said under my breath, qualifying it with, "Fake breasts. Wheels on a baby stroller. Big tears falling down a baby's face."

Poor kid. His face was turning red now as he continued to scream, red and sticky with tears, his misery highlighted by little snot bubbles coming from his nose.

"Snot bubbles," I added, glancing indignantly at the parents. Why weren't they doing something?

"There are better things for my life than this," the black-haired woman said in a heavily accented voice. Russian? Ukrainian? Definitely Slavic. I gave a little shudder at the accent. I was all too familiar with something similar. "I have him ten month. Now he is yours. I give him to you! Here is papers. You get custody papers with lawyer, and I sign."

"You can't do that!" the man exclaimed, grabbing at the woman's arm as she stalked off. He had an accent that sounded English, with something else mixed in.

I eyed him, intrigued despite the knowledge that it was far better not to get involved. He was tall, probably a few inches over six feet.

I didn't like tall men.

He also had long legs and broad shoulders.

I really didn't like broad shoulders.

Worst of all, he had the sort of face that made women stop and stare, all manly stubble and a little cleft in his square chin, and thick-lashed eyes that I personally would have killed for.

I *really, really* did not like handsome men.

"I don't know anything about taking care of a baby!" the man was saying in an angry tone, his hand on the woman's arm.

"Now is time you learn," the woman snapped with a toss of her thick hair. "Is too much for me! I have career!"

"Nastya, wait. You can't do this to me. I can't afford it right now—" The man started after her as she left.

My eyes widened as I looked from the couple to the baby, the latter now fast approaching hysterics, snot and tears dribbling everywhere, his strident crying making me want to cover my ears.

They were leaving? They were just walking away from the baby? I looked around in horror to see if anyone else had witnessed this. Weren't they concerned about some insane person grabbing the baby?

No one seemed to notice. No one seemed to care. I edged down the bench, closer to the baby. I should do something. I couldn't let the people just walk off and leave that poor, angry baby alone. But it was better to not become involved in a lovers' spat. That way lay disaster. Right? Right.

"Hey," I heard a voice call out, and, to my horror, discovered it came from my mouth. "Hey, you're forgetting your baby."

The man must have heard, or realized that he couldn't just leave the poor kid alone, because he turned around and marched back, a furious look etched on that handsome face.

I averted my gaze and slid back down the bench, pretending to be fascinated with the sight of my shoes.

The baby's cries went up in tone. I took a peek out of the corners of my eyes to see the man was now holding the baby, bouncing it up and down a little, obviously trying to jolly it out of the temper tantrum. The baby, like the man, had black hair and dark eyes, most likely his son. What sort of father didn't even know how to hold his own child?

"A very bad man," I told myself, and dropped my gaze again. I would not get involved. It wasn't my problem. He was probably one of those workaholics who had no time for their own children. I scorned those men. The way I saw it, if you made a baby, then you needed to own up to your responsibilities. It was just that simple.

I couldn't help but glance up, badly wanting to tell the man what I thought of him, but the sight that met my eyes held me arrested for a few seconds. The man's face was stricken as he held the screaming and writhing child, his expression not one of a heartless father who didn't have time for his child, but a man who was obviously as distressed as the child and, what's worse, had no idea what to do. He looked around desperately, clearly searching for some solution.

He looked utterly and completely lost, and as commuters streamed around him, men and women all intent on their own lives, ignoring the screaming child and helpless man, I felt a moment of kinship, of one isolated individual recognizing another.

"Don't get involved," I warned myself even as I was on my feet, moving toward the man. I stopped before him, saying softly, "Can I help?"

He turned a face of absolute agony to me, his dark blue eyes filled with panic. But even with those emotions stark on his face, some paternal sense must have kicked in, because he clutched the baby tighter, and started to shake his head.

"He's ... you know, he's really snotty," I said, pulling a little packet of tissues from my pocket and offering them to the man. "Maybe if you wiped that off him, he might feel better."

"Snotty?" the man repeated, looking at the baby as if he had no idea what to do about the matter.

"Oh, for heaven's sake ... here." I dabbed at the baby's nose with a couple of tissues, wiping where the snot had mixed with tears and dribbled down his mouth and chin. "He's really mad, isn't he?"

"He's not the only one who's mad," the man mumbled, grimacing when the baby screamed even louder, squirming and straining against the man's hold. "I don't know why he's crying."

I told myself to go sit back down, that it wasn't my problem, that I was not responsible for other people's parenting skills, or lack thereof.

"Well, you're not holding him right, for one," I said, exasperation driving common sense from my head. "I can't imagine it's comfortable to be held like you're about to drop him. Here, let me have him for a minute."

I held out my arms.

The man frowned at me, his long, narrow black brows pulling together when he studied me.

"Fine," I said, dropping my arms and turning back toward my bench. "I was just trying to help. Sorry I bothered you."

"God, I need help. I'm ... here." The man thrust the baby into my arms. I adjusted my hold on him, cradling him against my side, one hand rubbing his back.

"Shhh," I murmured to the baby, rocking from side to side. "I know you're pissed, but it's going to be all right. You just need to calm down. You need to find your inner peace."

"That's not how you talk to a baby," the man said, hovering protectively in front of me, as if he was going to snatch the child away.

"Oh really? You weren't doing any better." I gave him a sharp look and continued to murmur softly to the baby.

"I don't know anything about babies," the man admitted, his eyes moving between my face and that of the baby.

"It doesn't take a whole lot to know how to comfort one." I kept my voice gentle despite the sting of the words. Gradually the baby's cries became less strident, and he started making soft little hiccuping noises. "How on earth can you have a child and not know how to take care of him?"

"I didn't know I had him until an hour ago," the man said grimly.

I shot him a startled look. "As bad as a man is who doesn't have time for his kids, I have to say that one who doesn't even know he *has* a child is infinitely worse."

"I didn't know I had a son because his mother never bothered to tell me," he said, keeping his voice low as the baby started to go limp in my arms, making soft little wet snuffles against my neck when he relaxed against me.

"Oh. Well ... oh. I'm sorry, then."

"You're not a nanny, are you?" the man asked suddenly, his gaze sweeping over me, no doubt taking in my shoddy clothes and my duffel bag with its remnants of travel tags. "You're American?"

"Yes, I'm American, and no, I'm not a nanny. I don't know anything about children other than they need their noses wiped and you should rub their backs when they cry. What's his name?"

I thought for a minute the man was going to consult the wad of papers the baby's mother had shoved at him, but he merely put them into his pocket, making a little grimace. "Nastya calls him Piotr."

"That's Russian for Peter. Hey, Peter," I said softly, my lips against the baby's damp forehead. "You go to sleep now, and your daddy will take care of you, OK?"

"I don't know how to take care of a baby," the man said, running a hand through his hair. He looked around the train station again as if he expected to see a magic nanny shop appear before his eyes. When one didn't, his attention returned to me. "He likes you. Can you help me tonight?"

"No, don't fight it—just go to sleep. I promise things will look better after you've slept," I told the baby, still rubbing his back. The man's words grabbed my awareness, leaving me staring at him in disbelief. "Help you how?"

"I need someone to help me with him. With Peter. I'll call a nanny agency in the morning, but it's too late now to get anyone," he said with a glance at his watch.

His expensive watch, I noted. I also didn't like men who had money to spend on expensive watches. Those sorts of men tended to believe they could buy anything, including the services of a stranger.

"I don't know you from Adam," I pointed out, shaking my head.

"I don't know you either, but that doesn't mean I'm not willing to trust you." His gaze searched my face for a moment; then suddenly he gave me an odd half smile, one side of his mouth curling in an endearing way. A sudden flash of heat hit my belly at the sight of that smile. "Within reason, of course. I'd pay you. Double the going rate. Assuming you're not on your way somewhere? And if you were, I'd replace your ticket."

"I don't even know your name, and you're willing to trust your child to me?" I shook my head again. "You're nuttier than I thought."

"Not nutty, just desperate," he corrected me, holding out a hand. "My name is Theo. Theodor Papaioannou."

"Kiera Taylor," I said automatically, giving his hand a little shake before returning it to stroke the now quiet baby.

"How about it, Kiera? Will you give me a hand tonight? I'll pay whatever you want."

I couldn't help but recognize the desperation in his eyes. How could I not see it? Despite the knowledge that what he asked was way out of line, I considered it—I actually considered it for a few seconds. Then pain whipped me with the realization of what I was doing. When would I learn? How many times did life have to crush me to the ground before I got it?

"No," I said, carefully placing the now sleeping baby into his stroller, strapping him in before I stood up and faced the man. "I'm sorry. I wish I could, but it's just safer if I don't. Good luck, Theo."

He said nothing, just watched when I gathered up my purse and bag and, without a glance back, headed for the entrance of the station, where I could get a taxicab. It would damage my budget, but I couldn't stay there with that handsome, desperate man.

I made it five steps before I heard an almost inaudible, "Please."

I stopped.

I ordered my legs to continue walking. They stood firm.

Slowly, I turned back around. "Tambourines," I told Theo.

His eyebrows rose.

"Drums. The bell on those big horns."

"Musical instruments for five hundred?" he asked, a glint of amusement coming into his eyes.

"Swami Betelbaum, my meditation counselor, says it's good to think of round things in times of stress," I explained, staring at him.

The longer I looked, the less I liked him. He was too handsome, too big, too needy. Just ... *too.*

I couldn't do this. It was the height of folly. He was a stranger, and I ... I couldn't afford to trust anyone.

I opened my mouth to say no, but what came out was, "One night. I'll help you with Peter until you get a nanny tomorrow, although I really do not know anything about kids. I'm just a paralegal from Sacramento. Do you live here in Auckland?"

"No," he said, giving me a relieved smile that did far too many things to my insides to make me at all comfortable. "But I may be. I'm thinking of setting up an office here, and just got in to look around when Nastya tracked me down. I'm booked at a hotel not too far from here."

If he thought I was going to stay in close confines with him, he was nuts. He'd just have to get me a room of my own. "Whoa, hold on there. I am not staying with you in your hotel room."

He gave me another half smile. "It's a suite. There are two bedrooms."

"Which would be fine assuming I trusted you, but I don't." I eyed him. There was no way I would consent to spend the night with a man who looked that handsome. Handsome men were never, ever unaware of their appearance. They expected women to tumble into bed just as a matter of fact.

And why shouldn't you have a little fun once in a while? my inner voice whispered. That damned inner voice, the one Swami Betelbaum said I had to learn to ignore, for it would lead me away from serenity.

And I so desperately wanted serenity.

"The doors have locks. You may lock yourself into your room," he said, his mouth tight.

I realized that I'd offended him. And no surprise, I'd more or less accused him of being a rapist, or worse.

"Locked doors are nothing but an illusion," I said, suddenly so tired, I just wanted to curl into a little ball and let the world pass me by. How long had it been since I'd slept? "How do I know you're not some horrible ax-murdering serial killer who's luring me to his hotel room so he can chop me up into little bits?"

"I doubt if many serial killers take their ten-month-old sons with them on their killing sprees," he said with a hint of that sexy half smile. "If you like, I'll give you the names and numbers of people who will act as a character witness."

"Your ax-murdering buddies?" I said with a snort.

"Only one has an ax," he answered, the smile definitely there this time. "I can give you the name of a respected banker in Sydney, and my broker in Athens, and ..." His voice grew a little strained. "... my brother. He's a successful real estate developer."

"Uh-huh. I bet he'd say anything for you."

"No." The word was abrupt, but there was a lot of emotion behind it, emotion that I recognized—self-loathing, regret, and sorrow. "If anything, he's likely to tell you all sorts of unsavory tales about me," he finished, obviously trying to make light the situation, his eyes not meeting mine. "He's eminently respectable, though. He has a wife and four children."

One night. The thought danced with dizzying temptation in my brain. Misha would never be able to find me if I wasn't booked under my own name. I'd have a night where I could rest, actually sleep, without listening for the sound of my murderer creeping upon me unawares.

One night of safety. I wanted it so much, I could almost taste it.

"All right," I said, even as I automatically scanned the crowd. It had become second nature to me now. "But I don't want the hotel to know my name."

He gave me an odd look, but agreed, picking up my bag. I hesitated a minute, then took hold of the stroller and pushed it after him. He paused a few yards away and collected a laptop bag and a small overnight bag.

"I'm going to call your references, though," I warned him. "If anything seems wrong, the deal's off."

He inclined his head in acknowledgment and pushed the door with his elbow, holding it open for me.

I said nothing, but brushed against his arm when I passed through the door, suddenly very much aware of him as a man.

One that was far too handsome and self-possessed for my peace of mind.

TWO

Theo sat in the cab and wondered if life would ever be the same.

He had a son. A ten-month-old son. His gaze slid over to where the baby sat strapped into the seat between him and Kiera. A child, one that looked like him, so he knew that Nastya wasn't pulling a fast one. Not that he really thought she would. She might be many things, but her mind was too shallow to work along those sorts of devious routes.

The paralyzing sense of desperation washed over him when he looked at the baby sleeping next to him. How the hell could he be a father? He couldn't even straighten out his own life, so how was he supposed to raise a child who wouldn't turn out to be as big a failure as he was?

His brother, Iakovos, was the perfect father. Not him. Not the drunkard who almost killed an innocent woman and her two unborn children.

God, he wanted a drink. No, not just wanted it, he needed it, craved the sense of oblivion that would ease the pain that always seemed to be near, no matter what he did.

A son.

He looked at the baby again, trying to assess his feelings. Part of him, what he thought of as the good part, was moved by the sight of the child. *Your son*, the good side whispered to him, an alien wave of protectiveness gripping him hard in the chest. A son to be protected and nurtured, to be taught. A son who would grow up to be a better man than his father.

The baby slept with his head crooked to the side. Theo frowned. That couldn't feel good. Just as he was about to move the baby's head, Kiera leaned over Peter, adjusting him into a more comfortable position.

Her gaze met his, and he was aware once again of the condemnation she obviously felt for him. And why shouldn't she—hadn't she herself asked what sort of a father didn't know he had a son, let alone how to care for him?

"I really didn't know about him," he told her, feeling it necessary, for some reason, to explain. "Nastya called this morning, saying she was going to Italy, and she wanted to see me before she left."

"Italy?" Kiera asked.

"She's a model." Without thinking, he ran his gaze over her body, assessing and weighing the positives and negatives without being aware he did so. She was taller than medium height, a bit too thin for his taste, with hair that he had first thought was dark brown, but turned a rich auburn in the afternoon light. He couldn't get a good look at her breasts in the shapeless, baggy T-shirt she wore over a pair of leggings, but they didn't seem to be overly inspiring. Her face was heart-shaped, heavily freckled, and bore the faint mark of a dimple on one cheek. Her eyes … her eyes haunted him, even though he was consumed with his own troubles.

"What are you running from?" he asked softly, so the taxi driver couldn't overhear.

She jerked back against the door, eyes the color of the Aegean suddenly wide with fear. She didn't deny it; she just looked at him with those huge eyes, like a gazelle startled at a water hole. For some bizarre reason he didn't at all understand, he was aware that the newly born need to protect Peter extended to her, as well.

He didn't know her, he reminded himself. True, he'd be in possession of all the available facts about her and her legal history in the next hour, thanks to the text message he'd sent to his assistant while waiting for a cab, but that would give only the details about her life. He didn't know her as a person. And yet … there was something about her, some sense of fragility, as if she was so wound up, the least little thing would shatter her. The image of a startled deer poised to flee remained with him.

"What are you afraid of?" he asked.

"Lots of things," she said, her gaze dropping to her hands. "Sharks. Poison pygmy darts. De-decapitation."

His eyes narrowed on her as she stuttered the last word. She was plainly terrified of something. No, some*one*. Why else would she agree to stay with a stranger? Some motive was driving her willingness to help him out, despite the fact that she clearly didn't trust him. He'd never been the lesser of two evils, and he didn't like the feeling. He wanted to know whom she was afraid of before he entrusted his son to her.

His son. Would he ever get used to hearing that? Would he ever make even half as good a father as Iakovos? A sense of panic hit him hard in the gut before he pushed it down, telling himself that he didn't have a choice. He had a son now. He had to be a father even if he hadn't the slightest idea how to do that.

"I think I'll take those references now," Kiera said, holding out her hand for his phone, which he'd told her she could use to make calls.

What sort of woman didn't have a mobile phone in this day and age?

One who was running from someone.

He pulled up the address book, picked a number, hit dial, and gave her the phone. "This is Simon, my banker."

He listened in silence as she apologized for disturbing the banker and explained that she was calling regarding a business proposition she was considering undertaking. "What I really would like to know is whether you feel Mr. Papaioannou is a good risk."

He raised one eyebrow when she studiously avoided meeting his eye.

"No, no, of course not, I'm not asking for financial information—I just want to know, if you were considering a … some business with him, would you be comfortable doing so? Well … I don't think what sort of business is really pertinent. Either you trust someone or you don't. No, sir, I do not—"

Theo sighed, took the phone from her, and said abruptly, "Simon, she wants to know if I'm trustworthy. That's all," before handing the phone back to her.

Her face turned a delicate shade of pink, something that both amused and amazed him. He didn't think women still blushed. Certainly, the sort of women he usually dated had long since lost that ability. He couldn't even imagine Nastya blushing over anything.

"I see. Thank you for your help. I'm sorry to have bothered you."

She hung up the phone, biting her lower lip for a moment.

A surge of heat hit him when he looked at her mouth. She had the cutest little rosebud lips that just made him want to taste them.

"Cantaloupes," she finally said.

"Golf balls."

She shot him a surprised glance. He smiled.

"Oreo cookies viewed from the top," she answered in a challenging voice, then added, "That was really embarrassing, but if you don't mind, I'd like another reference." She handed the phone back to him.

He looked at his watch, and dialed a number. "Hello, Henry. Do me a favor and tell the lady I'm about to put on the phone whether or not you feel my word can be trusted. No, just do it."

She took the phone, her gaze still avoiding his. "Hello. Yes, thank you. You do. With … oh." The tiniest corner of her mouth curved in the beginning of a smile. "And has he … no, no, of course not. I see. Thank you very much."

"Have I what?" he couldn't keep from asking as she

handed him the phone, her cheeks still pink, but for a moment, her eyes held laughter.

"He says he would trust you to date his eighteen-year-old daughter, and he can't say that about anyone else, least of all the young man who *is* dating her."

"Satisfied, or do you want the last one?"

The smile in her eyes died when she leaned back over Peter, adjusting a lightweight blanket that covered him. "I'd like one more, if you don't mind."

"I don't, but it'll have to wait a few minutes," he said, nodding out of the window as they pulled up in front of an elegant hotel.

She looked worried, and as they got out of the car, Theo covertly checked his phone, knowing that even an assistant as proficient as Annemarie couldn't turn up a background check that quickly, but wanting very much to know what she'd find out about Kiera.

He wasn't stupid—he wouldn't place his son in what could be a potentially dangerous situation until he knew more about Kiera, but until then, he reserved the right to be intrigued by her.

The background report had better have information about whom she was so afraid of. He had a feeling he was going to want to have a word or two with whoever it was.

THREE

I was more than a little self-conscious walking into a hotel with a complete stranger, but two things reassured me: the first was that the hotel was large, with a steady stream of people moving in and out of the lobby, and the second was the fact that Theo got a call while he was paying off the taxi driver. That allowed me to edge forward into the lobby while he stood outside talking rapidly in Greek.

"Look, Peter, people. Lots of people. Aren't they interesting?" I pushed the baby in his stroller just inside the doorway, pausing to quickly assess the people in the lobby. No one showed even the slightest bit of interest in me. No one rose up to ooze menace and horror, or point a finger and demand the police arrest me. No one so much as looked our way, which did much to calm my already frazzled nerves.

At the very least, I'd be out of Mikhail's reach for a night.

"Sorry about that," Theo said, appearing suddenly beside me. He picked up his laptop bag and the baby's bag, leaving the others for the porter, startling me for a second when I felt the warmth of his hand on my back as we entered the lobby proper. "You two stay here. I won't be long."

The baby was starting to fuss again, having woken up just as we arrived at the hotel. I knelt down to check that he wasn't strapped in too tight, caught a whiff of something horrible, and wrinkled my nose at the deceptively sweet baby.

"Oh, man, I didn't even think of that," I told him, sending up a little prayer that Theo knew how to change a baby. "I'm sorry you're sitting in your own feces, Peter. I imagine it's very uncomfortable as well as being extremely stinky, but as soon as your daddy gets us to his room, I'm sure he'll clean you up and make you happy again. I wonder what you like to eat."

Peter, who had been sucking on his fingers, suddenly yelled, "No no no no" when Theo approached, pointing the accusatory wet fingers at him.

"He can talk," Theo said, a look of delight crossing his face. "I wonder what else he can say? Can you say 'Papa,' Peter? 'Papa'? Maybe I have a piece of candy… " Theo set down his laptop bag and started patting the pockets of his suit jacket.

"He's not a parrot, Theo," I said, and, when Peter's face started to crumple up into more tears, gave in to instincts I didn't know I possessed and took him out of the stroller, balancing him on my hip while I rubbed his back again. "I'm going to give you a little piece of advice that I hope you take to heart, baby. Never let other people project their expectations onto you. You do not have to say 'Papa' if you don't want to. Just because he's your father doesn't mean he has the right to demand things of you that you're not comfortable providing. You say 'Papa' in your own good time. And if you don't want to do that, you can just call him no no no. We are not here to judge you. Just find your inner happy place, and don't worry about other people, OK?"

Theo looked like he wanted to laugh, but he managed to keep a straight face when we went toward the elevator, a porter with our things on a wheeled cart following behind us.

"Oh, this is quite … large," I said a few minutes later, looking around the suite that Theo had booked. The living room alone could probably have fit my previous apartment into it.

Theo paid off the porter, opened the door to one bedroom, then strode across the living room to the other. "Do you have a preference which room you want?"

I shook my head, still taking in the elegant surroundings.

"I'll take this one, then. It has two beds in it." He collected his luggage and that of the baby, and took them into his room.

Hadn't he said something to his ex about not being able to afford the baby? How was he paying for this room if money was tight? He should have downgraded. Or was it a business thing? One of the attorneys in the law firm I'd worked for once told me that appearance was everything, and that if you looked like you had money, people believed you did. Maybe he was putting on a good front for business reasons?

Guilt pricked me. He'd promised double a normal babysitter's fee, and I had been willing to take it. "Tires. Olives. Aunt Talia's left earlobe."

Then again, what was I doing there? Was I really willing to help with Peter's care just for the thought of a night's sleep? "Sadly, yes, I am," I said aloud, wincing when another wave of baby stink hit me. "We're here, and we'll just deal with situations as they arise, right? Holy cow, baby. That is really powerful."

"Your room is there," Theo said, reemerging to nod toward the other door. "You should probably check that the lock works. I'll take Peter."

"Sure," I said, handing him the baby and hurrying toward my room. "He needs changing."

"What?"

I paused at the door to my room and saw the moment when he understood. His face twitched as he held the baby out at arm's length, saying something in Greek, looking like he couldn't believe that odor came from such a small child.

And then he looked up and started toward me.

I spun around, slamming the door shut, and locking it for good measure.

"Kiera." His voice was slightly muffled.

"Yes?"

"The baby needs changing."

"Yes, he does."

"I've never changed a baby."

"Neither have I."

"But you're a woman."

I gave in and giggled a little before opening the door. "I hate to break this to you, but just because I have a uterus does not mean I have instinctive knowledge regarding diaper changing."

"Please," he said, holding out Peter.

The baby's face started to crumple, like he was about to cry. Theo looked like he might cry, as well.

"He's your son," I pointed out.

"And I'm trying very hard to cope with that fact, but I'm new at this, and I need help. *Pleeease.*"

"Oh, very well, but we're doing this in your bedroom." I gave in to the inevitable, taking the baby and walking past Theo toward his room. "I want to be able to sleep in mine."

"I've got to make a couple of calls. Then we can order dinner."

I nodded and went into the bathroom attached to Theo's bedroom, spreading one of the hotel's thick blue towels down on a bath mat before laying the baby on top.

"I hope you don't have expectations about this experience that I can't meet," I told the baby, opening his bag and examining some of the contents. "I will do my best, but just keep in mind that this is a first for me. What do we have in here … ? Diapers, check. Some sort of ointment. Powder. Oh, a box of wipes. That looks handy. Now, let us get you undone. This unsnaps along there, excellent. And this looks like it comes off there, and then we remove that, and OH HOLY JESUS!"

The memory of the ten minutes that followed would live with me for a long, long time. Eventually, I got the baby's bottom mostly cleaned up by using half the box of wipes, and two extra diapers to mop up the overflow, leaving the floor strewn with debris of my battle.

Even with the fan going full strength, the odor in the room was enough to send Theo reeling backward when he came in to see how we were doing. "You're not done yet?" he asked, staring in disbelief as, covered in baby powder that had somehow exploded all over Peter, the floor, and me, I clutched a naked, squirming baby to my hip.

"Does it look like we're done?" I snapped, at the end of my tether. "Make yourself useful. Get a garbage bag and gather up all that. I got Peter cleaned up, but he still reeks. I think I'm going to have to wash his bottom."

"Do *something*," Theo agreed, flinching while he backed out of the bathroom.

Hope flared with the sight of the bidet. "Right, that's what its job is. Let's just try … oh, Lord, no!"

I must have held Peter in the wrong position to intercept the stream of water, because it merrily sailed through his kicking legs and got me dead in the chest.

Peter looked like he might cry again, filling me with panic and a newborn sense of determination. "All right, don't get stressed. Think of your happy place. Find your inner Zen, and relax there while I try to work out a solid strategy," I told the baby, and pulled off my sopping wet bidet-water T-shirt.

"He needs a shower," Theo said helpfully when he returned with a garbage bag, gathering up the debris.

"I'm going to give him a bath," I answered, running some warm water, the wet, naked baby still clutched to my side. I didn't dare set him down, not knowing how clean the floor was. Before the powder had exploded all over it, that is.

"He's pissing on the wall."

"What? Oh, Peter, no!"

I realized a little too late that turning around to see what the baby was doing was simply going to spread pee everywhere, and it did, right across the front of Theo's shirt as he was in the process of bending down to pick up a diaper.

Theo jumped back and swore.

"Oh, don't make such a big deal about a little baby pee," I snapped when he ripped off his shirt. "I had poop all over my arms. I had to wash them three times before I could stop gagging."

He looked up to answer and stopped, his eyes focused on my chest.

I looked down and discovered that my last clean bra, a sheer little number with pretty embroidery on the cups, had been soaked along with my shirt, and was now, in effect, translucent.

I felt hot and uncomfortable and damp, and yet, at the same time, oddly aroused by the look he was giving my breasts. But I'd die before I let him know that. "I'm sorry if the sight of my boobs offends you. I got wet trying to wash the baby in the bidet."

Theo dragged his gaze off my chest, giving the bidet a curious look. "You tried to give him a bath in the bidet?"

"I tried to wash off his bottom, yes. That's what it's for, after all. But he didn't like it, so we're just going to go with a full bath. You can leave now."

"I'll stay and help now that he's not ... I'll help give him a bath."

"You want to do it? Fine." I tried handing him the wet baby.

He backed up, holding his hands up. "I said I'd help. You can do it and I'll watch you so I can do it the next time."

"Either you do it, or I do it, but if I do it, you have to leave," I told him, removing from the baby's grip the toilet paper he had snagged.

"Why can't I stay?" Theo asked, frowning down at me.

I wanted nothing so much at that moment as to punch him in the knees. "Because my underwear matches my bra."

"That's nice to know, but does it have some bearing on bathing Peter?"

"Yes! He's a baby! He can't sit in the tub by himself, so I'll have to get in with him."

"So?"

I glared at him until he glanced back down at my breasts. "Ah. Well, it won't bother me."

"It would me." Did the man honestly think I was going to be all but naked in the same confined space as him?

"Fine. Then I'll get in the tub with him," he said, his hands on his belt buckle.

His pants hit the floor before I could turn hastily around to the tub, swishing the water in an attempt to distract myself. "Leave your underwear on."

"Why? Unlike you, I'm not shy."

"Just leave it on," I growled, closing my eyes until I heard a splash.

I opened them then, my gaze immediately falling on the sight of Theo's naked chest just a few inches from me. I stared at his chest. I closed my eyes again, then opened them back up. No, he was still there, still as gorgeous as the first look.

Dear God, the man was beautiful.

"Baby," he said, holding out his hands.

"What? Oh." I handed over Peter, busying myself with a washcloth and soap.

It was downright mean of him to flaunt that chest at me. What did he think I was, a nun?

The baby sat between Theo's knees, happily splashing the water, talking baby talk to it, chuckling when Theo helped him splash.

It took me three tries, but at last I was able to drag my eyes off the expanse of magnificent chest, whereupon I was relieved to see that Theo had kept on his black bikini briefs. At that point, I made a solemn oath while I tried to wash Peter. I would not look at Theo's groin. It held absolutely no interest for me. It didn't matter to me in the least what he had stuffed into his underwear. I simply did not care.

I looked, and almost fell into the tub.

"Careful," Theo warned, glancing up, his chest and face wet from his and Peter's play, his grin fading a little as he looked at me. "Are you all right? You look like you're going to pass out."

"Yes, I'm fine, totally fine. Why shouldn't I be fine? My … er … my hand slipped is all. It happens to everyone. It's a perfectly normal, everyday occurrence. People's hands slip all the time." I steadfastly returned my gaze to the baby. Dammit, I would not let Theo discombobulate me this way. He would love knowing that just a little bare chest, and arms, and biceps that made my inner self swoon, could so fluster me.

It struck me then that I didn't feel particularly threatened by Theo. I slid a quick glance at him while washing the baby's leg, wondering about that fact, prodding at it to see what it meant. I didn't know the man, and yet, here he was almost naked, and all I felt was an almost consuming desire to look at his chest. And legs. And arms.

I cleared my throat, feeling heat on my cheeks. I needed to stop thinking about Theo's muscles, and skin, and, oh Lord, his thighs! I would ignore him and concentrate wholly on the baby. That was the answer.

The baby had other ideas, and squirmed out of my grip every time I tried to pin him down to wash an arm or a leg.

"Sorry," I apologized when, as I tried to wash the baby's chest, he flung himself to the side, and I got Theo's calf instead.

"He likes the water," Theo said.

I tried to think of words to answer him, but my brain seemed to have shut down when I glanced along the long line of Theo's legs. He had dark body hair, not so much that I wanted to buy him a razor, but enough to make me very aware of the difference between his body and mine.

What on earth was I doing thinking about his body? Baby! Wash the baby!

I got hold of Peter's arm, intent on swiping his bottom with the washcloth, but before I could do so, he lunged forward to grab at Theo's bobbing toes, and I fell over the edge of the tub.

"Are you all right?" he asked. My face was smooshed into his stomach, my breath stuck in my throat when I struggled to get off him, my soapy hands on the hard muscles of his thighs.

I managed to push myself off him, but felt my face flaming with embarrassment. "Sorry, he doesn't want to be washed."

"If you're going to bathe me, as well, I'm taking my underwear off," Theo said, his eyes dancing when I tried to look anywhere but at his crotch.

I wouldn't look, I absolutely would not look…

His underwear appeared to have a couple of bulldogs stuffed into it.

Oh, dear God in heaven.

"Kiera? Did you hurt your stomach on the edge of the tub?" Theo asked I put a hand to my chest to try to get some air into my lungs.

"No, I'm fine," I said, realizing that my voice sounded like that of a frog. A female frog entranced by the package of a nearby male frog. I cleared my throat. "I … uh … I think the baby's clean."

"All right. Although it seems a shame, he really likes it."

I kept my eyes firmly on Peter, bouncing him in the water a few times while Theo got out of the tub, absently accepting the towel he handed me to dry the baby.

The loud, wet smack of underwear hitting the floor had me freezing in the act of drying him. For a moment, panic threatened to rise, but to my relief, it ebbed away and left only an odd sense of anger.

Theo said, "I'll have dinner brought up here, if you don't mind. It'll be easier on Peter."

"I don't mind," I said quickly, wondering where all the air in the bathroom had gone.

He stood behind me, naked. I could *feel* him standing there, wet and naked, and looking like he did, deliberately flaunting himself at me. How dare he stand there without a single stitch of clothing on, his skin all warm and wet and slick, just like he didn't know what effect he was having on me? Men who looked like him *always* knew the way women reacted to them. They ate it up.

The bastards.

"What sorts of things does he eat, do you think?" Theo asked. "There's some formula in the bag, but Nastya didn't say if he ate anything else. I suppose I can look that up online."

Well, I was not going to let him get to me. I would not give him the satisfaction of reacting to him, all male and naked and wet, with his two-bulldog crotch right there. He could stand there with his sleek muscles and tantalizing flesh for as long as he liked—I would die before I pandered to his ego so much as one tiny little morsel.

"Finger foods, I imagine," I said, drying the baby. "Cereal, maybe. Yogurt. Some easily chewed fruit. A little plain pasta."

"I'll get it ordered."

"And maybe—" I turned to look up at him, and stopped. He was drying his face and chest, the rest of him right there at face level.

I stared in disbelief at his genitals.

"Maybe what?" He looked down at me, a little hint of a smile curling his mouth as I continued to stare. "Like what you see?"

His voice cut through the fog in my mind.

I cleared my throat and, with an effort that bordered on superhuman, dragged my eyes up to his. "Not really, no."

His eyebrows rose; he obviously hadn't expected that response.

I cherished the anger that still boiled around inside of me. That anger would keep me safe. "I don't like men who are bigger than me. I don't like men who are handsome. I don't like men with big ..." I waved a hand at his crotch. "... big body parts. And I really don't like men who use their physical appeal to get what they want. Do you want to dress Peter, or shall I?"

"You can." He watched me for a minute while I dug

through the baby's bag, pulling out clean clothes and a fresh diaper. He said nothing more, but left the room.

Idiot, I told myself, watching him leave. *Hooo, even the rear view … no! Stop looking, you fool!* "I'm the worst liar in the world, Peter," I said softly, feeling flushed and hot and incredibly aroused. Annoyed! I felt incredibly *annoyed,* not aroused.

Dammit, Theo was the finest specimen of man I'd ever seen. Despite the fact that he didn't set off any of my mental threat warnings, I had to get out of there fast, or I'd be in way over my head, and I was tired of constantly feeling like I was swimming against the tide.

By the time I got the baby dressed, Theo was on the phone, placing an order for dinner.

I put Peter on the floor, pulling on my wet T-shirt, the feeling of it irksome, but better than having my boobs more or less naked around Theo. The baby no-no-ed me a couple of times, then crawled over to the bed, clutching the bedspread to pull himself up to his feet.

I knelt behind him, my hands out to catch him in case he fell, but although he seemed a bit wobbly, he bounced and slapped his hands on the blanket without tipping over. "Well, aren't you clever?" I said, smiling when he bounced on his chubby little legs. "You can stand."

"Of course he can," Theo said, thankfully dressed. "He can probably walk, too. We'll see after dinner."

Pride was evident in Theo's voice when he spoke, and was just as obvious in his eyes when he cast a conspiratorial look my way while, with the help of his grip on the bed, Peter bounced a few more times. But it was the look on Theo's face that made something deep in my belly warm, leaving me with a need, an aching want, to be, just for a moment, part of that look of pride.

That way lies foolishness, my inner self commented, and reluctantly, I let go of the need and want and annoying sexual interest. "I'm going to change into something a little less bath-time fun," I told Theo, getting to my feet when Peter sat down to play with Theo's shoes.

"If you think that's bath-time fun, then I have something to show you," was his reply, made with a half-lidded look that, despite my better self, sent the slow burn in my stomach into a raging inferno of lust.

Our gazes met, his teasing and mine wary. I wanted to tell him that I had spent the last nine months hiding from every shadow, every stranger ... but nothing had left me feeling as off-balance and worried as I was now.

Pure and simple, I was the prey to Theo's hunter, and there wasn't a damned thing I could do about it. So why wasn't I running away? I gave a mental headshake over the fact that I should be walking out the door right that second, and instead, I was finding excuses to remain.

I all but ran to my room to change, giving myself yet another lecture as I did so.

When I returned to the living room, my resolve to keep Theo at an arm's length once again firm—or as firm as it was going to get—I found him sitting on the floor along with Peter, a soft cloth book, a stuffed giraffe that Peter was beating on Theo's foot, and a yellow rubber bulb-shaped item.

"I was just sitting here thinking about all the things I'm going to have to do." Theo's expression was strained. "This is all so new to me, but I'm going to do it right. I *have* to do it right."

"It's bound to be a big adjustment for you both," I said, glancing around the room.

"That's an understatement. I keep asking myself what I think I'm doing taking on a baby when I know nothing about them, but then he no-nos me, and I melt inside."

"He is awfully cute." I eyed all the electrical cords coming from various lamps, and mentally *tsk*ed.

"I'm going to have to get him some proper toys," Theo said, watching when I moved over to where a glass coffee table sat. "This is all Nastya packed for him. At least he has a chew toy."

"A what?" I grunted when I shoved the coffee table back

until it was pushed up against one of the couches, and un-plugged the nearby lamps.

"He's teething, I think. At least he has some teeth, so I assume that means he's teething, and I thought you gave babies something to chew on when they did that." He held up the yellow rubber bulb with an odd poky bit at the end. "Chew toy."

"Makes sense." I eyed an end table, taking the lamp from it and setting it onto the small dining room table that sat between us and the tiny kitchenette.

"What are you doing?" Theo asked when Peter took the chew toy from him and stuffed it into his mouth, gnawing on it while he, too, watched me.

"If Peter fell, he could hit his head on the glass coffee table," I answered, nodding toward it. "And pull that lamp down on himself."

"Are you sure you're not a nanny?" Theo asked with another one of those sexy half smiles.

"Quite sure. I do, however, have common sense." I returned to my bedroom, taking a spare blanket from a closet, which I spread out onto the carpet, placing the baby and his toys on top.

Before he could answer, Theo's phone chirruped. He pulled it out, looked at it, and said as he got to his feet, "I have to check an important e-mail on my laptop. Can you watch him for a little bit? Dinner should be here soon."

"Sure." I smiled when Peter, no-no-no-ing madly, used my legs to pull himself onto his feet, and glanced up at Theo when he hesitated.

"Do you still want to make that third call?"

"I think that's best, don't you?" I met his searching gaze with one of calm control, now that I had my errant emotions in hand.

He shrugged and pulled up an entry from the phone's contact list, handing it to me. "Try the top number first. If he isn't at the apartment, try the second number. That's the house."

I took the phone, wondering what sort of person had both an apartment and a house, waiting until he went into the other room, and the baby was entertaining himself by trying to chew the colors off the book, before I hit the dial button.

"Hello. Is Mr. Papaioannou available?"

"No, not here. Kyrie Papaioannou away."

"I see. Thank you." I hung up and dialed the second number before I lost my nerve.

The greeting was in Greek.

"Hello. I'd like to speak with Mr. Papaioannou, please."

"He is expecting you?" the woman asked, her voice annoyed, as if she'd been disturbed.

"No, not really. I'm calling in regards to his brother, Theo."

The woman was silent for a few seconds. "You hold," she ordered.

I held.

A minute later, another woman's voice spoke. "Who's this?"

I didn't want to give my name but decided she couldn't do much with just part of it. "My name is Kiera."

"You're calling about Theo? Has he been hurt?"

"No, not at all." Was this his sister-in-law? She sounded worried. "I'm sorry if I startled you, but I was trying to reach Mr. Papaioannou. Theo's brother, that is."

"I see. Iakovos is out with our girls, teaching them to swim, not that I won't have to go out later and undo everything he's taught them, because gorgeous as he is, he can't swim worth a damn. But that really doesn't matter, does it?"

"No," I agreed, somewhat surprised by the turn the conversation had taken.

"I'm Harry Papaioannou, by the way. Theo's sister-in-law. Can I help you with something?"

"I hope so. This is going to seem like it's a very odd question, but I'd like to know if you trust Theo."

"Trust him?"

"Yes."

"Why?"

I made a face at nothing. "Well … because I want to know if I can trust him."

"Trust him with what?"

I had the worst urge to laugh. This had to be the most bizarre conversation I'd ever had. "With me, basically."

"Really," Harry drawled, sounding much more interested and a whole lot less suspicious. "Well, to answer your question, yes, I do trust him. He's had some issues in the past, but even despite those, I trust him. We haven't seen him since Nicky turned one, but … well, the answer is yes."

"All right, thank you."

"This isn't about that whole list thing, is it?"

"What list thing?"

"Dmitri told us that he heard that some magazine editor who has a man crush on Theo is pushing to get him on the list. The bachelor list."

"I … I don't know anything about a list."

"If you take my advice, don't let him get on it. Not only does Theo *not* need more women throwing themselves at him, but it's just a bitch once they're on the list. Women think that it's a hunting-season-is-open sign, for one."

"All right," I said, wondering if the woman named Harry was insane, or if I was. "I won't."

"Good. Is Theo there? Where are you? Why hasn't he called us in forever?"

I wasn't at all comfortable telling this woman where we were, not since I knew well how deadly it could be to have one's whereabouts known. Perhaps there was a reason Theo didn't maintain contact with his family. Regardless of his relationship with them, it wasn't my place to tell them where he was. "I'm sorry, but I can't answer that. I'll tell him you asked, though. Thanks for the information, and I'm sorry I disturbed you."

I hung up at the same time Harry demanded to talk to Theo, staring at the phone for a moment, wondering what I was doing sitting in a hotel room with a man who evidently didn't need more women throwing themselves at him.

He was trouble, pure and simple.

"Well?" Theo wandered in, squatting down next to Peter, his expression oddly guarded. "Did my brother tell you how unstable I am, and to get away while you could?"

"I didn't talk to him," I said, giving him back his phone. "I spoke with your sister-in-law. She said she trusted you."

"Harry," he said with a fond smile that warmed his eyes.

"I got the idea she wants you to call. She also said …" I shook my head at the oddness of it all. "I'm not quite sure I understand this, but she said something about not letting you be on a list."

His smile grew. "Oh?"

"Yes. Evidently it's bad, and I'm supposed to stop you."

"Did she say anything else?"

I got to my feet and, feeling the need for something to do that put a little distance between Theo and me, fetched the baby's formula and bottles. "Not really, just that your brother was teaching his daughters to swim and that she'd have to undo it all later."

Theo laughed. "That sounds like Harry."

I had to leave soon, I told myself. Entangling myself with this enticing man and adorable baby was not the answer to my problems.

The right thing, the reasonable thing, was to leave first thing in the morning. I barely knew Theo, even if I was oddly comfortable with him, and he didn't need me to help with Peter. Not really. He was just a little overwhelmed at finding himself a new father, and he felt better having someone else around to help him over the hump of learning how to take care of a baby.

I was just a convenient body, nothing more.

I just wished that idea didn't hurt so much.

Theo talked nonsense to Peter while the latter was sucking noisily on his bottle. Another wave of longing swept through me, this one with so much strength, it made me tremble. There was something in Theo's eyes, a sense of a man trying to keep his head above water, that called to me, like seeking like, my psyche wanting to comfort him even though I had no place doing so. I was broken, a danger to everyone I was near, my life such a knot of horror, fear, and despair that I doubted if I'd ever get it untangled, and yet, there I was wanting nothing more than to ease the pain that was so stark in his eyes.

God knew what I might have done at that moment if Peter hadn't finished his bottle and demanded that Theo admire it.

I bolted to my room while Theo interested Peter in a toy, leaving me with the firm conviction that I had to get away from the seductive man who had so easily consumed my thoughts before it was too late.

If it wasn't already.

FOUR

Theo was furious when he saw the e-mail from his assistant. Annemarie was efficient in all things, even when she was in Australia while he was in New Zealand, and she hadn't failed his request for an immediate background history on Kiera, or at least what could be found in a short amount of time. His body might desire her, but his body had made a lot of bad choices in the past, and he wasn't about to risk the safety of his son with a stranger who so readily agreed to go off with him without a backward glance.

Except it hadn't really been that way. He'd had to use every bit of his not inconsiderable charm to get her to agree to help him.

He looked down at the laptop screen, anger rising at the first sentence.

Subject Kiera Taylor has an arrest warrant issued by Wellington police.

She was a fugitive, a criminal. He was ready to throw her damned lies in her face, along with her soft looks and gentle way with Peter, not to mention the attraction to him that she fought, or pretended to fight. It was all false, all a lie.

Then he read the next sentences, and he slumped back, his mind chewing it over.

She is charged with theft of property of Mikhail Girbac, specifically a valuable piece of computer equipment. The warrant has not been served, and her whereabouts are currently unknown. I did a quick search, and it turns out Mikhail Girbac has three arrests for domestic violence, one for robbery, and one for involvement in organized crime, all in Australia. He also has robbery and assault arrests in New Zealand, but to date, no convictions. Kiera Taylor has no prior convictions or other pending charges in New Zealand or Australia. I will be unable to find out if she has a record in the US until offices open there.

He could just picture the situation: some man, probably a lover, beat her up, and she took a computer as retaliation. He filed charges, and she ran. That made sense with regard to her general air of fear and wariness. He hadn't failed to notice how carefully she'd searched the lobby of the hotel before she entered it.

The little gazelle was frightened, very frightened, but Theo wasn't a fool. She hadn't told him she was on the run from the police, and an honest woman would have done so. Desperate as he was for her help, it would be the sheerest folly to trust her with Peter's care.

Get me everything you can find on her, he e-mailed back to Annemarie. *Also get full details on Mikhail Girbac.*

He closed his laptop and, after a moment's thought, stuck it into its bag and pushed it behind the armchair. He didn't really think she'd steal it right in front of him, but out of sight, out of mind.

"I think he's hungry," Kiera said when Theo emerged from his room. She was in the tiny kitchen with a package of disposable baby bottles and the baby formula, reading the instructions. "Oh, good, it says I can give this to him at room temperature. I was worried about heating it up."

Peter distracted Theo for a few minutes by no-no-no-ing him, sucking happily on a cloth book.

"Do we just give it to him?" Kiera asked, kneeling next to them with the bottle in her hands. "Or do you have to hold him to feed him?"

"I don't know," Theo said, the familiar panic returning before he squelched it down. "Maybe if I hold him on my lap sitting up?"

They tried that, and to Theo's intense relief, Peter reached for the bottle, happily sucking from it, his eyes watching Kiera when she moved away.

"I'll just see if there's something that he can eat in here."

He watched Kiera search the mini fridge, amazed that someone who looked so innocent and genuine could so completely hide the truth. He wondered if she had been driven to run from her boyfriend, or if there was more to it. Perhaps she was the consummate con artist, and he'd just fallen right into her silky-skinned, seductive trap.

It was on the tip of his tongue to ask her about the warrant when she held up a miniature bottle of wine, and asked what he'd like.

"Nothing."

Kiera looked at him oddly, no doubt noting the strangled sound of the word. His gut clenched, but he hadn't been through hell and back again to let the need to drink control him. He made an effort to relax, using the coping mechanisms that he'd relied on in the past to get him through social situations where alcohol was present.

"You don't drink?"

"No."

She poured two of the mini bottles she'd opened into the sink, and came over to sit next to him. Peter had finished with his bottle, and was now holding on to the couch, trying to crawl under one of the cushions. "How long have you been sober?"

Theo shot her a questioning look.

"My father," she answered.

His gaze dropped to Peter. It took him a few minutes before he answered. "Five years, four months, twelve days."

"That's a good start," she said, her voice soft with understanding.

Theo wanted to wrap himself in it. "I made a lot of mistakes before I went into the clinic," he admitted, his voice gruff.

"But now you have even more of a reason to stay sober." Kiera nodded to Peter.

His gaze moved to hers, noting that her lovely eyes reflected the same thing he saw in the mirror when he was at a low point: doubt, fear, and pain. "My father had three children. It didn't stop him from drinking himself to death when my mother died. What makes you think one child will be able to keep me from following the same path?"

She considered him, then slowly shook her head. "You're not your father, Theo."

"No." He looked at Peter. "I'm not."

She reached out and put her hand on his, obviously trying to comfort him. "This is going to sound ridiculous since we just met, but despite that, I have confidence in you. You may be new to being a father, but I think you're going to make an excellent one."

He closed his eyes, turning his hand so that his fingers curled through hers, bringing her fingers to his mouth.

Sexual interest flared within him again, spreading a warm glow that started at his cock and rippled outward. He embraced it, welcoming the sensation, since it drove before it the need for a drink. With nothing more on his mind than a little precursor to seduction, he kissed her fingers, giving her his sexiest look, the one that never failed to bring women to his bed.

She stiffened and, with a murmured excuse, all but ran to her room.

"No no no," Peter said, watching her.

"Dammit," Theo swore at himself, angry that he'd allowed his lust to make him forget he had to treat her carefully. "I'm a fool, Peter. I scared her."

Part of him wanted to be irritated with the situation. What the hell had he done that was so bad? He didn't like being treated like he was tantamount to a rapist. He didn't like how she seemed to interpret everything he did as being a threat to her personal safety. He didn't like the fact that she didn't seem to like him at all. "Women don't dislike me, Peter. Some may not be overly interested in me, but they don't actively avoid me. I may have my own personal demons, but

I have never mistreated a woman. I've never given one the desire to run away from me. For God's sake, Harry broke my nose when I tried to kiss her. No, Peter, I don't like any of this. Kiera's afraid, and I'm willing to bet she was abused by that Mikhail person with all the domestic violence arrests. But why is she running? Why doesn't she get the police involved if she's that afraid?"

And just what sort of woman would be in such a bad mental place that she'd go with an absolute stranger to his hotel room? He knew the answer even before the question finished forming in his head: one who was deceptive, a liar, a thief ... or one who was wholly and completely terrified.

That last thought made him feel like the world's biggest jerk. If she truly was afraid of him, he could see how what to him was a perfectly natural flirtation might have been viewed in a completely different light.

It was a very disconcerting thought.

"No wonder she can't stand to be around me. Then again, maybe it's an act? Damn, I wish I knew. Either she's a hell of an actress and plans on robbing me blind, or she's desperate." He took the chew toy that Peter brought him, babbling something that only he understood. "And frankly, I don't like either situation. Much as I regret it, I'm afraid she's going to have to go. We can't put you at risk, old man, can we?"

He spent the next twenty minutes playing with Peter, the niggling unease that was worry about Kiera pushed to the back of his mind as he was alternately enchanted and terrified by his son.

"It's not so much that he scares me," he told Kiera when she finally emerged from her room. He was flat on his back, holding Peter above him while making a rough approximation of airplane noises. Peter screamed his delight, his arms and legs kicking wildly when he chuckled and no-no-ed happily.

She looked momentarily startled to be coming into a conversation that he had been holding in his head. "Oh?"

"It's that I don't know what I'm doing. What if I do something wrong? What if I mess up his life to the point where he hates me and has to spend years in therapy? What if I *am* my father after all?" He sat up, putting Peter down. The baby immediately no-no-ed Kiera, then crawled over to Theo's foot and began gnawing on his ankle. "This shouldn't have happened to me."

"Birth control goes both ways," Kiera said, giving Peter an empty toilet paper roll, smiling when the baby promptly put it in his mouth.

He cast her a questioning glance. "Was that innuendo?"

She looked startled for a moment; then a little frown pulled her delicately arched brows together. "Not at all. I just meant that it's not fair to expect women to always have to be the ones to take care of it. Maybe your Nastya got tired of being the one to get IUDs and shots and arm implants."

"That's not exactly what I meant…"

"Uh-huh. Just like you can't afford Peter?" The look she gave him was one of cool disdain.

Theo sent her a questioning glance. "I *what*?"

"In the train station you told your ex you couldn't afford Peter."

"Ah, that." Theo smiled at the baby. "I meant I couldn't afford the time to be a father, and the second I said it, I realized what an ass I was being. I won't say that it's going to be easy juggling a baby and my business, but I'll have to make it work. He's definitely worth the effort."

Their food arrived at that point, a waiter bringing in a cart full of a variety of dishes, followed by a maid with a high chair. Kiera glanced at the carpet and, picking up Peter while Theo directed the food to be placed on a small round table, went into his room. For one moment he wondered if he'd left his wallet out in plain view, but was ashamed of himself when she appeared with two towels in her hand.

"This carpet looks expensive," she told him when she laid the largest towel down under the high chair, plopping Peter down on it before swathing him, too, with a towel.

"For someone who isn't a nanny, you are remarkably good at this. I think this is yours." He slid a plate her way.

Kiera ignored her food to give Peter a couple of pieces of plain penne pasta before chopping up a slice of orange into very small pieces, which she placed on his tray. "You want to feed him some of that?" she asked, nodding toward a small dish of applesauce.

"Sure." He placed the bowl on the tray, only barely catching it when Peter smashed his fist into it, knocking the bowl into the air in an arc that landed with a wet splat on the table.

"The key words in that sentence being *feed him*, not give it to him," Kiera said, handing him the towel.

Theo mopped up the blobs of applesauce splattered on the table. "He can grab things. I thought he could use a spoon."

"Maybe. Maybe he still needs help. Do not allow your father's expectations of your ability with a spoon to make you feel in any way inferior," she told Peter, taking what remained of the applesauce and, with a spoon, managing to get some of it into his mouth. He talked happily, applesauce bubbling from his lips while he shoved a piece of pasta into his mouth. "You march to the beat of your own personal drummer, and never mind what anyone else is doing."

"Swami Betelbaum?" Theo asked, amused despite the grave misgivings he had of her. He supposed he owed her a meal, after what she'd gone through cleaning up Peter. Once that was done, though, he'd explain that he couldn't have her there after all, and would give her payment for a few days in compensation. Maybe a week's worth.

His gaze dropped to her breasts at the memory of her act of heroism in cleaning Peter, and found to his sadness that her chest was once again almost indistinguishable in yet another baggy T-shirt.

"Swami Betelbaum is full of much excellent advice. He helped me a lot getting a handle on panic attacks." She squinted at the variety of beverages that sat on the table. "I wonder if he can take other liquids than the formula. Do you suppose he's lactose intolerant?"

He paused, a forkful of steak almost to his mouth. "Swami Betelbaum? You'd have a better idea of that than me."

"Smart-ass." She made a face at him before nodding toward Peter.

He grinned, delighted by the fact that she had evidently relaxed despite her hypervigilance, although he was all too aware of the irony that he cared about her mental state when he was planning on sending her on her way immediately after dinner. "I don't know. Does he look it to you?"

"I don't know that there is a look, but I'm not going to risk it." She poured a little apple juice into a plastic cup and held it up for Peter. He pushed it away, and made grabby pincer hands at Theo, babbling earnestly. "I guess that answers that. I think he wants your steak."

"Well, he can't have it," Theo said, moving his plate a little. "No," he told Peter. "This is adult food. Not good for babies."

"No no no no!" Peter said, continuing to reach for it.

"I am very hungry," he continued, giving his son a stern look that he hoped exuded fatherly firmness. "I have worked hard today, and took one to the gut when I found out about you. I'd like to eat my dinner in peace. You will note that we have provided you with your own food. Please eat it. No, that is throwing it on Kiera. Do you see the look on her face? That says she did not enjoy a piece of pasta thrown onto her arm."

"Half-chewed, slobbery, applesaucy pasta," Kiera corrected him, removing the obnoxious item and wiping her arm, before mashing a couple of slices of cooked carrot with a fork and offering Peter a spoon of it. "I'm glad you're talking to him like he's intelligent, Theo. Swami Betelbaum said it's important to not underestimate people's abilities. And there, see? He likes the carrots."

Peter reached for him. Or rather, his dinner.

"Should I?" he asked Kiera, hesitant to deny his new-found son anything he wanted. For a moment, he had visions of ponies and dirt bikes and, later, a very fast sports car in his son's future. It was a nice vision, he decided, one that featured an older version of himself—slightly older, with perhaps one or two strands of silver at his temples in a distinguished, yet still attractive, appearance—beside his grown son. Oddly, his vision included Kiera, standing on the other side of Peter, her face full of pride.

"I don't see why not, although you'll have to mash it down. Maybe chop it up and mix it with some potato?"

"Hmm?" It took an effort, but he stopped imagining a delightful moment in which he told Iakovos how his son had graduated Oxford with top honors. Once again, Kiera intruded on that scene, standing next to him, her arm through his, while she told Harry about the many world-changing scientific discoveries that Peter had made before graduating.

"Is something wrong?" Kiera asked him, almost eating a bite of the lasagna she had requested for dinner, but putting it down untasted when Peter started banging the spoon she'd given him to play with on the tray, causing bits of applesauce, orange, and pasta to bounce onto the floor. "Yogurt, Peter? Do you like yogurt?"

What right did she have intruding on his private fantasies of the fabulous successes Peter would have in the future? It wasn't right that she, a thief, should demand that she be present at all of Peter's moments of triumph simply because she fed him and bathed him and put up with him throwing food on her without once complaining.

He felt disgruntled and aroused at the same time. Damn his libido. If this kept up, he'd have to find a woman to slake that particular thirst.

Except he didn't want a woman. Not one who didn't have a freckled, heart-shaped face, and eyes like the Aegean. He wondered what she tasted like. Was she salty, like the sea?

He cleared his throat, one eye on Peter, who now was smearing yogurt all over the high chair tray, happily babbling to himself. "So, what brings a paralegal from California to New Zealand?" he asked in what he thought was a very conversational tone of voice, not at all one that sounded like he was desperately trying to distract himself from thoughts of tasting her lips. And breasts. And belly. And hidden parts that he suspected would be as hot as the noonday sun.

She was silent for a moment, her fork of food still not having reached her mouth. Her gaze skittered over to Peter. It took her almost half a minute, but at last she said, "A man."

"Ah. Boyfriend?"

"Now former, yes." She stared at her plate, setting down her fork.

"New Zealand is a long way to come just to be with a man," he said, alternating between a desire to ask her outright about the warrant and to toss her onto the nearest bed to lick every square inch of her.

"Mistake number one," she said, tearing a roll apart and plucking out some of the soft inside to give to Peter. He mashed it into the yogurt/pasta mess on his tray before smearing it onto the top of his head. Her gaze met Theo's, anger and resentment making her eyes glitter with little blue and green sparks. "He was big, like you. And handsome, like you. And he had—" She gestured toward his groin. "Like you."

Theo wanted to be offended, but knew he had to treat her gently. She had survived something he couldn't even imagine, and he wanted to explain that he had not meant to upset her. "If you're referring to the episode in the bathroom, I apologize. I wouldn't have been so cavalier about removing my clothes in front of you if I'd known it bothered you. Although I will also point out that I may be big like this ex of yours, but I'm not him," he said, intentionally echoing her comment about him not being his father.

Her gaze dropped. "So you say."

"I'm going to let that insult pass, because I am an understanding man, and not a monster who uses his size and face and cock to intimidate women. Again, I'm sorry about what happened earlier in the bathroom, but I had no way of knowing that it would make you so uncomfortable. As for the rest, I can't help how I look any more than you can. Less, because it's a bit more obvious if I wear cosmetics."

Peter grabbed the bowl of mashed carrot that Kiera had left too close to him. He banged it on his tray, singing a song to himself, dipping his fingers into it and pointing at her.

"No one likes to admit they're a monster," she said, swallowing hard, her gaze still on the table. "What you think may make you the most understanding man on earth may not appear that way to someone else."

Peter snatched a handful of mashed potatoes from Theo's plate and, with a deep chuckle, stuck his fingers first in his mouth, then on his head.

"I didn't say I was the most understanding man. I simply meant that I can see now why you were upset earlier. Also, I assume you are referring to the fact that I mentioned my problem with alcohol." He was suddenly irritated. He didn't know how she knew about the less-than-savory things he had done when he was drunk, but it was clear she did, and it annoyed him. "Because I've apologized for groping Harry."

Peter upended the bowl of carrots, and put that on his head, too.

Kiera's gaze shot to Theo's, her eyes wary. "You groped your sister-in-law?"

"Yes." He shook a piece of meat at her that he had been in the process of chopping up for Peter. "But you needn't look like I'm the scum of the earth. Not only did I not know what I was doing because I was blitzed, but Jake beat the shit out of me for that, and as I just said, I apologized to Harry the next day."

"Jake?" she asked, looking confused.

"Iakovos," he said with an abrupt gesture. "It's Greek for Jacob. I call him Jake sometimes."

"Oh." She glanced toward Peter, her eyes widening, an odd little chirrup of laughter slipping out of her delightful lips. He looked to see what was so funny, staring in dismay at the sight. Peter was covered from the top of his head down to his once-clean shirt in carrot, mashed potato, and yogurt.

A blob of carrot fell from the bowl he'd inverted over his head, and plopped down onto the tray, which was almost unrecognizable. "I think he's going to need another bath."

He looked with regret at his partially eaten steak, putting his fork down. "This fatherhood thing is a lot more involved than I thought it would be. No, don't bother getting up. I'll give him a bath now that I know how."

"Hang on. So long as he's filthy, let me try to get a bit more food in him."

Ten minutes later, Theo took the still babbling baby to his bathroom, stripped them both, and had his second bath of the day. Another wave of panic hit him while Peter played in the water. What the hell did he know about raising a child, let alone taking care of a baby? How was he supposed to do this on his own? Even if he had a nanny, he'd still be responsible for Peter's welfare and happiness, and a million other things that he couldn't face.

He felt totally and completely out of his depth, but he knew he had to keep it together for Peter's sake. He just hoped he'd be able to do that without losing control completely.

Peter splashed and babbled and kicked his little feet for a bit, but when he started slumping against Theo's leg, gnawing slowly on his kneecap, Theo decided bath time was over. "Sleepy? Good. I don't think you should see Kiera leave. I wouldn't want to traumatize you when you're this young."

It took a good five minutes to dry Peter, and then he had to look at all the things in the diaper bag that were evidently supposed to be spread on him, to decide which were applicable. "You don't have a rash, so we'll put that one aside. Doesn't powder cause women to get UTIs when used down there?" He eyed the baby powder, then looked down at Peter, who had fistfuls of Theo's chest hair and was using it to get to his feet. He was pleased to see that Peter hadn't been circumcised. "But just in case it's the same for baby boys as women, we'll give it a pass." In the end he got Peter diapered and clad in a one-piece garment that looked appropriate for sleeping.

"No no," Peter said, putting his fingers in his mouth and gnawing.

"I'll get your chew toy," he promised, and opened the bathroom door.

Kiera stood at the low dresser across from the door, half turned away, his wallet in her hand, and a look of startled horror on her face.

Rage filled him, rage at himself for being so stupid, so blind to the truth about her, and rage that she could return his kindness with such duplicity.

"What the hell do you think you're doing?" he roared, setting Peter on the floor, stalking over to where she stood frozen, her gazelle eyes huge. He snatched his wallet from her hand, frustration with the whole horrible day turning what would have been a simple gesture into a grand wave of his hand.

Kiera gasped and dropped to her knees, her hands protectively clasped over her head.

He stood looking down at her, stunned by her automatic response, looking first at his hand, which was raised to the level of his head, then down to where she gasped words in between terrible little heart-wrenching sobs.

"I'm sorry—I didn't take anything, I swear. I just wanted to make sure you were the Theo who you said you were—"

Her voice held a level of terror that he had never, in his entire life, heard uttered by another human being. Carefully, she dropped her arms, but she scuttled backward until she was pressed into the wall, her whole body clearly trying to make itself smaller and less of a target.

He lowered his hand slowly, feeling as if he'd been kicked in the gut by a mule. She watched him with eyes now dark with fear and, when he made no move toward her, hesitantly got to her feet and backed out of the room, still murmuring an explanation and apology. She took two steps back, then whirled and ran to her room, slamming the door behind her. He fancied he could even hear her turning the lock.

Everything he knew changed at that moment. The world ceased to be a place in which he was comfortable, where he knew who he was, and what it owed him. Instead of that familiar life, a new reality resolved itself, one where a lovely, vulnerable woman had been so mistreated that she had groveled before him at the slightest gesture of his hand.

He had a child who needed his love and care, and now … he looked at the closed door, imagining he could feel the waves of fear rolling out of her room. And now he had Kiera.

For the first time in Theo's life, he moved his own happiness, welfare, and desires out of their places of primary importance, and replaced them with those of a delicate, frightened woman and a baby who deserved a father.

He picked up Peter, suddenly needing to hold him, to feel the baby's warmth against his chest. He needed to feel like he wasn't the monster he'd seen reflected in Kiera's eyes. "What the hell did her ex do to her?" he asked Peter in a whisper. "What the ever-living hell did he do to her?"

The baby gurgled sleepily into his neck.

"And what am I going to do with you? How am I going to be as good a father as you deserve? I'm not Iakovos—I'm not sure I can do this."

Peter hiccuped, and the feeling of the baby dozing against him with such trust filled Theo with a sharp stab of love, followed immediately by the bone-deep determination to do whatever it took to give Peter a happy life. "I don't know how I'm going to do it, but I'm going to be the father you need. I'll get another assistant if I need to, although Lord knows Annemarie is almost superhuman in her ability to cope with things. So that's that, right? We'll do this together. Just take it easy on me for a bit until I get the hang of things, all right, old man?"

He thought then of Kiera in her room, clearly terrified of him, and a second resolve formed, this one deep in his belly, accompanied by a burn that made him feel suddenly invincible. He laid Peter down in the crib he'd had the hotel bring up, covering the baby with a blanket as he promised,

"We're going to make it right, Peter. Somehow, we have to show her that she can trust us, and then we're going to make things right with her. Because she needs us, and I'm starting to think we may need her, as well."

Theo sighed to himself as he called down to the front desk to ask if they had a printer he could use. Had it been only that morning when his life was uncomplicated and easy? He felt like that time was a million years past.

And yet, for the first time, he felt oddly satisfied with life. He had a goal—two goals—and by God, he was going to see them through. This time, he wouldn't mess up his life. There was too much riding on his success.

FIVE

"Pizza," I said, sitting on the bathroom floor, my back against the wall while I clutched my knees to my chest, trying desperately to keep from hyperventilating. "Coins. Some melons. CD-ROMs. Fists."

My stomach twisted at the last word. I tried desperately to calm the wild beating of my heart, the false item bothering me. I owed it to Swami Betelbaum to banish that, at least. "Not fists," I said, trying to erase from my mind the image of Theo's angry face. That beautiful face, made terrible by his anger.

And why shouldn't he be angry? It made perfect sense to me to verify that he was the man for which he'd given me references, but I knew to the very depths of my soul that he wouldn't see it that way. Men like him didn't like to be challenged. Or questioned.

My breath caught in my throat again, threatening to strangle me. "Globes. Yo-yos. Records. Potpies."

How could I be so stupid? I'd allowed myself to be lulled into a false sense of security with Theo just because he seemed so nice. So needy. And so grateful for my help with Peter.

"This is what you get for that level of idiocy," I said aloud, and with an effort got to my feet. I stared at myself in the mirror for a moment, not liking what I saw. "Swami Betelbaum would be disappointed," I told my reflection, then cracked open the bathroom door to peer out into my room.

I hated the fact I was such a coward that I couldn't just walk out into the room like a normal person, but that was well beyond my abilities at the moment.

The room was as I'd left it. Theo wasn't in it, storming and raging at me, nor was he pounding on the door, demanding I leave immediately, both of which I half expected. I sat on the bed for thirty minutes, just sitting and thinking, trying to make a plan, trying to come up with a way to explain to Theo what I'd been doing, but my mind refused to cooperate.

Too many nights spent without sleep. Too many days spent looking over my shoulder.

The best my scattered mind could come up with was to wait until I was sure Theo was asleep, and then slip out of the suite.

But where would I go?

"Hurn?" A noise caused my head to snap up, the startled exclamation a half snore. I must have been on the verge of dozing off despite sitting bolt upright on the end of the bed. My gaze moved to the door, staring with surprise at a white thing that fluttered and squirmed under the bottom of it.

It was a piece of paper. It wriggled and jerked, crumpling up a bit as a silver blade shoved it through.

Was that a table knife? Theo had a knife? Panic wanted to return, wanted to grip me in its breathless, heart-pounding grip, but the white, crumpled thing lying halfway under my door seemed so out of place, it drove me to stand up, instead. With a glance to make sure the door was still locked, I approached it silently, holding my breath in case he could hear me.

There was no noise. I examined the white thing. It appeared to be an envelope. With my fingers twitching a little, I gave it a tentative pull. It gave without much of an effort. I looked at it, turning it over. Scrawled on the front in a bold script was my name.

"Theo wrote me a letter?" I whispered aloud. "Is it a formal demand that I leave?"

I really didn't want to read it. I knew what I'd find there: slurs, angry words, condemnation, and finally a demand that I take myself off. He might even threaten to call the police on me. "Mercury. Venus. Earth. Mars."

Calling myself all sorts of names, I sat on the bed and tore open the envelope, several sheets of paper spilling out from it onto the blanket.

The first thing I picked up was some sort of a picture. I looked at it in surprise. It was a photocopy of a Greek driver's license issued to Theodor Christos Orien Papaioannou, with an address in Athens. The picture of Theo wasn't great, certainly not doing his handsome face any favors, but it was obviously him.

"What the ..." I looked at the next sheet. It was a printout from some sort of a financial company, giving a biography of him. The picture there was better, but his smile in it smacked of an awareness of himself that raised all sorts of warnings in my head.

A third sheet appeared to be a bank statement from a New Zealand bank. The account numbers had been blacked out, but the amounts were enough to make my eyebrows rise. At the top, someone had written in the same bold hand as the envelope, *Just in case you have concerns about my solvency.*

"So much for me offering to pay for my share of dinner," I said to myself before turning to the last page, the one that was filled with that unique handwriting.

Kiera, I'm more sorry than you can know that I frightened you. You have every right to make sure I am who I said I am, and it's my deep regret that I didn't think of that earlier. I'm enclosing a few printouts that I hope will reassure you that I'm not an ax murderer, or rapist, or cult leader determined to have you join my harem of twenty-two nubile wives, even though I would make you my prime wife, and would even dismiss the other twenty-two if you insisted.

I am happy to provide further proof of my identity if you would like it. You don't have to see me—you can just write on the back of this that you want more. Peter and I are going to sleep. My door will be closed, but not locked. I've left my wallet out on the table in the living room. You may go through it to your heart's content. Just in case you wonder about the pictures in it, the one of the woman is my sister, Elena, and the babies are my nieces and nephews. Thank you for taking care of Peter. He's in his crib with the chew toy, making adorable little sleepy noises.

I'm sorry. I'm really sorry.

Theo

I blinked back tears that pricked my eyes at the first few sentences, more than a little amazed that he wasn't furious with me, not even the littlest bit. He'd understood. And, what was more amazing, apologized. "Dammit, he's being nice, and I don't want that," I said, angrily wiping my eyes. "I can take everything but him being nice."

I read the note again, sniffing back the runny nose that always seemed to accompany tears. After thinking for a few minutes, I wrote on the back of the paper, *Don't let him sleep with the chew toy. He could choke on it.*

It took a few deep breaths, and a review of all the round brands of crackers that I could think of, but at last I unlocked the door and peeked out.

The living room was empty. Theo's wallet sat in solitary splendor on the table. I grabbed it and tiptoed to his door before kneeling and placing my note on the ground. The wallet sat on top, just in case Theo wouldn't see the note alone.

It took me a solid minute of psyching myself up to do it, but I tapped twice on his door, then raced back across the living room to the safety of my own bedroom, closing the door and locking it before eyeing my suitcase. I'd left it packed, so it was ready for me to sneak out in the middle of the night, but now …

I sat on the bed again and touched the page with Theo's driver's license. "I much prefer this picture, where you're delightfully tousled and informal, over the suited, well-groomed you in the financial report."

Silence filled my room for another ten minutes; then I made a decision.

"I'll stay," I said, feeling suddenly very brave. Swami Betelbaum would be proud of me, I thought when I nodded to myself, just as if he could see me connecting with another human being. Swami Betelbaum was very big on connections with others. "Theo apologized. He wasn't angry after all, and he was sorry for misunderstanding what I did. That's a good sign. That's a sign that he doesn't think he's always right, and can't ever be wrong." I sat for another minute before I said the words that I'd never thought to speak again. "I trust him."

But for how long? an inner voice asked.

I ignored it, not wanting to let it taint this strange new feeling of being in control, and climbed into bed fully clothed. I knew most people found it odd to go to bed ready to leap up and dash away at a second's notice, but I'd found it reassuring to know that if I had to run from Misha in the middle of the night, I would be ready to do so.

"Twenty-two nubile wives." I snorted, thinking about Theo's note while looking at the light from the city that snuck in through the curtains and flickered on the ceiling. "In your dreams, Theo."

Portentous words, as it turned out.

It started just as it always did when I was exhausted: a vaguely unpleasant dream, one with random images that flitted across my mind's eye, morphing and changing, before it settled into a replay of the scene in Wellington. The whoosh of the air-conditioning in Misha's apartment provided background white noise, above which he screamed at me, punctuated by the sounds of breaking glass while he raged, destroying anything that came within his reach.

The dream me cowered before him, trying to understand why he was so angry, my question about that receiving a backhand in response that knocked me backward into the wall. Before I could shake the stars from my head, he was on me, one hand around my neck, throttling me as he shoved his face in mine, spittle flying when he told me in exquisite detail what he would do to me if I dared ever betray him.

The fear that swamped me in the dream was awful, but it was nothing compared with what I had felt at the time: fear and the sick knowledge that there was no way to break free from Misha. He had too many friends, too many people who owed him favors.

The dream shifted to me snatching up my few precious possessions—a couple of books, clothing, the tiny Zen garden rocks I used because they were round—all of that went into a duffel bag. There was no sense of the futility, the hopelessness, that I'd felt when I crept out of the apartment, praying I'd be a long way away before Misha found me gone, but I'd felt it at the time. And I had felt it two weeks later, after my time at a shelter for battered women had come to an end. I still felt dregs of it even now.

A shadow fell across me, and in my dream I knew—I knew without a shred of doubt—that Misha had found me. He was going to cut me up the way he'd promised if I ever left him, and a scream rose within me, one filled with the knowledge that I had failed to escape after all. He had found me, and now I would pay the price.

I thought at first the pounding was the blood in my ears, but suddenly I was awake, blinking and looking wildly around the room. It was empty.

"Kiera? Dammit, open the door!" The pounding sounded again over Theo's muffled voice. I rubbed my face.

"What? What's wrong?" I called at the same moment that a horrible fear gripped me, one that was every bit as terrifying as that in my dream.

Without thinking, I ran to the door, twisting the lock before jerking it open. "Is it Peter? Is he all right? Dammit, I told you to take his chew toy away from him while he was sleeping!"

Theo stood before me, one hand raised to pound on the door. I flinched and took an instinctive step back at the sight of the raised hand, but for once my panic was directed outward. I pushed past him and ran to his room, my heart beating a frantic tattoo as I stood next to the crib, panting slightly.

Peter lay on his back, one little fist next to his face, sound asleep. I searched the crib, but didn't see the chew toy. "What's wrong with him?" I asked in a quiet voice, lifting the light blanket to make sure that his little chubby legs weren't twisted. He looked perfectly fine.

"Nothing that I know of. Should there be?" Theo's face was a study of worry as he twitched back the blanket I'd dislodged in my search. "I put him on his back. I thought that's what I was supposed to do?"

"You are. Jeezumcrow, why did you scare me like that?" I couldn't help but gently stroke Peter's black hair, now straight, but showing signs that it might curl.

"I scared *you*?" He looked outraged, speaking in a gritty whisper. "You almost gave me a heart attack screaming. I thought someone was killing you."

In an instant, two things occurred to me: Theo was stark naked, and I had been dreaming again.

"I ... I ..." I had a hard time dragging my gaze from the expanse of bare chest that stood before me. I'd seen men's chests before, but Theo's went beyond nice straight into the realm of gorgeous. He was muscled, but not obscenely so, his chest hair softening the definition somewhat, but not so much that it obscured any of the lovely curves and valleys. I had the worst urge to reach out and put my hand in the middle of his chest, allowing my fingers to tease the soft black curls. I swallowed back what seemed like a gallon of saliva, trying to get a hold of my wits. "I dream sometimes."

"Only sometimes?" One corner of his mouth quirked. I didn't know if it was because he caught me ogling his chest, or if something else about me amused him. "I dream all the time."

I took a step back, looking anywhere but at the glorious masculinity that stood before me, taunting me, begging me to touch him, and making my body suddenly come to life with a demand that I apply it to Theo's body immediately, if not sooner. I made an effort to gather my thoughts, my pride insisting that I act like the most amazingly handsome man I'd ever seen wasn't standing before me, absolutely uncaring that he was as bare as the day he was born. "You don't want to have the sorts of dreams I get. Shouldn't you ..." I made a vague gesture toward an opened suitcase that sat on a rack.

"Shouldn't I what?" He didn't approach me, but he didn't have to. I could feel him pushing all his male nudity on me. And suddenly, that incensed me. How dare he stand there being comfortable with the fact that he was so gorgeous, it just about made my tongue cleave to the roof of my mouth? He probably did it on purpose. He probably got naked every chance he could just so that he could make women stand there with their tongues cleaved, unable to look away from that glorious chest. And arms. He had very nice arms, not veiny and overly hairy, but solid. Muscled. The sort of arms that you wanted on a man. And his hands—I had to stop thinking about that, knowing full well I had a weakness for men's hands.

"Kiera?"

"Hmm?" He was looking at me like I was the one standing there being outrageous.

"What should I do?"

And his thighs. My gaze skittered over his penis, thankfully not in an aggressive state, and allowed myself to take in the sight of long thigh muscles. I *loved* men's thighs. And there was Theo flaunting his thighs at me.

"Fine. I'll wait until you're done. If you're finished with my chest, can I cross my arms?"

Anger grew in me, a protective sort of anger intended to guard me from what my body wanted. And because my lust had led me astray before, I encouraged the anger, cherished it, fanned its flames higher, because if I wasn't angry, then I'd just stand there and stare at the man, all but drooling on him.

And that was what he wanted, the sexy-chested, nice-armed, molestable-thighed bastard.

"Should I turn around? I'm told my ass is nice."

"Yes," I said without thinking. I had to keep my anger hot. It was important that I do that... The thought dried up on my brain when Theo turned around, allowing my gaze to sweep upward from nice calves to the backs of those thighs that I suddenly wanted to lick, only to have my eyes stagger to a halt on his behind.

Holy Mary, Mother of God, I was in trouble. My jaw sagged a little at the sight of that behind. The glimpse I had before was nice, but this ... my brain had a field day admiring it. It was lighter than the rest of him, with lovely swoops and curves that called to my hands. I swore to myself, my hands positively itching to hold the sweet, sweet line of his butt cheeks. More than a little dazzled, I let my gaze start at the top and run downward, just to see if I'd mistaken the beauty of his behind.

The muscles of his broad shoulders tapered down to his waist, and on down to his butt. No, I thought to myself, doing a little mental headshake, I wasn't mistaken. His behind was glorious. I wanted badly to kiss the two little dimples that sat above it. Hell, I wanted to kiss all of him, front and back.

"Is that enough? I hope so, because it's a bit boring just looking at the wall." He turned back around, but must have noticed the stunned expression on my face, because he reached out a hand as he stepped forward.

Instinct had me backing up until I bumped into a chair.

He stopped, lowering his hand, the playful expression that had lit his eyes with mirth fading. He studied my face for a moment, then strolled over to the suitcase and donned a pair of jeans. He turned back to me, asking, "Better?"

I nodded, feeling like there wasn't nearly enough air in the room.

"Can I come closer to you? It's hard to whisper across the length of the room."

A little warmth grew in my belly. He was asking permission to come near me? I shook my head at the idea. No man had ever asked me what I wanted.

"All right, I'll stay here," he said, obviously misinterpreting the gesture.

"No, that headshake was for me," I told him, and, calling myself a coward, moved forward until I was about a foot away from him. "No one has ever asked me if they could approach me. I'm not ... I'm not some weird germophobe, Theo."

"No, but I did frighten you earlier." He lifted his hand, slowly, and I knew he'd made the movement deliberate so as not to scare me again. His fingers brushed a strand of hair off where it was stuck on my lip. "If I promised you right now that I will never hurt you, would you believe me?"

I didn't answer. He was making such an effort to be nice, to not frighten me, that I didn't want to answer that kindness with the truth.

"I didn't think so." His thumb brushed my bottom lip for a brief second. "Regardless, I swear to you that I will never raise my hand to you in anger. I hope that someday you will believe that."

I sighed, wishing that was true, but having heard too many similar promises from Misha to believe it. "I appreciate that," I said at last, feeling I had to make some acknowledgment of his promise.

"Do you want to tell me about the dream?" he asked, allowing his hand to slide down to my arm. He frowned as he looked at it. "Do you ... er ... this may not be any of my business, but do you always sleep fully clothed?"

"Yes." I made a vague gesture. "If you sleep like this, all you have to do is put your shoes on and you're ready to go."

"Go where?"

I met his gaze, then let it drop. Unfortunately, it fell right to his chest. "Wherever you have to go."

"Kiera."

I glanced up at his eyes again, marveling at just how handsome he was. He had a long, thin nose; a jaw, now shadowed with stubble, that was angled in such a way that made my stomach feel hot; a chin that had the barest hint of a cleft in it, which I wanted badly to nibble on; and dark blue eyes that were almost navy in color. My tongue returned to cleave-mode at the sight of the black stubble, my fingers damn near tingling with the need to touch his face. There was something about his upper lip, the way it pressed into the lower one, that seemed to hold an unholy fascination for me. Men's lips weren't supposed to be that delicious looking, were they?

Dammit, he was deliberately being sexy again, even with his pants on.

"I'm going to touch you, Kiera. I'm going to put my arms around you. I'm going to hug you. Nothing more. All right?"

I tried to fan my anger again, feeling it was far preferable to the lustful thoughts that were filling my head at the sight of him, but that all failed when Theo closed the distance between us, his movements deliberate as he put his arms around me, gently pulling me to his chest, his hands on my back in an impersonal way that nonetheless sent a little skitter of heat down my spine and straight to my hidden parts, pooling there in a way that made me highly aware of them.

"Why?" I asked, unable to keep from breathing in his scent. It was a combination of tangy lemon and something woodsy, like cedar.

"I couldn't help myself," he said. "Mind you, I badly want to hug you in a manner that would have you looking at my chest like you did a few minutes ago, but since that sort of hug would be of a sexual nature, and I can see you don't want any of that—"

"I don't?" someone said, and after a moment, I realized the voice came from my mouth. Dammit, I hadn't authorized it to say that, and yet, I was lying if I tried to deny it.

Swami Betelbaum had a whole lot of things to say about

people who lied to themselves, and none of it was complimentary.

Theo froze in the middle of the impersonal hug. "You didn't like me naked."

"Oh, I liked you naked," I admitted, assessing what was going on, more than a little amazed by the circumstance. There I was in the arms of a man, the arms of a half-naked man, one I had just met, and rather than feeling vaguely nauseous, my whole body was trying hard to get me to press it up against Theo. "But you knew that. You were deliberately being naked at me, with all those muscles, and the chest, and the hands, and not a ton of body hair, which I'd expected because you're Greek, and I thought all Greek men were, you know, hirsute, but you aren't overly hairy, which I think you were *also* doing deliberately just so I'd notice."

"My mother was English," he said, his voice sounding odd. He released me to step back, amusement dancing in those pretty dark blue eyes. "That helps with the need to wax everything off. As for being deliberately naked at you—I don't know what to say. I told you I wasn't shy."

"Well, as to that, if I had a body like yours, I wouldn't be shy either," I said.

"If you had a body like mine, I wouldn't even now be fantasizing about kissing you," he answered, and I couldn't help but smile a little.

"What … uh …" I cleared my throat, feeling all shades of awkward even though I tried to adopt a nonchalant pose. "What are you doing in the fantasy?"

"Kiera Taylor," he said in a faux-shocked voice, his eyes wide. "Are you flirting with me? A man who was a few minutes ago naked in your presence?"

I felt a giggle rise in me. "I'm not a sexless freak, you know. I just don't like …"

"Men who are pretty, have big bodies and sizable cocks, not that mine is unnaturally huge or anything. Not porn-star big. Just a normal size, one suitable for the job at hand. So to speak."

"I don't know about that," I said, my gaze dropping to the front of his jeans. "It seemed pretty beefy to me."

"I want badly to both leer at you and adopt a modest mien, but since I suspect you wouldn't see either in this dim light, I will simply tell you that in my kissing fantasy I have my hands on your hips, and am teasing you into opening your mouth to me by kissing along your sweet, delectable lips, nipping that plump lower lip that I badly want to taste, after which, with a sigh of pleasure, you open up to me, allowing me into your sweetness."

I stared at him, the images he was evoking dancing enticingly in my mind, my tongue having cleaved once again to the roof of my mouth. I tried to be angry about that, but couldn't. "That's … that's a pretty specific fantasy. What am I doing in it?"

"Ah, now, your participation is very important," he said, his voice grave, but his eyes full of warmth and amusement. It was an oddly arousing expression, and I couldn't help but take a step closer to him. "I would like to say that you ripped off my clothes and demanded to have your wanton way with me, but you were not so easily swayed by my charms. Instead, you chose to toy with me by putting your hands on my ass, lightly dragging your nails up and down my spine."

A little tremor shook me at the thought of my hands on that ass. "Do I bite you anywhere?"

One of his glossy black eyebrows rose. "Do you want to?"

"Yes," I answered without thinking. My eyes went to the cords in his neck. "There's a spot … it just struck me that it might be nice to bite … not that I'm a vampire or anything … but that spot on your neck is kind of … interesting."

"Then you may bite it," he said after a moment. I couldn't help but notice that his hands were fisted. "I will happily yield my neck to you. Er … was there anything else you wanted to do in my fantasy?"

"Your chest," I said, my body demanding that I walk it over and rub it against him. In fact, before I realized I was doing it, I moved forward again. What the hell was this madness? I never felt instant attractions for men, certainly not after the experience of Mikhail, but Theo was … different.

No man is different. They're all the same underneath, the voice in my head said.

"What about it?"Theo's voice went rough about the edges. "Do you touch it in my fantasy?"

"Oh, yes," I breathed, taking another step, leaving me so close to him that my breasts touched his chest with every breath I took in. "I would definitely be spreading my fingers across it, touching all those lovely thick muscles, and kissing your nipples."

"My nipples would like that," he said, his voice outright husky now. His fingers spread wide, then twitched, but he kept his arms at his sides, and for that, I was profoundly grateful.

Men who looked like him, the ones who probably had to pry women off them with a spatula, were not known for their restraint. They were arrogant, assuming they had the right to do whatever they wanted without first asking. And yet here was Theo, making an effort to keep himself in check.

Because he knew I'd been frightened. A little piece of ice that had built up around my heart cracked, and broke off.

I cleared my throat again. "And then there's your belly."

His stomach contracted. "What do you want to do to it? Please tell me it involves your tongue. And your breasts. Both, possibly at the same time if you are especially flexible."

"I'm not particularly so, although I'm fast."

He blinked at me.

I gave a little laugh. "I didn't mean that the way it sounded. Theo?"

"Yes?"

"I'd like to kiss you." I swallowed hard when the words left my lips, but I felt strongly that I had to find an outlet for all the feelings he had stirred in me with just a few words. I had to know if he was a man I could trust, and that meant I had to leave myself vulnerable to him.

Just a little. Just to see what he did with it.

"Kissing you has been on the top of the list of things I've wanted to do for a long time."

"We met this morning," I pointed out.

"An eon ago," he agreed, and reached for me.

I froze for a moment, but allowed him to pull me until I swayed into him, my mind overcome with the sensation of that delicious hard body pressed against my own. I'd never been one to feel overly feminine, but the way my body molded to his made me appreciate the softness that was inherent in women. "I want to kiss you," I repeated, a warning note in my voice.

His eyes were on my mouth.

"That is, I don't want you to kiss me. Well, not at first. Does that make sense?"

"No," he said quickly, but the corners of his lips quirked. "Don't let that stop you, though. Can I leave my hands on your hips?"

"Yes," I said, tilting my head up. I was a tall woman, but Theo was taller than me by about five inches, not so much that I couldn't stand on tiptoes and kiss him, but enough of a difference that it made me feel even more feminine. My lips brushed his in the lightest of touches.

"Would you mind if I touched your breasts, too?" he inquired as I kissed first one corner of his mouth, then another.

I thought about it for a moment, testing to see if that made me feel panicky.

My breasts certainly were go for Theo's hands. They all but clamored to be placed into them, and the sooner the better. "All right," I said.

I continued feathering little kisses across his mouth. His lips were relaxed, parted ever so slightly, leaving me feeling hot and restless. "How do you feel about tongues?" I asked, shifting my hips so that the aching part of me was pressed tighter against him.

"I approve of them in both utilitarian and sexual use," he answered, his lips touching mine as he spoke. His hands, which had been resting on the curve of my hips, moved, his fingers spreading when they slid upward. His thumbs brushed the undersides of breasts that were suddenly far too sensitive for my peace of mind.

"OK. I'm going in," I said, my hands on his shoulders as I leaned even harder into him, my tongue teasing the space between his lips.

I made tentative little dabs into the warmth of his mouth, the act intimate, but it felt right. *He* felt right.

Until he gets angry, and then he will use your attraction to him to punish you, the dark voice spoke in my head.

"You won't try to boss my mouth around?" I asked, the voice in my head stirring a tendril of doubt that was making the pleasure I experienced fade a little.

"I will do whatever you want me to do," he said. "And not that I'm not enjoying this to the utmost, which I am, even though you may well just kill me if you tease me anymore as you did with that last pass, but I would like to point out that if at any time you'd like me to take over, I will be happy to do so."

I nipped his bottom lip, my hands sweeping down his sides, the muscles underneath the silky flesh lying in thick bands. I wanted badly to grab his butt with both hands, but I reminded myself that not only had I just met him that day; I would much prefer to have the butt naked before I groped it. "All right, I'll let you take over, but I reserve the right to have you stop at any time."

"I agree to your terms," he said in a no-nonsense manner, and slowly moved his hands up over my breasts until he cupped my face, angling my head slightly to one side. His lips were gentle on mine, but more persistent than I had been with him. He teased, he nipped, he sucked my lower lip into his mouth until I moaned, and moved against him again, feeling the growing length of him on my pelvic bone. Then he was inside my mouth, his tongue sweeping in, but it was an invasion my entire body welcomed, my fingers digging into his shoulders with the pleasure of it all.

"I've never—Lord, your chest—I've never been one for French-kissing," I said when we came up for breath. "Tongues are … you know, slimy … but this is …"

"Good?" he asked, smiling down at me.

"Very."

"I'm happy to hear that. Can I suggest we sit on the bed and continue?"

My gaze swiveled to the bed, assessing my feelings. "I'm not going to have sex with you, if that's what you're thinking."

"I wouldn't presume," he answered, gently tugging me as he backed up to the bed. "Remember when I swore I wouldn't ever strike you? You can add to that my solemn promise that I will never force you to do anything you don't want to do."

I wanted to believe him, oh, how I wanted to believe. But I'd been fooled before, with dire consequences. Still, I trusted my ability to escape should he lose control, and allowed him to pull me down onto his lap. He kissed me again, his hands sliding under my T-shirt, the long, blunt fingers seeming to be made of fire when they stroked and teased my breasts.

"Kiera," he said, the word almost a moan as he cupped both of my breasts, his mouth hot and suddenly very demanding on mine. "If you knew what you do to me. What your breasts do to me. And your hips. And legs. You have very long legs. I want very much to show you the pleasure we could have together with your hips and breasts and your legs wrapped around me."

I gave in to the desire that I had tried to fight for what seemed like such a very long time, and nuzzled his neck before gently biting on that tendon that sang a sweet siren song to me.

Beneath me, he froze; then suddenly, I was on my back, and he loomed over me. My breath caught in my throat, but it wasn't panic that flooded my brain—it was sexual need, a desire so strong, it overwhelmed me, almost making me shake with want.

"That, my tempting little gazelle, is not playing fair. Let's see how you like this."

He pushed up my shirt, revealing my breasts. He paused, glancing up. "Bra on or off?"

Off, my body shrieked at me even as my back arched. *Off, off, off!*

"On," I said, knowing I had to have some control of my desires.

He nodded, then dipped his head down, his hands on the undersides of my breasts, his breath steaming the valley between them. I moaned softly as he nuzzled, he kissed, he rubbed them with stubbly cheeks, the sensation both soft and extremely arousing, and by the time his tongue got into the action, I knew I had to stop him or I really would end up fulfilling his fantasy of ripping off all his clothes and having my way with him.

Slowly, very slowly, I slid out from underneath him. My breath was ragged, my body one giant erogenous zone that yelled rude words at me for removing it from Theo. "Thank you," I said, trying to keep my voice steady.

"For kissing you?" he asked, rolling over so that he leaned back on one arm.

I would not look at the bulge in his jeans. I absolutely would not look at it.

I looked. "Jeezumcrow, Theo, it looks like you have a bulldog stuffed down your pants. Doesn't that hurt?"

He looked down in surprise, then up to me, his laughter filling me with a sense of joy that I hadn't experienced in a very long time. "It hurts like hell right now, but there's not much *I* can do about it."

I froze for a second, wondering if he was trying a passive-aggressive maneuver to make me indulge in oral sex.

He sighed, then stood up, his hands on my arms. "It doesn't hurt, not in the sense you mean, but I'm not going to apologize for an erection that was honestly earned. You're a very desirable woman, Kiera. I will never force myself on you, but if you're upset by seeing the fact that I very much want to get you into my bed, then I will apologize, and do my best to sit with a pillow on my lap. Or a blanket. Or Peter, although the way he bounces, that might not be the most comfortable of erection shields."

"I'm not offended. If I was someone else, I'd be on you like honey on a stick, but I have some issues with trust."

"I understand," he said, and I had an odd feeling he did. Perhaps it was because he'd made mistakes in his past, too.

I started to leave, biting my lip when I thought of the room that waited for me. One filled with nightmares and sorrow, a lonely, cold, empty room. What I wanted to ask was insane. I should never in a million years consider it. And yet, I had put myself in his hands, and he stopped without a word of complaint when he obviously wanted more from me. He had respected those boundaries. "Would you mind if I slept in here? In the other bed? I ... I don't get the nightmares when someone is around. I was in a few different women's shelters, and I never had them there."

He peeled back the blankets on the other bed and gestured to it before turning back to his own, and dropping his pants. "Be my guest, but be warned, my brother tells me I snore. It's the basest lie, of course, but just in case you hear a noise that in anyone else might be considered a snore, you needn't be worried."

I giggled, checked on Peter, then climbed into the bed fully clothed. He opened his mouth like he was going to comment on that, then shook his head and got into his own bed.

It was nice, I decided a half hour later. Peter occasionally made little snorts in his sleep, rustling as he moved. Theo was silent in his bed, and at one point, when I looked over, I could see him lying on his back, his hands behind his head as he stared up at the ceiling. I wondered what he was thinking, decided that was not a suitable thing for contemplation, and rolled over.

An hour later, I was still awake, my body humming like electricity was flowing through it, feeling itchy and restless and unhappy. Theo must have fallen asleep, because he was completely quiet. It looked like he was sleeping on his belly. I turned again, punching my pillow before flipping it over to a cool side.

No, I told my inner voice. *No, we are not going to do that. It was bad enough that we asked to be here.*

My inner voice pointed out yet again Swami Betelbaum's dictates on the importance of being honest with oneself.

Fine, I snarled, and got out of bed, whispering, "Theo? Are you awake?"

"Yes."

"I'm … I feel … oh, hell. Can I sleep with you?"

I could feel the surprise in the silence that followed. "I'd be delighted," he said finally, his voice sounding choked. He rolled over onto his side, so he was facing me.

"Thank you," I said, and, grabbing my pillow and the sheet from my bed, settled myself on top of his blankets, wrapping myself in my sheet, carefully nudging one of his pillows aside to make room for mine. I turned my back to him, and wriggled backward until I could feel the pressure of his body. Then I sighed in relief, pulled the sheet up under my chin so that I was more or less burritoed into it, and promptly fell asleep.

SIX

Theo was in hell. Not only did Kiera dash his hopes when her idea of sleeping with him turned out to be just that, but at some point during the night, she must have extricated herself from the cocoon of sheet that she'd used to keep her luscious body from its rightful place next to him, and was now splayed across his chest, one of her legs pressed between his. Her mouth was open a little, her breath warm on his collarbone.

He wanted badly to strip off the leggings and T-shirt she wore, so that he could stroke all that glorious flesh that he knew lurked beneath, but he'd made a solemn promise to himself that he would not do anything to frighten her. It had almost killed him when she insisted on torturing him with shy little kisses, but it was a hundred times worse when she allowed him to take control.

The fire she stirred in him was almost enough to scorch the sheets. He slid a hand down her back, and under her T-shirt, his mind moaning with the feeling of her warm, satiny flesh.

"Mmrf?" she murmured into his collarbone, then stiffened. His hand stilled, but he left it where it lay on her bare back, waiting to see how she would react to their intimate position. She lifted her head and squinted at him through the curtain of dark hair. "Theo?"

"Right here."

She looked down at his chest, and he felt her breath catch. She pushed back a bit, but it wasn't to peel herself off him as he thought she would. Instead, she spread her fingers across a pectoral. "So very warm. I want to ... I think I want ..."

She bit her lip, clearly too shy to put into words just what it was that she wanted.

"You may touch whatever you want to touch," he told her, hardly daring to breathe lest he scare off his little gazelle. "With your hands, mouth, or any other body part."

She blinked at him, her blue-green eyes so serious. He liked them much better when she was laughing, or giggling while he teased her. "Oh. Well. Am I crushing you?"

"Not in the least. Do you mind if I touch you, as well?"

She thought about that for a minute. "I think that would be nice."

"Good." He wanted to strip her bare so he could have access to all of her, but contented himself to appreciate what she was willing to give. She bent her head and kissed the middle of his chest, her hands making long stroking motions that ran from his collarbone down to where the sheet covered his belly.

"I've never met anyone who has such a nice chest," she said, kissing one of his nipples. "You have an actual six-pack, Theo. I've never known a man with an actual, bona fide six-pack."

"And I suffered like hell for it," he said, laughing, trying to unhook her bra with just one hand, but unable to do more than make awkward tugs at it. "When Jake made that top ten bachelor list, I figured I would give him a run for his money. We shared a personal trainer, but she was half in love with him and made me work like a dog four hours a day, while she allowed him to swim laps for half an hour."

"You put me in a really difficult situation, here," she said, letting her fingers trail down his belly, pushing the sheet a bit until it was on his pelvic bone. "I suspect you have way too much regard for yourself already, and yet, I really do want to tell you just how nice your chest and stomach are."

"If I let you get by without complimenting me on that, will you let me take your bra off?"

"No," she said, and he gave a mental sigh, pulling his hand from where it was still trying to manipulate the damned hooks. She smiled, and to his utter surprise—and complete joy—she pulled her T-shirt over her head and, with a deft move, took her bra off, as well. "But since you've been so nice as to let me touch your chest, I think it's only fair you get to do the same."

"Oh, thank you," he said, possessing himself immediately of her breasts. They weren't too large, not surprising given that the rest of her was finely made, tall but willowy. "You have just made my day. Possibly my week."

She laughed, the sound deep and throaty, one that went straight to his groin. He pulled her down over him so that he had access to those tempting, satiny breasts, enjoying her gasp when he took one delicious nipple in his mouth, swirling his tongue over the taut tip. The taste and heat and feel of her filled his mind, making him crave more. She groaned and arched, her hands clutching the sheet. "Glorioski! Do the other one!" He obliged, his body tensing with the sensation of her.

He wanted badly to make love to her, but he would let her set the pace. If she wasn't ready for it, then he'd wait. Even if it killed him.

One part of his mind idly wondered where the plan to give her the boot had gone. He told that part to go screw itself, then, unable to keep from touching her, slid his hands down to the waistband of her leggings.

"May I?" he asked, hoping she didn't hear the heavy throb of need in his voice. He didn't want her to think he was an animal, unable to control his base desires, and yet, just the taste of her breasts made him want to plunge deep into her depths and claim her as his own.

She panted a little as she looked down, then got to her feet right there on the bed, pulling up first one leg, then the other as she divested herself of the tight black cloth.

He couldn't help himself—he flat out ogled her legs, from the tips of narrow, long feet up to sturdy ankles, calves that curved out in a flare that reminded him of her hips, on up to her thighs, her satiny, enticing thighs that he wanted to bury his face in. He traced a line up both legs, from ankles to the backs of her knees.

She hesitated, still standing over him; then suddenly with an annoyed noise at herself, she removed her underwear. His eyes widened at the gesture. Was she signaling what he thought she was signaling? Any other woman stripping herself buck naked would tell him exactly what she had planned, but with Kiera, it could simply mean she was testing him, making sure she could trust him. He hadn't missed the calculating glances she had slid his way earlier, and knew that her trust issues extended to lovemaking.

"Why are you goggling at me like that?" she asked, her hands on her hips. That just made him look at her hips and admire the flare of them, their sweet curves making him hard enough to hew marble. "Is it my pubic area? I don't wax down there because it hurts like a motherfussing pus bag, but I do trim when things get unruly." She bent over to look at her pubic mound. "I didn't think it was time to prune again, but if it offends you—"

"Gods of all the pantheon, Judeo-Christian, and Islamic worlds, no!" he said, his body tighter and harder than he ever remembered being when she dropped down to her knees, straddling his hips. She reached behind and twitched the sheet off the lower half of his body, her eyes on his as she leaned forward and kissed first one, then another nipple before nibbling a path upward to his mouth.

"Make love to me, Theo," she whispered.

Words choked in his throat. He wanted to thank her, to get on his knees and promise her anything, but instead, he did a quick mental calculation.

"Shall we do it this way?" he asked, pulling his knees up a bit, his hands full of her breasts.

She pursed her lips. "Are you letting me be in charge because you know I'm a bit skittish when it comes to men, or is this your favorite position?"

"Both. Neither. What was the question?" His cock positively ached with the need to embrace her heat, but he let her take the lead.

"What about foreplay?"

"What about it?" he asked, more than a little desperate. He wondered if it would be unseemly to beg her to take pity on him and impale herself on his cock.

"Do we need it?" She looked down at his penis. "Did we already do it? I'm ready to go if you are."

"I can honestly say that I was ready yesterday," he answered, sending up fervent little prayers that he'd survive the experience of Kiera making love to him long enough to give her pleasure.

She giggled and, positioning him, started to sink down.

He groaned as the tip of him slipped into her, but she paused, asking, "Oh. Do you have any … er … illnesses? I have a birth control implant, but I suppose we should be adult and address that."

"No diseases, venereal or otherwise. I am allergic to penicillin, though."

She smiled, giving her hips a little wiggle as she continued to descend upon him. "I'll remember that should you come down with pneumonia. Theo, this is very … is there an end to you? You seem to go on and on, and yet you promised me you weren't porn-star big."

"Almost there," he gasped, his hands sliding down her hips to her thighs. "Dear God, woman, stop doing that swivel or it will be all over! No, not that one—that one is—nrng—it's the other one I object to. Yes, that one. Stop doing that this instant. Do it just once again, and then stop it."

She giggled again, and did both a left and right swivel as she moved up and down on him.

His eyes crossed, his hands convulsively clutching the sheet beneath them, expending every last iota of energy he possessed to keep from moving his hips. He knew he would never be able to stand the sensations if he were to thrust into her, filling her, taking her gasps into his mouth. He just had to lie there dormant, and think of horrible things to distract himself from the tight, velvety grip that moved upon him and left him on the verge of a climax.

"This is so very nice," she murmured, leaning down to kiss him. "I didn't know you would feel like this inside me. You are so very there." She moved with a little faster rhythm.

Theo was quite sure he would die with the pleasure, and then she leaned down and gently bit his nipple. The streak of pure sexual pleasure that made his chest burn was too much for him.

"Is there a reason you aren't helping?"

He opened his eyes, desperation filling his voice. "You don't mind if I move?"

"Of course not. It's much better when you get in on the—THEO!"

He flipped her over without dislodging himself, her legs draped over his arms as he growled into her mouth. "You didn't say I could move! I was trying to be a considerate lover! It was your job to tell me that I could—oh, God, don't tighten like that."

"Kegels," she said, her breath as tortured as his own. She dragged her nails up his back, and matched his thrusts, biting the cord in his neck. "Now, Theo, now!"

"Thank God, I didn't think I could last much longer," he said, panting in between each word. He tried a couple of swivels of his own, but it was an effort that he knew he wouldn't fully get to explore. She quivered beneath him, her body tightening in ripples that just about made him see stars as he gave in to his own climax.

It seemed to take forever before he could catch his breath, his mind stuck in a postorgasmic haze that consisted only of Kiera and his exhausted wreck of a body.

"That was pretty damned amazing," Kiera said when he rallied enough strength to roll off her. He didn't think at first he'd be able to, since his muscles all seemed to have turned to wet noodles, but he was a gentleman, and gentlemen didn't crush their lovers into the bed just because said lovers had wrung them like a wet towel.

"You can talk?" he asked, glaring at her. "Why can you talk and I'm almost dead? I don't have any muscles left, and my brain shut down when you damn near squeezed my cock off—please continue doing the Kegels, by the way—and you can talk? Women!"

She giggled, lifting a hand as if she was going to stroke him, but it fell languidly to the bed. "I'm pretty boneless myself."

With a great effort, he managed to roll over onto his side and look at her. Her eyes were closed, but there was a little smile that sat on the corners of her lips. He knew he shouldn't ask, but his curiosity got the better of him. He picked his words carefully nonetheless. "Would it insult you if I asked what made you change your mind?"

She opened her eyes and looked at him, confused for a moment before she realized what he was asking. A little blush flooded her cheeks under the freckles, delighting him. "Oh. Well, Swami Betelbaum is very big on not lying to yourself. And after you were so … understanding … earlier by stopping when I wanted you to stop, I realized that I was lying to myself if I didn't admit that I really did want to keep going. So, I decided if you were still interested, then I'd go ahead and let my libido romp all over you."

"I like your libido," he said, moving his hand to her arm, then up to her face to brush back a loose strand of hair. "It can feel free to romp on me any time it wants."

She looked at him silently for a moment, the laughter in her eyes dying. "Theo, I want to tell you something. It's hard, but … well, this kind of makes us close, and I don't have anyone else to tell. I get so tired of going around and around with it in my own brain. Maybe you can see something I can't see."

He raised his eyebrows, wondering if she was going to tell him about the warrant.

"You probably guessed this, but my relationship with my ex wasn't good." Her eyes were shadowed with pain.

"I assume by the way you reacted last night that he was abusive."

Her gaze skittered away, and she scooted over, pulling up the sheet she'd brought over from the other bed, wrapping it around herself. "Yes. He almost killed me one day when he caught me using his computer. It took me a couple of days to recover, and when I did, I knew I had to get out or the next time, he'd shut me up for good."

"Ah?" Theo was filled with a fury that made him want to fight. He knew from the years of therapy that he didn't have to give in to his desires, and thus, instead he acknowledged the feelings, gave them a long, hard look, and admitted to himself that he badly wanted to find and beat this man who had mistreated his delicate gazelle.

"I didn't take anything of his, only my stuff, some books, and my clothes, and a couple of little knickknacks that only have meaning to me. But he went to the police and told them I took his computer. They sent a letter to the women's shelter where I went that I was to report to the station and turn myself in. I didn't."

"Why not?"

"Misha has friends there," she said bleakly.

"Misha being … ?"

"Mikhail, my ex. Misha is the diminutive of that name. I'm pretty certain that it was his police friends who helped him track me to the last two apartments I rented."

"Dirty cops?" Theo asked, his sense of outrage growing even greater, which was a miracle considering he was already so furious he wanted to pound this Mikhail into a pulp.

"Yes."

"Then I don't blame you for not turning yourself in," he said, stroking the bare arm nearest him, mentally drafting the conversation he would have with his attorney.

"That was in Wellington. I managed to get out of there without him finding me, but I had to use my bank card here in Auckland, and I think he followed me. He's ... there's no other word for it than hunting me. I don't know why, other than he wants to punish me for leaving him, but he almost caught me before I left Wellington, and he swore to kill me if I didn't give him back what I'd stolen."

"You said you didn't take his computer."

"I didn't." She knelt next to him, her hand on his arm. "All I took were my things. Just what would fit in my duffel bag. I double-checked it to make sure I didn't have anything that was his by mistake, but it's just my clothes, a couple of paperback books, a hairbrush that was my grandmother's, and a desk Zen garden that Swami Betelbaum recommended. I didn't even take my phone, because Misha paid for it."

"Have you talked to an attorney?" he asked, wondering if he oughtn't bring in a second lawyer to deal with her situation. If he had his personal lawyer working on the custody agreement for Peter, he could get a second one going on Kiera's case.

"Yes. The women's shelter set me up with a pro bono lady. She said that I needed to turn myself in, and we could talk after that, but Misha has a lot of friends, and he isn't shy about using them." Her eyes held a silent plea. "With some of them in the police, if I turned myself in ..." She shuddered.

"Then we won't do that," he said.

"We?" she asked, suddenly wary again.

He took her hand and kissed it. "I owe you for helping with Peter."

"Theo, what we just did ... that was nice. Really nice. The nicest I've ever experienced, but it doesn't mean we have any sort of a future together, if that's what you're thinking. And I apologize if I'm presuming that what is probably very common casual sex to you is something more to me. Because it's not."

"That is a very hard sentence to parse," he said slowly. "But I think there was an insult in there aimed at me."

"No," she said, pulling her hand back. "Not an insult,

just a recognition that you no doubt have a crap-ton of sexual partners, and that flings like what we did are just that—flings."

"Do you know," he said, frowning, "that got even more insulting. I find myself feeling like I should defend my history with women, and at the same time reassure you that our recent activity was something profound."

"Of course you don't have to reassure me," she said quickly, hurting his pride a little. "I wouldn't expect that at all."

"But you think me perfectly capable of what? Serial one-night stands?"

She must have seen something in his eyes, because she suddenly hugged him. "No. It's just men who look like you—well, you have to admit that women are probably all over you."

"You're not making it better," he told her, rising above the pain that she didn't think what they had was worth exploring more. He wasn't under any delusion that she was madly in love with him any more than he was with her, and yet, there was an attraction between them, a feeling of rightness that he experienced with her that he wanted very much to nurture. But she wasn't coming from the same emotional space he was, and he had to remember that her reactions were influenced heavily by her past.

"I know," she murmured into his shoulder. He was somewhat amused to find she was rubbing his back in the same manner she had done for Peter the day before. "I'm sorry. I can't seem to open my mouth without saying the wrong thing."

"I don't know about that." He let his hands slide down to her ass, giving it a little squeeze. "I'd say you were very adept with your mouth. Mine certainly enjoyed yours."

She moved away, another of the delightful pink blushes on her cheek. "My point, before I more or less called you a male nympho, for which I apologize, is that I can't stay with you. Assuming that's what you'd want."

"I think it is, yes," he said, surprising himself by admitting it. But then, why should he be so surprised? Both his father and brother had fallen almost instantly in love with the woman of their choice, and although he'd never understood that, he was beginning to see how it might happen.

"If my situation was different—" She bit off the sentence. "But it isn't, and I can't risk Misha finding out about you and Peter. It's just that simple."

He realized then that she truly believed that it was inevitable that this ex, the brutish thug Mikhail, would find her. And he knew without a single shred of doubt that she would outright refuse to remain with him simply because she wanted to protect them.

None of his romantic partners had ever tried to protect him. It was an odd feeling, both heartwarming and annoying.

"I think you're jumping the gun, as you Americans say," he said without giving a hint to the mental plans he was forming and discarding. "And I have an idea how we can both help each other, but first, I need to make a few calls."

"Help each other how?" she asked, suspicious.

"Several ways, and none of them including the smutty things you are thinking," he teased, delighted when she looked amazed that he'd read her mind. "The most urgent of which will take place today."

"I have to get going," she said, giving another shake of her head. "That was our agreement."

"Yes, but I reserved the right to extend that agreement. Didn't you read the fine print?"

"Theo," she said with a little scowl and what was no doubt going to be a reprimand on her lips.

"There are four nannies who will be arriving here in the next—" He picked up his watch from the nightstand. "—in the next six hours, and I would greatly appreciate you helping me interview them."

"I don't know anything about nannies," she protested.

"No more than I do, but two heads have got to be better than one, eh? In exchange for this help, I will set my lawyer onto the situation with the warrant."

"I didn't tell you my tale of woe in order to guilt you into helping me," she said. "Advice, yes, I'm happy to have your advice, but I can't afford an expensive lawyer."

"That's where the mutually beneficial part enters into the agreement," he said, getting up when he heard Peter gurgle. "You help me find a competent nanny, and I'll pay you in my lawyer's fees."

"That's hardly a fair exchange—oh Lord."

Theo held his son at arm's length, a foul stench wafting on wings of the air-conditioning. "The boy is going to turn into a dolphin if he has many more baths. Would you—"

"Nope," she said, gathering up her clothes, and, with the sheet wrapped around her, dashed to her own room.

"Coward!" he yelled after her, his heart singing despite the foulness that Peter had managed to create. "You, sir, are repulsive, but since we have to woo Kiera into letting us take care of her, I guess it's a bath for both of us."

He didn't wonder when he had decided to take care of Kiera. He simply knew that she needed him, and he'd be damned if he let her down. She'd just have to accept that about this, he knew best.

SEVEN

"You are the biggest of all the fools who ever fooled around," I told my reflection, wiping a circle in the steam clinging to the mirror while I brushed out my wet hair. "You can't stay with him. Even if he wanted you to. You know this. You know what will happen if you do. And yet, here you are, tempted by a delicious man and adorable, if stinky, baby. This is all shades of wrong, so why are you even considering staying another day?"

My reflection made a face, which didn't help me at all try to reconcile the happenings of the morning. The issue of steaming hot sex with Theo aside—and I knew full well that a relationship with him was not at all something I should be thinking about—the real problem was the knowledge that I was a danger to Theo and Peter.

"I know Misha well enough," I told myself while I dressed. "He wouldn't hesitate so much as a second to use anyone for his own purposes, and would, in fact, take exceptional joy in hurting someone who was close to me."

I'd had enough proof of that over the years, seeing with the wisdom of time away from the abusive relationship just how he'd manipulated me into abandoning my friends and ostracizing my family until I was left with no one but him.

"Bowling balls, wheels of Gouda cheese, owl's eyes," I murmured, taking my few toiletries out of the bathroom to my duffel bag. I eyed it, wondering if I dared put my trust in Misha being unable to find me for a day or two, just a couple of days that I could spend helping Theo. And enjoying Theo. And learning about him, like why he was on the outs with his family, and what he was going to do with Peter, and a million other things that I wanted to know about him.

"Maybe if I stay in the hotel room, Misha won't have an inkling of where I am, or even if I am still in Auckland." I gnawed my lower lip while I thought about that. The urge to crawl out from under the burden of Misha was strong, but I knew what would happen if I let my guard down. "Rotelle pasta. Pushchair wheels. Life Savers."

Theo tapped at my door and opened it a couple of inches, Peter in his arms. "Can I leave him with you for a few minutes? I badly need to shave unless you want to end up with some serious whisker burn, and I'm hesitant to do it with this little devil underfoot."

"Sure," I said, stuffing my things into the duffel bag. Just the sight of Peter made the decision for me. I had no choice. I couldn't put their lives at risk simply because I wanted to spend time with them.

"Thanks. Breakfast here or at the restaurant downstairs?"

"Oh, here, don't you think?" I said quickly, feeling like a huge coward. I tried to justify it when I took Peter, who was babbling happily to himself. He promptly grabbed a clump of my still-wet hair, and put it in his mouth. "Peter's kind of messy."

"In more ways than one," he said with a grin, then allowed his gaze to move along my body in a possessive manner that sent little zings of electricity skittering along my skin, sinking into my deepest parts. "I'll get breakfast ordered."

I followed him into the living room, picking up the small package of oyster crackers that I'd saved from the selection of baby-suitable food that had been brought up the night before. "Do you like crackers, Peter? I know they aren't the breakfast that you are expecting, but you may consider them an appetizer, and it's good for you to broaden your expectations. As Swami Betelbaum says, the wider you open your eyes, the more likely they are to fall out and go exploring on their own. In a metaphysical sense, of course."

I could have sworn that Theo snorted while disappearing into his room.

By the time Theo returned, Peter had drunk half a bottle of formula, eaten exactly three crackers, spilled onto the floor in succession two small cups of water that I offered him in case he was thirsty after the crackers, dragged most of my clothes out of the duffel bag and flung them around the floor when I went to get a towel to mop up the water, pulled the Bible from the top of the nightstand, and, finally, gotten into the cubbyhole at the bottom of the nightstand and withdrawn a stack of hotel stationery and informative tourist pamphlets.

"What the hell happened in here?" Theo asked in amazement, surveying the ruins of what had been a tidy room. He looked at his watch. "It's only been twelve minutes."

I sat on the floor trying to repack my small cosmetic bag with the things that Peter had spread on the floor while I'd dashed into the bathroom to use the toilet, and shot Theo a glare. "Your child is evidently an octopus."

Theo smiled with what I very much feared was pride, the smile cracking a little when Peter turned to him and pointed, no-no-ing. "Erm. Is there a reason you put lipstick on him?"

"I just thought it looked good smeared on his forehead," I snapped, lying flat on my stomach to reach under the dresser in order to snag the small round compact of loose powder that rolled under it. The compact was empty. "Great. Now I'll have to tell housekeeping there's a pile of powder under there."

He eyed me when I stood up, no doubt noticing that the very same lipstick that Peter had smeared on himself also appeared in child-finger-sized blobs on both of my arms, one of my boobs, and my left earlobe. His lips twitched.

I pointed at him with a tampon I had wrestled out of Peter's grasp. "Don't you dare!"

The twitching became more pronounced.

"I swear to you, Theo, I will not be responsible for my actions if you even think about laughing. Your child is an octopus. A strange mutant child-octopus hybrid!"

"I'm sorry," he said in a choked voice, "I'm going to have risk it. It would harm my spleen to keep it bottled up."

"Gah!" I snarled, and, throwing my things on the bed, marched into the bathroom to clean up for a second time that morning, the sound of Theo's whoops of laughter following me.

"I have appointments this afternoon that I can't miss," Theo told me an hour later, when having breakfasted (and cleaned up Peter for the third time that morning), I sat on the floor playing a rousing game of Stack Things on Kiera. "I've rearranged all my morning meetings for the nanny interviews, but I can't miss the afternoon ones, including signing the custody paperwork my lawyer is filing so that Peter is legally mine. Would you mind watching him for me?"

I was immediately torn between a spurt of pleasure that I had an excuse for not leaving, and the dread feeling that I was not only being foolish to remain in one spot for longer than a day but also endangering them.

"Please," he said, squatting down next to us, Peter gnawing on one of his fingers. I studied Theo, noting that the dark blue suit he wore almost matched his eyes, that his shoes were highly polished, and his shirt was so sharply pressed it looked like it could cut bread. His hair was combed back in what I was starting to think of as his slick, professional look. I much preferred the tousled, informal Theo. "I know we have some things to talk about, and I'm happy to do so once I'm done with these meetings, but it would make me feel better to know that you'll be with Peter while I'm away."

"You'd trust your child to someone you just met?" I asked in what I hoped was a light tone.

He studied me for the count of ten. "I'd trust my child to you, yes."

A warm kernel blossomed in my belly, and spread outward. "I'll stay with him," I said despite intending to tell Theo I had to be on my way after the nanny interviews.

"Thank you." He leaned forward over Peter's head and gave me a swift kiss, then smiled, his breath hot on my lips, and kissed me again, his mouth moving on mine in a way that had all my intimate parts taking notice. My breasts instantly felt heavy and uncomfortably confined in my bra. "You, my fair little gazelle, are far too enticing for my peace of mind."

"Gazelle?" I asked, wanting to fan myself, but refusing to feed his ego any more than I already had.

He flashed one of his heart-stopping grins as he picked up Peter and blew a raspberry on the baby's stomach. "You remind me of a gazelle at a watering hole, all long legs and graceful lines, but oh-so watchful of everything going on around you."

"Gazelle," I said again, considering it. I decided it wasn't objectionable. "If I'm watchful, it's because there are blue-eyed lions like you prowling around in the shadows."

A knock sounded at the door just as he was going to say something that I knew would be outrageous and laden with sexual innuendo. I got hastily to my feet, smoothing out my T-shirt.

A woman at the door murmured something, handing Theo a sheet of paper. He read it, then held open the door for her.

I took an instant dislike to the woman, who looked like she was in her mid-thirties, with curly blond hair, and a coolly confident manner that instantly made me feel like I was dressed in rags, that my hair was ratty and unkempt, and that I was a gawky, graceless beanpole.

"Maureen Renshaw," Theo said, handing Peter to me before gesturing the nanny to the couch opposite. To my secret pleasure, Theo sat next to me, one arm draped casually over my shoulders. "This is Kiera and Peter. The latter is ten months old, and is the most charming baby on the face of the earth."

Peter bounced on my legs, grabbing a handful of my hair and putting the ends of it in his mouth while he watched his father, his chuckles emerging along with little spit bubbles.

"All new parents feel that way, to be sure," Nanny Maureen said, giving us what I thought of as an insincere smile.

"I assure you that in this case it's the truth. Peter has a very cheerful disposition," Theo said, taking a couple of tissues and pulling my hair from Peter's grasp, wiping the slobber from it. I snagged one of the baby's toys and allowed him to snatch it from my hand, and start beating Theo with it, all the while no-no-ing him. "He hasn't cried once since we got him, has he, Kiera?"

"Since you got him?" Nanny Maureen asked, her eyes narrowing.

"Nope. He's been as good as gold if you forget him screaming himself into a snotty fit at the train station, but I think we can excuse that. It was a trying circumstance, and he couldn't find his inner peace."

"Er …"

"Custody of my son has recently been granted to me by his mother," Theo said in a voice that I had never heard. It was clipped, his British accent even more pronounced, as if he were a lord and he'd been forced to chastise a serf.

"Oh, then this is not baby's mum?" Maureen gave a little sniff after sending me a glance filled with disdain. She turned to Theo, and smiled a brittle, hard smile. "I'm sure I can help you bring baby the order and structure to his day that is obviously lacking in his life."

"Whoa, now." My words were out before I even considered the wisdom of getting riled up by this woman. "He's not obviously lacking for anything. He's very happy, as Theo just said. He's smart, and curious about things around him, and likes baths. That's not a baby who is lacking quality of life."

"I'm sure your … *companion* … means well," Maureen said, ignoring me to address Theo. "But judging by the bad behavior she is all but encouraging baby to exhibit, I can see that I will have my work cut out instilling in baby the good habits that all responsible parents desire. You wish for live-in help, yes? Luckily, I've just completed an assignment with a charming Asian couple who decided to return to India, and am free for the three months you specified. Obviously, we can negotiate longer terms should they be needed."

I wanted to tell her exactly what I thought of her, but before I could, Theo was on his feet, offering his hand, thanking her for coming, and telling her he'd be in contact with the agency shortly. He had her out the door before I could explode.

"What a self-righteous, pompous twit," I said, pulling my hair once again from Peter's mouth. "I'm not teaching him bad habits, am I?"

"Not in the least," Theo said, smiling down at us before glancing at his phone. "You're as good with him as if you were his mother. Better, because I don't think you'd ever dump your child on his father without so much as a tear shed."

"Oh, hell no." I snuggled Peter, kissing the top of his head, and wondered how Nastya could have abandoned her own child. I decided it wasn't worth getting upset about, since clearly she had made the right decision. Peter would have a wonderful future with Theo, a much better one than he would have with a mother who was too busy with her career.

A little pang twanged in my heart at the thought that I wouldn't get to see Peter grow up to be a happy child, but I shoved that down, way down. There was no sense in crying over something impossible.

The second nanny interviewee was named Susan, and I knew in thirty seconds that she wouldn't do. She all but purred at Theo, eating him up with her eyes, and was so completely unaware of Peter and me that at one point she stepped on my foot in her attempt to sit next to Theo. She got a polite handshake and escort to the door, where she lingered, sending Theo all sorts of messages with her eyes.

"That was disgusting," I said when the door closed, then cast Theo a sympathetic look. "I'm sorry."

"For what? She wasn't your pick from the agency's offerings."

"For the fact that you have to put up with that sort of behavior. I can only imagine how annoying it is."

He smiled and leaned down to kiss me before he answered the next knock on the door. "That's why I'm counting on you to save me."

Number three didn't even get in the door. She just stood and stared at Theo, gulped a couple of times, then turned around and walked away without a word.

Theo turned to look at me, one eyebrow cocked.

I laughed out loud.

He rolled his eyes.

The fourth candidate, one Lauren Moscat, was just about perfect. She was in her late thirties, informed Theo that she was in a relationship with a longtime partner, and had a degree in childhood education. She didn't talk down to me, and even appeared delighted when Peter needed his diaper changed.

"Oh, let me. I'm an old hand at a dirty bottom," she said, taking Peter to the bathroom Theo indicated.

I exchanged a glance with him. We both followed her in, standing in the doorway and watching as Peter was expertly cleaned, powdered, anointed, and diapered without so much as one bit of poop smeared anywhere. She even deftly managed to whip a diaper over his penis when he started to pee straight up into the air.

"What do you think?" Theo asked in a whisper, pulling me back to the living room.

"She certainly seems to know how to diaper him without going through a whole boxful of wipes, which is miles ahead of us. And Peter likes her," I answered, reluctance giving my words a leaden feel. I didn't want to admit that I was bereft at the idea of never seeing Peter again, but honesty made me acknowledge that fact to myself, and add, "I think she's probably a very good nanny, and she doesn't seem to give a hoot about how you look."

"For which I'm grateful." He cast a glance toward the bathroom when Lauren appeared with Peter in her arms, the baby chuckling and wiping his slobbery fingers on her hair.

I felt as if I'd taken a physical blow.

I sat silent while Theo chatted with the nanny for another ten minutes, trying to summon up a genuine smile when he offered her the job. Lauren accepted with alacrity.

"Well," Theo said, glancing at his watch before turning to me. "I've got time for lunch if we make it fast. What do you say to that?"

"I'm happy to watch Peter if you two would like to have a little peace and quiet," Lauren said, making silly noises at Peter, which delighted him. "I'll go to the agency and formally accept the contract afterward."

"That sounds perfect," Theo said, taking my hand before I could protest. "We'll be down in the restaurant if you need us."

"But—" I felt the usual flood of panic at the idea of going out into a public space, but it was regret at leaving Peter with Lauren that was uppermost on my mind.

"You deserve a break, sweet," he said, twining his fingers through mine.

We walked in silence down the long hallway to the elevator. Each step seemed longer than the last one until we finally stopped a couple of yards in front of the closed elevator doors.

I looked at Theo, wondering how I could say what I wanted to say. It wasn't my business. I'd already decided that I had to leave. And yet …

"Why do I feel like I'm doing something wrong?" Theo asked, frowning down into my eyes.

"Because it is wrong," I said, relief easing the tension in my shoulders.

"She's perfectly competent. He'll be fine with her," he pointed out. "Her references—which my assistant verified—are excellent."

I just looked at him.

He looked back at me.

Without a word, we both turned and went back to the suite. I felt a surge of rightness when I took Peter from a surprised Lauren. Theo explained to her that we had changed our minds, and that he would naturally pay her the full amount of the three-month contract in compensation for the sudden change of plans.

I nuzzled Peter, holding on to him when he pulled himself up to stand, his little chubby legs wobbling while he sang a song to himself and beat on the couch with the hairbrush he had managed to extract from my purse.

"Lunch here?" Theo asked, having finally gotten rid of Lauren.

"Yes, please," I said, sitting back with a sigh of happiness. I knew full well it wasn't a happiness that would last, but I decided to heed Swami Betelbaum's advice and simply embrace the moment, for once letting the future worry about itself.

EIGHT

The packages started arriving while Peter and I were snuggled together on the couch, watching a documentary on the coral reef, which I felt was more suitable for his development than one of the mindless, perky children's shows.

"So, you see, this is the result of our abuse of the planet," I finished summarizing as the program showed horrible stretches of bleached, dead coral. "And this is why we need to listen to scientists, and not politicians. I know you don't understand the difference now, but you will someday, and I hope you can draw upon this experience—who is that?"

I clutched Peter at the sound of a knock at the door, fear sending a jolt of adrenaline through me, making sweat prickle on my palms. Had Mikhail found me? I was here alone with Peter—there was no way I could explain the baby to him. He'd go ballistic, and quite possibly do something unthinkable.

Nausea swept me, sending me to my feet lest I throw up on the baby. I looked wildly around the suite. Where could I hide him? Where could I put him that he would be safe? His crib? He might fall out of it. And if Mikhail dragged me off, that would mean Peter would be by himself until Theo came home.

A sob caught in my throat at the horrible decision to be made. At the sound of the second knock, I dashed with Peter into Theo's room, putting the baby into his crib with the toy he had clutched in his grasp.

"Stay there. Stay quiet. I won't let anyone hurt you," I whispered, kissing him on his dear little head before closing the bedroom door and trying to compose myself. My hand was on the door handle when I saw the small panel to the right of the door. A video camera! I touched a button and immediately a flickery screen lit up, showing one of the hotel staff standing outside the door, looking bored. Behind him was a cart that was loaded with items.

So relieved I could almost cry, I opened the door.

"Mrs. Papaioannou?" the clerk said, not waiting for me to answer before he wheeled in the luggage cart. "Your husband had some items delivered for you. I'll set them here, shall I?"

"Oh, yes, thank you." I wanted to correct him as to my identity, but decided that I'd live with being called Theo's wife if it meant one fewer person knew I was there. I hurried over to my purse, extracting a few bills, then added another when I remembered the class of hotel. My funds were severely depleted, meaning I'd have to use my bank card soon, but I pushed that thought aside.

The clerk unloaded several large cardboard boxes, three plastic carrier bags, and what looked like a giant giraffe with a swinging torso.

"Thank you," I said, giving the clerk a tip before thankfully closing the door. I fetched Peter and showed him the boxes. "It looks like your daddy found a little time to do some shopping in between the meetings. Should we wait for him to open them?"

Peter crawled over to the giraffe and began to no-no-no at it, patting it and chewing on it.

"Right. That's a no. Let's see what I have to do to get it set up."

An exciting half hour followed, but at last the giraffe was up on its four legs, the carrier bags of baby clothes were unpacked and stacked neatly on one of the couches, and the diaper supplies had been moved into Theo's bathroom.

Peter whooped with joy while the giraffe did its thing, swinging him back and forth with a soft, electric hum.

"You ride 'em, cowpoke—crapbeans!" Fear once again sent my adrenaline into overdrive at another knock, but this time I had the presence of mind to check the security camera before I went into a full-fledged panic, and saw the same clerk with yet another luggage cart full of things.

"Someone is intent on spoiling you," I told Peter before opening the door.

"Your husband has more things for you," the clerk announced, rolling past me without waiting for me to ask him in.

"So I see." I dug out the last of my money, standing silently by the door as he unloaded what looked like a small pirate's chest, a half-dozen carrier bags, and a giant box clearly containing a stroller that converted into a car seat. I handed the clerk the tip as he left, then said, eyeing the large box, "You have a perfectly fine stroller and car seat, but I guess your dad didn't think it met his exacting needs. Right. Well, let's see what he has for you now."

The pirate's chest turned out to be a toy box, which, given the number of toys I found in two of the carrier bags, made sense. Another bag contained several more items of clothing for Peter. I shook them all out, smiling over Theo's choices. "Your dad has a pretty good eye, although I think jeans for the under-one set is pushing it a bit. Oh, look, shoes! Let's see what's in this bag…"

I stopped and stared as I lifted out of the bag a delicate lace bra in pale pink. "I don't know how he thinks he's going to get you into that, but I very much want to be there when he tries."

Several pairs of silky underwear followed, as well as two more bras, a couple of bodysuits in champagne lace and black silk, and a very pretty navy blue polka-dot satin cami and sleep shorts set. "Mm-hmm," I said, moving on to the next bag. This one contained several pairs of leggings in a variety of colors, a handful of blouses in varying shades of sheerness, and a soft cashmere sweater in apricot.

"Your father," I said to Peter, who had been released from the giraffe, and was now happily wallowing around in a veritable toy store of baby things, "is going to be getting an earful from me. Don't look at me that way; I know his intentions were good—although, really, some of that lingerie has wicked thoughts written all over it—but nonetheless, this is not going to do at all."

The other bags contained plain black heels in three different sizes, and a pair of tennis shoes in the same. "This has really left me speechless—"

I paused at the knock before saying with a shake of my head, "He couldn't have. There's nothing left in the city."

A look at the camera showed the clerk again, but this time he had a mound of luggage on the cart.

"Uh," I said, opening the door. "Are you moving someone else in? Because I don't know if there's any room that isn't being occupied by the toys, baby things, furniture, a stroller, toy chest, and the giraffe."

"This lot is empty," he said, jerking his head toward the luggage, and unceremoniously dumping it in front of Theo's bedroom.

"Well, of course it is. Sorry, I'm out of cash. I'll tell Theo to hit you up the next time he sees you," I said after he unloaded.

The clerk shrugged, and wheeled out his now empty cart.

It took almost an hour to spread out the luggage set that Theo had bought, holding clothes up to Peter to make sure they fit him before I clipped off sales tags, and fold and put everything away. The clothes intended for me were a different matter.

I was still trying to decide what to do with them when the door clicked as the key card was inserted, and Theo entered.

"Ah, good, the things got here," he said, smiling at the sight of Peter surrounded by toys. He was stacking a set of plastic bowls, talking softly to them while periodically chewing on a rim. "What do you think of them, old man? Did Papa get you nice toys?"

"Peter," I said serenely, smiling when Theo sat down on the floor despite his fancy suit and showed the baby how a car could be zoomed around the blanket. "Remember that you are not responsible for your father's expectations of pleasure in things he has chosen for you. You may like or dislike regardless of whether he thinks they are nice. It's your choice."

"Jealous because I didn't get you anything?" Theo asked, tipping his head to the side in a way that made me want to grab his head and kiss the breath out of his mouth.

Until his words sank into my head. I glanced at the carrier bags of lingerie and clothing that sat on the couch. "You didn't … uh …"

"I didn't what?" he asked, his eyebrows going up.

A cold sweat made me feel sick, so sick I was sure I was going to vomit. Misha had found me. He'd found me, and this was his way of toying with me. I staggered to my feet and ran for my room.

"Kiera?"

I made it into the bathroom, panting and clutching the toilet, tears burning the back of my eyes, the fear making me shake uncontrollably. What had I done? How could I have endangered Theo and Peter like that?

"Kiera? God, sweetheart, I'm sorry. I'm so sorry. I didn't think. Come here. Let me hold you. I'm a brute. I'm a horrible, thoughtless brute." Theo pulled me into his arms, his body warm and solid and infinitely comforting. "I can't apologize enough. I was just trying to tease you. I didn't think about what it would do to you. I've ruined everything, didn't I? You hate me now, and you won't let me make love to you in all the ways that filled my head during the interminably long meetings, and I'll die alone, with no one to tell me how disgustingly handsome I am, and why my belly should be outlawed. Kiera? Please, love, tell me you forgive my stupidity."

The heat of his chest against mine allowed me to relax despite the initial flare of anger when I realized he'd been teasing me. I sagged into him, acknowledging that my response had been extreme, and he wasn't responsible for that. I reached up with a still shaky hand and pulled his tie free, unbuttoning his shirt so I could have access to his neck. "Die alone, Theo? Really? Do you think all the herds of women who want your disgustingly handsome face and perfect body will let that happen?" I gently bit the tendon in his neck, making him moan and pull my hips tight against his.

"I'm counting on you to keep me safe from them," he murmured into my neck, kissing a hot path to my jaw.

I slipped out of his arms, well aware that I was all too vulnerable to his charms. "I don't think that's wise while the Master of Toys is still awake," I pointed out.

"Ah. Good point." He made a wry face as we returned to the living room. "Now that I've made an ass of myself, will you tell me what you think of what I sent? I guessed on your size—you're about my sister's height, but aren't as bulky as she is—but I wasn't sure of your shoe size. And ... er ... bra size."

He sat down on the floor again, looking at me oddly when I held out my hand for him.

"Up," I told him, finding a little kernel of bossiness that I didn't know existed in me.

He rose, one eyebrow up in question.

"The carpet has all sorts of packing residue on it from the toys and giraffe. Your suit is way too nice to get dirty crawling around in all that with Peter. If you boys want to play, you have to put on your grubby clothes."

"I don't have grubby clothes," he said with dignity, bending down to kiss Peter on the head and saying in a faux whisper, "I get the idea she means it, old man. We'd better do as she says, eh?"

"Yes, and this one needs a change," I said, lifting up Peter.

"Sorry," Theo said, raising his hands while walking backward to his room. "There is nothing I would love to do more than get elbow deep in baby shit, but unfortunately, I can't right now. Not with my nice suit on."

"Oh, that's cheating," I yelled after him, then took Peter in to be changed, cleaned, and stuffed into one of the new outfits, giggling as I did so.

The argument started later, after we'd eaten (in the room again, although Theo offered to take us to a restaurant where he'd heard families were welcome), and Peter had a bath, and was happily snuggled in bed with a stuffed kiwi bird that was almost as big as he was.

"Would you like to model some of this?" Theo said, pulling out one of the teddies, draping it across his chest.

"No."

"Not your color? How about this one?" He pulled the satin cami. "I thought this would go well with your hair."

"I'm sure it does, but I don't want to try it on either. I don't want it, Theo."

"No?" He wrinkled his forehead, sighing. "Well, I admit that I picked it out because I wanted to see you in it, but it's your choice. You can pick out something you prefer instead."

"I'm not going to, because I don't need anything. I have clothes. Thank you for thinking of me, but I don't need any of it."

His wrinkles deepened into a frown. "Why don't you want them? I realize they may not be exactly to your taste, but you don't have very much, and I thought you'd enjoy a few new things."

"You thought wrong," I said, standing, watching him closely.

His frown grew. "You have only one pair of shoes."

"So?"

"They're nice, but they aren't very dressy. I thought you'd like a pair of something a little fancier for when we go out."

I took a deep breath, feeling like I was standing on the edge of a razor. "I don't like heels."

"Why not?"

"Because it's impossible to run in them."

He sat still for a moment, his eyes troubled. "Do you think you will ever have the need to run from me?"

"No," I said without thinking. I don't know how Theo had done it in such a short time, but I trusted him where I didn't trust anyone else. "But I may have to run when you aren't around."

"Ah. We're back to that discussion." He patted the couch. "I had hoped we could delay it until I told you about the idea I had midway through the most boring meeting regarding the development of a tiny piece of land to the north, but I see that isn't likely."

"Theo, I'm not going to take the clothes you bought for me. Thank you for thinking of me, but I have money. Not on me, but I have some money that I got when my parents died, and my brother sold their house. I'm not insolvent, even if I look like a bag lady."

To my surprise, a smile curled the corners of his mouth. "It's Harry all over again."

"Pardon?"

He was silent for a moment, then reached beneath the couch cushion and pulled out a long velvet box. "I don't suppose I could tempt you with this?"

I looked when he opened the case. A beautiful tennis bracelet lay within, glittering with green-blue stones. It looked like it cost as much as my new car that Mikhail had forced me to sell. "That's lovely. What sort of stones are they?"

"Teal sapphires."

"They're very pretty, but no, thank you."

He was silent for a moment. "Would it make any difference to know I bought them for you at the jeweler across the street, and they aren't a leftover from another woman?"

I shook my head.

"I had an idea it wouldn't. Well, at least I have one thing I can relate to with Iakovos."

I let my confusion show.

"He has to get down on bended knee and beg his wife to take any jewelry he wants her to have." He thought for a moment. "For that matter, she won't let him give her anything else either. She keeps telling him she's not after him for his money. You wouldn't believe the prenup argument they had."

"She sounds like a sensible woman," I said, warming slightly to this unknown sister-in-law.

He grinned. "She'll love you, if only because you give me endless hell about things."

"I don't mean to give you hell, Theo," I said, feeling a little pang of guilt. "I just don't want to take things from you. Not material things."

"Ah. Well, that brings up a subject that I wanted to discuss with you. If I promise not to slip this bracelet on your wrist even though it almost matches your stormy eyes, would you sit next to me and let me put my hand on your thigh?"

"Why my thigh?" I asked, but sat down beside him, my body humming at his nearness. I told my libido to get a grip on itself, but it ignored me, making several plans of what it wanted me to do to Theo.

"Because if I touch you anywhere else, we won't have this very important conversation."

"Very important?" I was distracted momentarily by the warmth of his hand through my leggings. "Did you talk to your lawyer about the warrant?"

"Yes, but I'll save that for later. While I was signing the custody papers, which includes a name change for Peter, since Nastya didn't see fit to give him my surname, it struck me that an answer to both our problems was staring me right in the eye."

"You want to adopt me?" I asked in horror.

He laughed. "In a way, yes. I want you to marry me."

I stared at him in outright disbelief. "You *what*?"

"Don't look so horrified, my startled little gazelle, and hear me out."

"I will not. You're downright crazy!" I said, trying to take my thigh back from where he was caressing it.

"In many ways, yes, but not about this. No, Kiera, listen to me." The laughter went out of his eyes when he slid his arm around me, pulling me tight to him. "You said that you thought your ex had a friend in the police, yes?"

"Yes, but—"

"Which makes sense if he's been able to track you. All he has to do is have his friend pull reports of a Kiera Taylor. The same goes for your bank cards, assuming he can get access to that info."

"He can," I said, rubbing my arms against the chill that made goose bumps prickle on them. "He has done it in the past."

"Marry me. Change your name to Papaioannou. You can use my bank cards until we get you your own. Your ex won't be able to follow you, because Kiera Taylor will disappear."

I was shaking my head before he finished. "A name change wouldn't solve anything. He's sure to be watching for that."

"Would he watch for you to be married?"

"No," I admitted slowly. "He doesn't think I have enough value to attract anyone else."

Theo smiled. "That's the perfect solution to the problem, then."

"Far from it. Marriage is...*marriage*. If I'm not going to take a couple of bags of clothes from you, what makes you think I'll accept access to your bank accounts? I'm a lot of things, Theo, but mercenary isn't one of them."

"I know you aren't mercenary. If you like, we can ..." He paused, obviously trying to find a solution. "You can write me a check for the balance in your accounts. I'll put that same amount in a special account for you, one with your new name. It'll be your money, just moved to an account where your ex won't think of looking."

"That seems reasonable," I admitted, relieved that I wouldn't have to use my bank cards after all. "Or it would be if the idea of marrying you wasn't harebrained. Theo, did you not listen at all when I told you that it's just too dangerous for me to be around you and Peter?"

"I listened. And I agree that if you posed a real danger,

I would make sure that Peter was well away from you. But I don't think there's a problem."

"Misha could be here in Auckland—" I started to protest.

"And that's where my plan really shines," he said, smiling. "After we get married at the local registrar's office, we go off to my sheep farm."

"You have a sheep farm?" I asked, wondering why anything about him surprised me. "Here? In New Zealand?"

"I do. It's very private. You have to take either a boat or a helicopter to get to it, and that makes it the ideal place for the new Mrs. Papaioannou to live without worry that a vicious brute will track her down. You'll like the farm. It's small but very picturesque. The man I bought it from lives there still with his wife and daughter, taking care of the sheep and house for me."

The idea danced in front of my mind with tantalizing clarity. "Spinning wheels," I said, telling myself I was a fool to even think I had a chance of safety. Still, if Theo had an isolated farm … "Sheep's hooves. Rolled-up bundles of wool."

"Plump little breasts," he said, bending down to kiss the tops of my breasts where they were visible rising above my shirt. "The round, perfect globes of an ass."

"Oh, this is ridiculous," I said, dismissing the image of the three of us on some wild, idyllically rugged sheep farm. "I can't believe you're offering to marry a woman you met the day before."

"That's what we Papaioannou men do," he said with a half grin.

I thought about it. I really thought about it, but in the end, I shook my head. "Thank you for offering, but there are just too many issues with it. Like what happens when you meet a woman you really want to be married to? What will happen when I have to leave you? What will your family think?"

"All of that is unimportant," he said, his eyes earnest. "What matters is your safety, and Peter's happiness."

"If you're thinking of me being his nanny—"

"I'm thinking of you being his mother. Well, stepmother. But mother in all the important senses of the word."

I gawked at him, outright openmouthed gawked at him. "Me? Who you met yesterday?"

His grin flashed, making my innards melt. "I told you, we Papaioannou work fast."

"That's not fast—that's insane. No, Theo." I stopped him from going on. "Thank you, but no. I'll … I'll stay with you until you get a proper nanny, one who doesn't make you fire her five minutes after hiring, but that's it. And I'm not going to take clothes or shoes or tiny bits of lace that would probably get stuck in my butt crack. OK?"

He didn't like it, but he didn't argue anymore. "I'm willing to call a truce if you are."

I watched him for a few seconds. "Because you want sex?"

"Because I don't want to argue anymore, not when it's clear you've made up your mind." He leaned forward and nipped my lower lip. "Although if you wanted me to make passionate, steamy love to you, then I am more than happy to do that, too."

I didn't even ask myself what the wise course to follow would be. I simply held my arms open and said, "Yes, please."

Theo's body curled around me kept my dreams at bay that night, although I woke up at one point in the middle of the night to find him standing over the crib, just watching Peter.

"Is he OK?" I asked, sitting up.

"Yes. I was just watching him sleep." He stood there for another minute, then got back into bed with me, reaching for me, tucking me against his beautiful chest. "I alternate between being furious with Nastya for keeping his existence from me, stealing his first ten months away, and wanting to get on my knees with gratitude that she's giving him up to me."

"She's given you full custody?"

"She said she would. Evidently her mother took care of him since he was born. Nastya said she'd only seen him a half-dozen times, and now her mother is ill in the hospital and not expected to live much longer."

"Poor thing," I said, feeling a pang for a woman who clearly tried to do her best for her grandchild. "Can you get her name and address?"

"I suppose so. Do I need to? She has no legal rights to Peter."

"No, but she must have loved him, and if she's in the hospital and near the end of her time, she would probably like to see him. Or at least some video of him. Maybe you could FaceTime her."

He was silent for a moment; then he heaved a big sigh. "And this is yet another reason why I need you in my life. I didn't even consider what she was going through, but you're absolutely right. I will put my assistant on to locating her, and at the very least, we'll do video calls with her."

I smiled into his chest, relaxing as the pull of his heat sank into me. I might not be able to stay with Theo, but I was determined to enjoy the time I had with him.

NINE

Theo wasn't impressed by the way the day started. First, he slept past the time he wanted to get up, mostly because having Kiera pressed up against him at night seemed to serve as some sort of a sleep aid. Never one to sleep soundly through the night, he had found her presence oddly comforting, and even though he woke up once to use the toilet, and then checked on Peter, he had fallen back asleep almost immediately with Kiera in his arms.

He thought the morning might be salvaged when he encouraged her to ride him like a rented mule, but just as her rhythm started going a little wild, and his hip thrusts upward were decidedly of the racing-toward-the-finish manner, Peter woke up and started crying.

"Poor little mite," Kiera said a few minutes later when they peeled back his diaper to find his ass red and angry. "I'd cry, too, if I had that all over my bottom. Right, where's that tube of rash ointment?"

Theo hovered over her as she read the instructions, cleaning the baby's ass before anointing the red cheeks. By then Peter had stopped crying, but his face was red and he looked as out of sorts with life as Theo felt.

Breakfast was trying, with Peter not wanting any of the food they offered him. Kiera managed to get a little formula and yogurt inside him, but after an hour, they conceded defeat.

"That's as good as it's going to get, I think," Kiera told him, wiping Peter's face and sticky hands with a damp cloth. "His bottom must really be hurting if it's making him this cranky."

Theo glanced at the clock. They really should have been out of here almost two hours before. "But a few more minutes won't hurt. Are you packed?" he asked Kiera.

"Yes. I'll finish with Peter's things if you can watch him."

Theo nodded, dialing a number and holding his phone to his ear with one hand, while offering Peter's chew toy to him with the other. The baby sat on his lap, looking disgruntled as he chewed in a desultory fashion on the toy.

"Hello? Pappamaumau residence," a familiar voice said into his ear.

"Hullo, Harry," he said, smiling despite the dismal morning.

"Theo!" she shrieked, damn near bursting his eardrum. "Iakovos, it's Theo! No, you can't have this phone—go get your own. Theo, where are you? Why did a strange woman ask me if I trusted you? Why haven't you called us in forever?"

"Theo," a deep male voice said, one that brought back so many memories. "Why are you worrying Harry like that? Who was the woman? And where the hell are you?"

"I didn't mean to, someone I'm trying to convince to marry me, and New Zealand."

"Marry you?" Harry said on a gasp. "Oh, Theo, I'm so happy for you! I want to hear everything! How did you meet her? Who is she? Why isn't she being convinced? Wait, did you tell her about the list? Is she annoyed about that? Just tell her that as soon as she marries you, you'll be off it."

"I didn't realize I was on one," he said, a little stunned by the flow of Harry's conversation. Iakovos always likened her to a storm, and he could see why. She was an unstoppable force once she got going.

"Number ten with a bullet," Harry said with a disgusted note in her voice.

"Ten is a decent start," Iakovos said. "It's no three, but you have to start somewhere."

"Three," Harry drawled, annoyance dripping off the word.

Theo had to laugh. "I would love to talk to you both about Jake's past history on the list, but I am very short on time, and I have an important question to ask you."

"Is something wrong?" Iakovos asked.

"Kind of. Is a diaper rash serious? I don't know if we should stop by the doctor or if Peter is just angry with us because his ass hurts."

Silence greeted his question for a good twenty seconds, at which point Harry said, "Diaper rash?" at the same time Iakovos asked, "Peter?"

"You have a baby?" Harry asked, her voice filled with incredulity. "With this mystery woman who called?"

"I have a baby. Not with Kiera, though, although I suppose Peter will be hers, too, if she marries me and becomes his stepmother." He took a deep breath and, before Harry exploded with questions, quickly ran through the history with Nastya, skating over how long he'd known Kiera, presenting her instead as a longtime girlfriend. "What we want to know is whether diaper rash is serious."

Kiera pulled a suitcase into the living area, looking around to see if she had missed anything before coming over to take Peter.

"That depends. How bad is it?" Harry asked slowly.

"They want to know how bad his ass is," Theo told Kiera. "What would you say on a scale of one to ten?"

"Six?" she asked.

He nodded. "He has a level six ass."

Harry made an odd noise like she had choked on something.

"How old is he?" Iakovos asked.

"Ten months."

"Ah. He's probably teething. If you have some ice, you can rub that on the gum where the tooth is coming in."

"There is teething gel you can get, too, although we never had much luck with it," Harry added, and spent the next five minutes offering advice for both Peter's ass and gums. It was much harder to get them both off the phone, and he was able to do so only by swearing on the grave of his mother that he would call them in the next week.

Twenty minutes later they emerged into the lobby of the hotel, Kiera pushing the new stroller with Peter, Theo carrying his briefcase and laptop case, and two hotel employees pushing luggage carts filled high with luggage, and Peter's toys, and swing.

"I don't know how you think you're getting all of that into one car," Kiera said, glancing quickly around the lobby.

"I don't. I called for two cars. Wait here. I'll see if they're outside."

She shot him a grateful look and moved over to a corner, manipulating the stroller so it was behind the luggage carts. His assistant called as he verified the two cars were waiting for him.

"I'm sorry to disturb you, Theo, but it's about the office that you rented in Auckland. There's been a mix-up, and the one you chose is not available, but the company has one available at a sister site two blocks away. Shall I tell them you'll take it? The rent is comparable, and I'm told the building is nicer, since it's newer."

"That's fine," he said, stepping into the lobby and gesturing for Kiera.

"Let me just go over the changes to the lease," Annemarie said smoothly.

"That's not necessary. I'm sure it'll be fine."

"I know you aren't interested in the fine details," she said firmly, "but it's important you know what you're getting into. Starting with the security system put into place in the building. It's very high-tech, with a twenty-four-hour complement of guards who monitor anyone who comes or goes in the building—"

"First car," he told Kiera, nodding to the black sedan

that was waiting. He gestured to the hotel porters to put the luggage in the second car, one eye on Kiera while she unsnapped the baby's car seat from the stroller and leaned into the back of the sedan to strap Peter and his seat in.

Midday was a busy time at the hotel, and he had trouble hearing Annemarie over the sound of the cars pulling up and leaving, voices calling to one another, and the hum of traffic on the street beyond. Annemarie's voice droned on detailing information he hadn't the slightest interest in, but long experience with her had taught him that he'd just have to let her work through it before he could hang up. He glanced toward the car with Kiera as the men finished loading the last of the luggage, handing them a healthy tip, his eyes narrowing. He didn't see Kiera at all in the backseat, and yet the stroller was sitting outside the waiting car.

He walked toward it, Annemarie's voice continuing in his ear. As he got closer, he could see Peter's round head where it bobbed in the back, but there was no sign of Kiera. He opened the door, and was shocked to see her crouched down in the footwell, her eyes huge and filled with terror.

"What's the matter?" he asked, hanging up his phone without regard to what Annemarie was saying.

"Get in the car," she hissed, gesturing him in.

"What? Why are you down there? Did something frighten you?" He glanced around but didn't see anything out of the ordinary. Ahead of them, two men stood next to a car, one supervising the unloading of luggage, while the other consulted his phone. Behind them, a Japanese family was pausing for a selfie with the doorman. People streamed into and out of the lobby, but nowhere did he see anything that could have caused such a response in Kiera.

"Just get in the car," she whispered, her voice throbbing with emotion.

"All right," he said, turning to fold the stroller down so he could put it in the front seat.

"No, leave it! Just get in!"

"I just bought this. It's a very nice model," he said, examining the various knobs and switches on it, trying to figure out how to make it fold up.

Kiera made a sobbing noise that went straight to his heart. "If you get in the car right now and leave the damned thing behind, I'll marry you."

That got his attention.

He looked in at her, glanced around one last time, and made his decision. He got in the car, telling the driver to go.

Kiera closed her eyes, her hands shaking as she allowed him to help her out of where she'd wedged herself. Peter started to cry, obviously feeling just as awful as both of them.

"What happened?" Theo asked when she got onto the seat on the far side of Peter. He dug Peter's chew toy out of where he'd stuffed it in his pocket, giving it to him before looking over his head at Kiera. "Did someone say something to you?"

"No," she said, craning her neck to look behind her, then slumped back in the seat, her eyes closed. "He was there."

Rage filled Theo, enough rage that he almost told the driver to turn around. He had to struggle with his temper for a few minutes, using all the control techniques he'd been taught at the clinic, eventually calming down enough to ask, "Where?"

"Ahead of us a couple of cars." Her eyes turned to him, filled with so much fear, he wanted to pull her onto his lap and kiss her until she forgot it. He wanted to kill the bastard who did this to his beautiful, brave gazelle. He wanted to make Kiera understand that she would never have to worry now that he was in her life.

"Are you sure?" he asked.

"Yes." She shivered. "Theo, he was so close to seeing me. Armen was there, too, his enforcer. They were together, right there, right in front of me. Either one of them could have seen me!"

"But they didn't. It's all right, Kiera. They didn't see you."

She didn't seem to hear him. "I'd just put Peter into the

car when I caught the sight of Misha coming out of the car. He had his phone in his hand—otherwise he would have looked up and seen me. Armen was getting luggage out … Oh my God, he's here. He found me. Melon balls. Mozzarella balls. Those cheese balls with shredded nuts on them."

"He hasn't found you. You're safe with me. Kiera, look at me."

"Doughnut holes." Reluctantly, she met his gaze.

"Are you safe? Right now, are you safe?"

She rubbed her arms again, but nodded. "Yes, I'm safe."

"I won't ever let that change." He raised his voice. "Driver, we're going to the registry office before we go to the airport." Theo spoke deliberately despite the fury that filled him. He texted a fast apology to Annemarie, telling her to move his afternoon meetings to the following day.

Kiera fussed over Peter, who was looking like he wanted to cry, and held the chew toy for him to gnaw on, but Theo could feel the frightened little glances she shot at him. He reached across Peter, taking her hand and giving it a squeeze.

"You can stop looking like a warthog just fouled the water hole, little gazelle," he said softly. "I won't let anything happen to you."

"You don't know him," she said almost inaudibly.

"No, but I have the resources and the desire to keep you and Peter safe, and that's just what I'm going to do. There's no way he can get to the sheep farm, and we'll head there as soon as we apply for a marriage license."

"Via the airport?" she asked, wrinkling her forehead.

"Yes. We'll take a helicopter." He smiled, trying to instill in her a sense of comfort. "Trust me, Kiera. I know it's hard, but try. I swear to you I won't let him near you."

She nodded, but her gaze dropped. She obviously didn't believe him, but he figured that trust in him was simply something she'd have to learn over time.

The process of filing for a marriage license went surprisingly easily. Theo had an idea that Kiera might balk when it came down to the legalities, but she filled out the form without a word other than to point out that they would have to wait three days before they could be married.

"We'll be safe on the farm," he reassured her. "And it will give me time to get my bank to issue you new cards. We won't be able to do anything about the license being record-ed, but I doubt if even your ex's friends would think to look at marriage records for you."

"I'm sure he wouldn't," she said with a twist of her lips. "He always told me that I'd never find anyone else."

Theo didn't say anything to that, knowing her nerves had suffered a shock. Instead he escorted her out of the of-fice. "Do you have a preference for marriage venues? I will get my assistant working on it immediately."

"There was a sign. …" She cleared her throat and slid a glance at him out of the corners of her eyes. "The registry office does marriages. Would you mind—"

"Not at all. So long as you're certain that you don't want a proper wedding."

She shuddered, and he didn't know if it was the idea of marrying him or of a public ceremony that caused it. He prayed it was the latter.

"You're not afraid of flying, are you?" he asked, more to change the subject than anything else.

"Me? No." She looked surprised for a moment before her brows lowered, and she reached across Peter to pinch his thigh. "Just because I have a few issues doesn't mean I'm afraid of everything, Theo."

He grinned, wishing he could have finished what they had started that morning. "Tonight," he said softly, "we are going to practice the wedding night acts."

"Do we need practice?" she asked, but he saw her pupils dilate at the idea.

"No, but it's always good to be prepared." His gaze swiv-eled to where Peter, still looking out of sorts, banged his chew toy on the car seat, two fingers in his mouth. "So long as a certain young man allows us to get the required time in."

"Poor little guy," she said, fussing with the straps holding in Peter. "I know how awful a toothache can be. I'll put more of that teething gel on him once we stop."

Theo brushed a hand over Peter's hair, but said nothing while Kiera talked to the baby, telling him that he just need-ed to make up his mind to not let the pain ruin his day. There were many things he needed to plan, one of which was to engage the firm of detectives Annemarie had recommended to dig deeper into Mikhail's past.

"Your farm must be really remote if we have to take a he-licopter to it," Kiera said a short time later when she snapped Peter's car seat into the back row of seats. "I have to say that I'm excited to see it. I love sheep. Do you shear them, as well? Before I met … before, I used to spin yarn, so I have a love of all things fleece."

"Yes, they are sheared, although I haven't been here during the time of the year when that happens. They're heir-loom sheep, actually, some rare breeds that are kept alive by aficionados. I've only had the farm for a few years, but the former owner does an excellent job taking care of it for me. Buckle up."

He signed the flight plan, consulted briefly with the he-licopter pilot, and got in, the pilot beside him.

Kiera looked up from the back, her eyebrows raised as she watched him put a headset on. "You're not … you have a pilot's license?"

"Have had since I was twenty-one," he said, turning to wink at her. "Don't look so horrified. I've flown this particular helicopter before, so I'm more than a little familiar with it."

"But …" She glanced at Peter, and he could hear her saying softly, "Helicopter wheels. Dials."

He started the engine, checking to make sure there was oil pressure before turning on the alternator, and engaging the clutch. The whole cab vibrated as the belts tightened, and the rotors started spinning, but Peter didn't seem to mind either the noise or the movement. Theo was pleased by that and made a mental note to point out to Jake that his son had taken to flying like he was a bird.

"The shape the blade thingies make when they are spinning," Kiera said loudly. "Parachutes when they are deployed."

Theo raised his voice so he could be heard over the sound of the engine, saying, "Actually, the parachutes on board are rectangular. Everyone ready? We're off, then!"

It wasn't a long flight, but a pleasant one, and although Theo had been to the farm only a couple of times, he very much enjoyed swinging out from Auckland over the coastline, and then heading in a northeast direction to a small cluster of islands.

Kiera busied herself with Peter at first, keeping a watchful eye on Theo, as well, a fact that had him smiling to himself, but after a while she relaxed, and even pointed out the window at things for Peter to notice.

He knew the moment she realized just where the sheep farm was located, because she suddenly plastered herself to the window, staring down on the oblong island that was part of a cluster of over a hundred islands. Theo admired the island, feeling a sense of pride in it. He'd always thought of Matuarikawaiti Island as being stingray shaped, with a wide, curved south end—where the buildings sat on the shallow bay—the land rising and narrowing to a rocky tail that swung to the west.

"The sheep farm is on an island?" Kiera yelled over the noise.

"The sheep farm *is* the island," he answered, pointing. All along the spine and the gently sloping south end, tiny white dots were visible against the greenery of the island.

Kiera said nothing more until they had landed, Theo and the pilot pulling out the most important of the luggage that traveled with them. The pilot promised to bring the rest, and Theo got Peter and Kiera off the helipad, and down the path leading to the beach and the house that waited for them.

"OK, this is amazing," Kiera said, looking around with astonishment. "Peter, look! Baby sheep!"

Peter, in Theo's arms, looked less than impressed, and rubbed his face with a slobbery fist.

"I think he wants a nap," Theo told her.

"Probably. He's no doubt tuckered out with all the mouth ouchies." Kiera tossed her purse and one of the small suitcases into the replacement stroller they'd picked up before going to the airport, and wheeled it after Theo. "I can't believe your sheep farm is an island. Wait, you said you bought the farm from someone else? Do you own the island, too?"

"Yes." He waited for her to stop gawking at the scenery before saying, "My brother owns an island in Greece."

"And?"

He grinned. "I kind of felt I had to have one, too."

She stared at him like he had dancing lambs on his head. "You're crazy. You know that, right?"

"Yes, but you love that about me," he told her, and gestured toward the nearest building. "This is our house. It used to be some sort of a lodge, but Richard—he's the manager and former owner—had it redone for a holiday let. I think you'll like it. It's not huge, but has three big bedrooms, a loggia that lets you see the most spectacular sunsets, a nice-sized kitchen, and there's even a pool. Peter will like the pool."

She eyed first him, then the baby. "Hmm."

"What?"

"He can't take a bath by himself, Theo. How do you expect him to do in a swimming pool?"

"We'll get him one of those floating things. And one of us will be with him at all times." He gave her his best smile, the one Harry said could charm the socks off a nun. "You'll see. It'll all work out perfectly."

Just as they reached the house, three people emerged from it.

"Richard," Theo said, freeing a hand to shake the one offered by the older man. "The place looks wonderful. This is Kiera and Peter. Kiera and I will be married in three days. Sweetheart, this is Richard Dart, his wife, Anne, and their daughter, Melanie."

"A baby!" Anne beamed as she tweaked Peter's toes. "He's so adorable. And you're engaged! That is very good news. Peter is the spitting image of you both."

"He's not my baby, actually," Kiera said, shaking hands with both Richard and Anne. "But I agree he's adorable. He's a bit cranky right now, though. We think he's teething."

"May I?" Anne said, holding out her arms.

Theo duly deposited Peter with her, and turned to nod toward a house that sat a little way down the beach. "That's Richard and Anne's house. Beyond it is the bank of solar arrays and batteries that we use for power. You'll notice the roofs are flat—we collect and store water there. The island is completely self-sustaining with regards to amenities."

"That's amazing," Kiera said, her eyes dazzled. "Everything here is just … so wonderful. I don't blame you for wanting to own the whole island. It's a paradise."

Theo took pride in her reaction. Although he liked the island well enough, he hadn't ever thought about living on it. Now, seeing it through Kiera's eyes, he began to think it might just be the haven he was looking for.

"The wharf needs a bit of work," Richard said, nodding toward a long wooden dock that stretched out toward the mainland. "Pontoons on the end are cracked. I had it in my notes to tell you at the next call, but since you've come out instead, I'll show you the damage."

"Can I hold Peter?" Melanie asked her mom. "He's so round and cute, and omigod, he can say words! Babies are just the end!"

Peter no-no-ed her a couple of times, making her giggle when her mother handed him over.

"Our Melanie is taking early childhood education at uni," Anne told Kiera. "She loves babies. I'm sure she'd be happy to watch Peter sometime if you two wanted a night on the mainland."

Kiera looked mildly terrified at that thought, but Theo thanked Melanie, watching for a moment to make sure the girl was dealing well with the baby in his unhappy state.

To Theo's surprise, she soon had Peter gurgling a wet little chuckle, and she even suffered him to put his slobbery fingers on her cheek.

Theo showed Kiera around the beach, gardens, and pool before climbing to the loggia. He noticed that although Kiera appeared relaxed and was chatting pleasantly, she stuck closely to Melanie. It warmed his heart that the woman he had decided upon had taken to his son so quickly.

Kiera might not think they had any future together, but he fervently hoped that between Peter and himself, they would bind her to them so that she never wanted to leave.

TEN

The next few days flew past with a speed I found worrisome. For a woman who had spent many a night huddled in a cot in some shelter or other, fear making me feel each passing second of long, sleepless nights, the fact that time could slide past without effort made me wonder if I wasn't allowing the peace of Theo's island paradise to blind me to the very real threats that Misha posed.

He was out there hunting for me. I knew it in my bones. It wasn't a coincidence that he was in Auckland. I could feel that black presence that hung over the entire city like a storm cloud.

Thankfully, Theo never pressured me to go to the mainland with him. Bless him, he knew just how close we'd come to having Misha see Peter, and each morning he put on one of the gorgeous GQ-cover-worthy suits, kissed the baby on his head before kissing me in a way that made my blood steam and my legs go boneless, then took either one of the boats or a helicopter over to Auckland.

"What are you wearing for your wedding?" Anne had asked after we'd been there three days. "Theo said you were marrying at the registry office, but you'll still want to wear something nice. Perhaps you'd like Mel and me to help you shop for something a little ..." She eyed my leggings and shapeless, faded tee. "Something a little more dressy?"

"Oh. Er …" I considered my clothing situation. All I had in the dresser in the master bedroom was four pairs of leggings, one pair of jeans, a handful of T-shirts, and assorted underwear. I told Theo to return the things he'd bought for me, but since he had only just the night before solemnly presented me with a bank card in the name that was not yet mine—and which he had couriered out at what I assumed was great expense—at least I had money that I could spend without Misha tracking me.

"I suppose I should have something a little more formal," I said slowly, my eyes on where Melanie was out on the grass, playing with Peter. The girl had turned out to be remarkably good with him, and I was getting to the point where I didn't feel the need to hover over her.

"There are a number of nice shops in Auckland," Anne continued. "We could pop over for lunch, get you a dress, and be back before Theo gets home. What do you think of that?"

I thought it sounded like the sheerest folly, but Theo was being so nice about everything, I didn't want to shame him in front of his friends by marrying him in leggings. Maybe if we drove straight from the dock and went directly to a shop, and back, it would minimize the risk of seeing Misha. "Do you know of a shop in particular?"

"I know of an excellent one. There's a restaurant nearby—"

"I think, if you don't mind, we'll just do the dress shopping and leave lunch for another day," I interrupted, moving past her to go out through one of the bank of French doors to the lawn where Peter and Melanie played. I had a sudden urge to hold him, to let him suck on my hair, and to hear him no-no me happily.

"If you like," Anne said, giving me an odd look, but after a moment she shrugged and called to her daughter.

Two hours later we arrived at the marina in Auckland.

"Is the car there?" Theo asked, his voice warm in my ear. He'd given me a cell phone the day before, as well, assuring me it was registered in his name. "Are the windows tinted? I told them I didn't want a car without tinted windows."

"It's here," I said, pushing Peter's stroller down the dock toward where there sat one of the ubiquitous black sedans that drove rich people around. I ignored the fact that by marrying Theo on the following day, I would technically be one of them. "I can't see through the windows, so we're good on the tinting. Thank you, Theo."

"My sweet little gazelle, I would move heaven and earth in order for you to marry me tomorrow, and arranging for a car is but a drop in the vast ocean of my devotion."

I giggled at his dramatic delivery.

"Are you gracing me with your presence for lunch?" he asked. "I have a meeting, but I can move it."

"No." I hated feeling so cowardly, but my skin felt prickly just knowing Misha was in the area. "I think the shopping will be enough of an outing for Peter and me."

"As you wish, although I would like you to see my office. It has a glorious view, and a couch that is large enough for you to strip me down and do all the things to me that I know you want to do."

"Ooh," I said, unable to keep from shivering a little at the promise in his voice. "I love it when you let me seduce you. Maybe we could see it tomorrow, after the wedding."

"An excellent idea. Happy shopping."

"Happy meeting ... er ... ing."

He laughed and hung up, and after making sure no one was lurking near the car, I wheeled Peter to it, allowing Melanie to help me stow the stroller.

Peter was in a bit of a subdued mood, which meant his teeth were hurting again. I rubbed a little of the teething gel on his gums, offering him his chew toy, which I'd tucked in my purse.

"What ... what are you giving him?" Anne asked, looking over her shoulder to make some comment or other.

"It's his chew toy. Sometimes he likes to gnaw on it. I think it makes his gums feel better," I said, tucking it into the diaper bag when Peter pushed it away in favor of a couple of linked plastic rings.

"A chew toy? But that's a ..." She looked startled for a moment, then gave a little shake of her head, and continued to narrate which businesses in town were worthy of patronage.

I was relieved to see that the shop she'd picked out was on the other side of the city from where I'd seen Misha. The driver found a spot about half a block down, and I made everyone wait in the car for a minute while I scanned the street.

"Sorry," I said once I'd made sure there was no Misha-shaped man lurking on the sidewalks. Since the street contained clothing boutiques, small cafés and bakeries, and an art gallery, I was fairly confident that this area didn't have any of the sorts of businesses that would attract him.

I got Peter out and into his stroller, tucking my phone into my purse before slinging it across my body.

"Now, you just have a good look around," Anne told me as Melanie claimed the stroller and started pushing it down the sidewalk toward the shop. "Don't worry about us. We'll keep Master Peter occupied while you try on whatever takes your fancy."

"Thanks," I said, worried that I sounded ungrateful. I kept scanning the street while I headed for the shop, Melanie and Anne behind me.

"Oh, look at that darling ladybug outfit," Anne said, pausing at the shop next to the one we were headed to. "It would be so cute on Peter. It even has little antennae on a headband!"

I smiled to myself, opening the door to the chic boutique, and mentally trying to form an explanation to Theo of why his son was dressed as a ladybug. Little bells tinkled as I entered, the relative darkness of the shop making me stop while I took off my sunglasses.

At the counter directly ahead of me, along the right-hand wall of the shop, a man stood, holding up a piece of paper bearing a woman's face for the clerk to examine.

My face.

"No, I can't say I've ever seen her," the clerk said.

My gaze met that of Armen, and for a moment, the world stopped. The look of surprise on his face must have matched my own, but I was faster. I spun around and was through the door before he moved.

I emerged into the blinding noon sunlight. To my right, Anne and Melanie stood with Peter still in his stroller, the two of them still window-shopping the baby store.

My feet moved of their own accord, turning left and racing down the sidewalk even as the bells jingled, and I heard Armen's shout. I wove through the people who wandered down the sidewalk shopping on their lunch hour, dashing around first one corner, then another, my heart in my throat. I prayed that Armen hadn't seen me with Peter just a few seconds before, and put all my faith in Anne and Melanie to keep him safe.

I risked a glance back when I spun around another corner. Armen had his phone to his ear as he ran, his face red with anger. I leaped across a crosswalk against the light, glancing off the back end of a car that sent me staggering to the side, but I was up on my feet and running before Armen gained so much as a yard on me.

Don't panic, my brain chanted at me. *Focus on your breathing. Remember how you used to run. Don't waste your energy on anything that doesn't carry you forward easily.* The muscle memory of years of high school and college track slowly warmed up, and I managed to steady my breathing, and lengthen my stride despite the people on the sidewalk. I wanted badly to circle back to make sure Peter was all right, but instinctively, I knew I had to lead my hunter away from him. I ran to the south, the number of pedestrians strolling on the sidewalks lessening, allowing me to get into my stride, my arms moving in a familiar rhythm as I focused only on running, on putting distance between myself and Armen. He might be a big ugly goon, but he didn't have the stamina that had been trained into me.

I was just wondering how far south I could lead him before he gave up the chase, when a car squealed to a halt in front of me, right in the middle of an intersection. We were in front of a bank, and I had been about to make a right and head west for a bit, when Misha leaped out of the car and lunged for me, getting his hand on my shirt even as I shied back.

"You goddamn bitch," he swore, his eyes narrow with rage, little flecks of spittle on his lips, as he threw me against the wall of the bank, the back of my head cracking against it with enough force to stun me for a second.

Panic flooded me, making me want to curl into a ball, which I always hoped would save me from the worst of the beating, but which never did. Instead, I tried to get to the door of the bank, but Misha had me in his grasp, twisting my T-shirt under my chin, almost strangling me. "Where is it? Where is flash?"

My brain tried to make sense of what he was saying. I was dimly aware of a couple of people passing by us, some of them making comments, but only one man stopped, concern and hesitation evident as he asked if there was a problem.

"Fuck off," Misha snarled at him, and evidently one look at the furious face was enough for my would-be Samaritan. "Where is it?"

"Your flash?" I tried to claw his hands from the twisted wad of shirt that was closing my throat. "What flash?"

"USB flash stick. You stole from me. You stole flash."

"I didn't. I don't know what you're talking about. I don't have a flash drive, any flash drive," I protested, praying that someone in the bank saw us, and had called the police. At least Misha couldn't kill me right there in public.

As if he read my thoughts, he dragged me across the street to the car, still holding me by the throat. I squawked and tried to fight him, but he simply dragged me, ignoring the comments of the people nearby. I knew if he got me in that car, I was dead. I would never see Peter again. I would never get to swim naked in Theo's pool on his private island that he got so he could impress his brother.

I'd never get to marry Theo.

And suddenly, I knew that I wanted all of that. I wanted a life with Theo. I wanted to wake up to find him snoring in my hair, one leg thrown over me. I wanted to watch Peter grow up. I wanted to tease Theo mercilessly every time a woman made googly eyes at him. I wanted the life that I'd never thought I could have.

With a strangled snarl, I stopped trying to drag my feet, instead throwing myself onto Misha, taking him by surprise enough that he was off-balance for a few seconds. My purse strap tangled around his wrist, allowing me to slip out of it. It was just enough time for me to dash back across the street and race straight into the bank. A couple of employees stood pressed against the door, clearly watching us.

Misha threw my purse into the car before he stalked forward, but just then Armen ran up, and the two men held a conference. Misha gave the bank a long, ugly look that I knew was meant for me; then he got into the car and pulled out to a squeal of oncoming vehicles' brakes.

Armen placed himself opposite the bank, leaning against the wall of another business, obviously waiting for me to come out.

"Excuse me." A woman's polite voice rose a little so she could be heard over my harsh breathing. "Are you in trouble? Would you like us to call the police on your behalf?"

It was on the tip of my tongue to say yes, but I remembered in time that there was a warrant hanging over my head. Even without Misha's dirty buddies, the police were not my friends.

"No, thank you. My fiancé will help me. I don't suppose there's another exit?"

She glanced out the door to where Armen was lounging. "There is, although we are not supposed to let customers use it. It leads to the trash area in the alley."

"Please," I said, letting her see the anguish in my eyes.

She made an abbreviated gesture, turning and shooing the couple of other employees back to their desks. "Very well, but do not tell anyone I did this. It's very much against the rules. This way."

My throat burned, and my legs felt like I'd run a hundred miles, but I pushed down the fear and horror and the mental images of what Misha would do to me if he caught me again.

The woman led me through a labyrinth of offices before opening a small door that had a number of signs warning about leaving it unlocked. "The alley," she said, about to open it.

"Hang on, please," I said, and eased the door open a crack. I couldn't look to the right, but I had a good view of the alley that stretched away to the left. Sitting at the end of it, blocking the sight of passing traffic, was a car.

Misha was waiting for me. I was about to ease the door closed again, my heart turning to lead and falling to my stomach with the knowledge that I was trapped, when a parking police car pulled up behind Misha. As the woman got out, clearly about to have a word with him, he slammed his foot on the gas, the car jerking forward.

"Thanks so much," I said hurriedly to the woman, and, after a moment's thought, raced down the alley in the direction where Misha had been. He might go around the block and head for the opposite end of the alley, but with luck, I'd make it to the far end and be gone by the time he arrived.

I made it out of the alley without any problem, and ignored looks of people when I took off, heading to the west, toward the suburbs, feeling it would be easier to lose Misha there. As soon as I hit a row of houses, I ran into the first backyard that I could find, hiding between a fence and a shed, collapsing down onto the ground, doubled over with the need to get air into my lungs, and the desire to vomit.

I was safe for the moment, unless the homeowner had seen me trespassing, but even if I was safe on that front, I had to emerge at some point so I could tell Theo where I was.

I reached into my jeans for my phone, but the pockets were empty of all but a couple of New Zealand dollars. With horror, I realized I'd put my phone in my purse before going into the store ... and Misha now had my purse.

"Aspirin," I whispered to myself, pulling my knees to my chest as I tried to calm my mind. "Valium. Codeine."

In the end, I decided I'd give Misha an hour to drive around looking for me before I'd poke my nose out and try to find someone willing to let me use their phone. Then I'd call Theo, tell him the horrible tale, and let him spend the rest of the night trying to reassure me that he would protect me from the evil that was Misha.

The question was, did I have the right to ask him to do that if it meant putting himself at risk? The second Misha realized Theo was protecting me, he'd make it his business to find out everything there was to know about him. I'd seen him target the families of rivals before and knew he was ruthless when it came to getting what he wanted.

A USB flash drive? I shook my head, wondering why he thought I'd stolen something like that. I conducted a mental inventory of my belongings, and saw nothing that even re-motely resembled a flash drive.

After what I deemed to be an hour, I crept out from my hidey-hole, watching both the house and the road, but no one shouted at me or confronted me. I started jogging down the road, hoping I looked like someone out for a little exer-cise, and not a desperate woman. I kept going north in the residential area until it turned commercial, pausing when I unexpectedly found a library.

"Hi," I said to the receptionist. "I know this is probably really against the rules, but could I use your phone?"

"There is a pay phone in the lobby," she said without looking up, nodding to the left.

"Oh. I didn't realize those were still around. Uh ..." I felt in my pocket. "I don't suppose you could break a dollar for me? It's kind of an emergency."

She sighed, clearly put out at being interrupted, but held

out her hand. "We keep a pay phone for people who do not have mobile phones."

"Thank you," I said meekly, and, after a quick look outside to make sure Misha wasn't lurking, went to the pay phone, the coins clutched in my hand.

It was then I realized I hadn't memorized Theo's cell number.

I banged my head on the phone booth wall for a moment, before I remembered his office. He was at his new office, and I was certain that it had phones. It took ten minutes for me to get the phone number, but at last I dialed it, doing a little dance of impatience. "Papaioannou International," a cool female voice greeted me.

"Hi, my name is Kiera Taylor—"

"We are out of the office at the moment. If you know the extension you want, you may dial it now. Otherwise, leave a message and we will get back to you at the earliest possible time."

I wanted to cry. I just wanted to sit right down and cry. Theo wasn't there? I looked at the clock on the wall above the librarian's desk. It was only a little after one. Maybe he was off at his lunch meeting? He had to go back to his office before long. Especially if Anne called him to tell him I'd gone crazy and ran off without a word to them.

"I'm going to have to go out," I told the phone, and hung it up.

The next hour was hellish, the sound of every car that stopped quickly making adrenaline rush through me. I felt itchy all over, as if a thousand eyes were on me. I tried to keep to streets with lots of pedestrians, figuring the more people around me, the better. Misha was sure to think I'd go for the less traveled streets, so it made sense to go to the most populous area. Fortunately, the address I'd memorized from the phone inquiry was located smack-dab in the business section of town.

"Thank God," I breathed when I saw the building rise up before me. I hesitated, but there was no sign of Misha. I joined a couple of other people in business suits who entered the building, trying to smooth down the wrinkled wad of T-shirt where Misha had throttled me, slapping a smile on my face as I approached the building's reception desk.

"Hello. Can you tell me what floor Papaioannou International is on?" I asked a receptionist.

The woman tapped on a keyboard with elegantly manicured nails. "That would be the seventh floor. May I have your name?"

"Oh, you have to call them?"

She nodded, her hand poised over the phone.

"Sure. My name is Kiera Taylor. Theodor Papaioannou is my fiancé."

"How lovely for you." Her gaze raked over my sweaty, filthy, rumpled self. "They do not answer. Ah, I see here a note that the phone system is in place, but the physical phones haven't yet been hooked up. A Ms. Annemarie Chanter has left a note stating that they hope to have the phones installed tomorrow. I will send up a message instead."

"Thank you." I stood at the desk, feeling all shades of out of place. Around me, men and women with well-cut suits and business attire passed through security, showing their badges and walking through a weapon detector. One or two of them glanced my way, but I knew for most of them I was invisible.

"I have sent a message," the receptionist announced. She didn't look any too pleased to have me there, but gestured toward a bank of white leather benches. "You may wait over there if you like."

"Thank you." I didn't like being so exposed, and hesitated before asking, "I don't suppose you could just … you know … let me through so I could go up to my fiancé's office?"

She pursed her lips again and tapped on the keyboard, making hope rise within me. "Your name again?"

"Kiera Taylor."

"I'm afraid you are not on the list of employees of Papaioannou International," she said, nodding toward the couch.

"Thank you," I said tiredly.

I waited a total of five hours, my unease driving me to visit the bathroom frequently enough that the lady at the desk must have thought I had a bladder infection. I used the time there to wash my face and hands, and try to get the worst of the dirt and wrinkles out of my shirt. My hair was a tangled mess, pulled back in a ponytail, in no way contributing to the image of me as worthy of being in such a fancy office building, let alone affianced to a man as gorgeous as Theo.

After the fifth hour, I gave up. Clearly either Theo had had a change of plans or Anne had gotten through to him, and he must be out trying to find me.

"What's it going to be?" I asked myself. "Marina to hire a boat that you don't have the money to pay for—and probably run smack-dab into Misha or Armen, because they're smart enough to watch the ways to get out of Auckland—or tackle this tomorrow?"

My heart broke at the realization that the following day was supposed to be my wedding day. With no other options, I hurried through the dusk toward a residential street I'd seen coming in. I'd simply have to find a spot to sleep outside, perhaps hidden by another shed. Luckily, the weather wasn't dangerously cold at night, although I knew it would be chilly.

It took another hour before I located a house that had no lights on and possessed a shed in the backyard. I had to skulk around the fence, figuring I'd have to climb it, but the gate was open. I slipped through it, being as quiet as possible so as to not arouse anyone in the house, or neighbors, and went to investigate the shed. It was filled with lawn equipment, a couple of rusty bikes, a few plastic bins with labels that indicated they were household miscellany, and, blessedly, a ratty sweater hanging over a gardening apron.

I curled up next to the bikes, donning the sweater, and using the apron as an abbreviated blanket.

"You could be in Theo's arms right now," I told myself. I was angry, both at myself and at Misha. He'd ruined every moment of my life when he was in it, and now he was doing the same when he was no longer a part of it. I spent a bit of time worrying about Theo, knowing he would be concerned for me, and then the truly hellish thought hit me that he might try to find Misha to accost him.

I dozed off about midnight to my best estimation, ignoring the rustling sounds around and behind me. Rodents were the least of my worries, and New Zealand, unlike Australia, had no venomous snakes or insects other than a couple of very rare spiders, so I didn't fear for my safety in that regard.

By what I guessed was two a.m., I couldn't stand it. I had to be moving, had to do something to get in contact with Theo. Maybe I could steal a boat and sail it to his island? I shook my head even as I loped down the deserted streets, heading for the marina. "Even if I wanted to, I don't know where the island is. I'll just have to find someone there and convince them to take me out."

The only areas of town that had traffic on the street were those that catered to nightclubs. I kept to the shadows as much as possible, pausing at every intersection to look for Misha or Armen. I was painfully aware that I was dehydrated, and that my stomach growled despite the frequent waves of nausea that hit me whenever I thought of Theo confronting Misha, but I pushed onward toward the marina. When I was a few blocks away, I slowed down, using vehicles, buildings, and whatever structures I could to pause and examine the entrance of the marina, looking for signs of Misha lying in wait.

And that's how the police found me—lurking behind a car, peering around it at the lighted marina entrance.

"All right, then," a man's voice said behind me, startling me into a panicked shriek. "On your feet. Put your hands on the fence behind you, please."

I spun around to find two policemen, one of whom held a notebook while the other was speaking softly into a shoulder radio. "Um. Hi."

"Hands on the fence, please," he repeated, gesturing toward the wooden fence behind me. I did as he said, wondering how long it would be before Misha's police buddy told him that I'd been taken in.

The cop with the notebook patted me down in an impersonal, professional manner.

"Can I ask why you're doing this?" I asked as soon as he was finished.

"We've had reports of a woman casing the area. Name?"

Reluctantly, I told him.

"You're American? Do you have your passport?"

"No, I left my purse behind," I said, realizing just how lame that sounded. "I don't have anything with me."

"Just so." He pulled a plastic zip handcuff from a pocket and moved behind me, taking my hands with him. "Have you had any alcohol or drugs tonight, Kiera?"

"No," I said miserably. I was so tired, so exhausted and hungry and thirsty, that the fight was gone out of me. Misha had won. I just hoped the police would let me write a letter to Theo before Misha got ahold of me.

"Are you willing to take a sobriety test?"

"Why not?" I said.

The second policeman said something about them arresting me for suspicion of loitering with intent to perform a felony, and hustled me into a car, driving me through the streets I'd so carefully crept along.

I was fingerprinted, photographed, tested for alcohol and drugs, and finally interviewed about what I was doing before being informed that since I had no ID, I would be held.

"There's also the matter of this," the policeman interviewing me said, sliding across a picture of a car.

I blinked at it, wondering if my brain was so far shot that I was hallucinating.

"What's that?"

"It's the car you stole this evening."

"I *what*?" What fresh hell was this?

"Mr. Papaioannou said he did not give you permission to take the car, and as it's worth a good deal of money, I'm afraid this will be considered a felony." The policeman looked over the top of his glasses at me. "That doesn't look good given your current warrant."

"Theo said I stole his car? He doesn't have a car."

"On the contrary, he purchased this car"—he consulted another sheet of paper—"yesterday."

I put my hand to my head, my brain whirling with one horrendous thought after another. Theo said I stole his car? How could he do that to me? Was every man I met going to accuse me of stealing something? A few tears leaked out as I said, "I don't understand any of this. I didn't take a car. If I had, do you think I'd be running around on foot?"

"Cars such as this sell on the black market for a good deal of money." He tapped the paper with his pen. "It appears from this warrant that you have dealings with a known member of organized crime."

I slumped in my chair, beaten. There was nothing more I could do. Theo had put the police on to me knowing that Misha had a contact here. He did it deliberately.

Pain laced me so deeply, it made me gasp. Everything I believed was wrong. The world wasn't a place of handsome men who murmured soft words in my ears and meant them—it was a place of pain and betrayal, and never-ending despair.

I was escorted to a holding cell. I entered it exhausted, feeling battered, bruised, and beyond the reach of hope.

Two other women occupied the cell, but both were obviously sleeping off indulgences. I took a free bunk, and curled up into a fetal ball, crying silently while I willed myself into oblivion.

ELEVEN

Theo entered the police station in a red haze of fury. "Five hours? She's been here for five hours and you didn't bother to tell me?"

The officer who had met him at the door had obviously been told by the commissioner to suck up to him, no doubt helped by the generous donation to the commissioner's pet charity that Theo had made the night before. "I'm sorry, Mr. Papaioannou, but it's our policy to process people in the morning—"

"Get her," he snarled, stopping by a desk, his gaze moving around the station. He knew he was being an ass, but after the night he'd had, filled with images of the most horrendous variety, most of which involved finding Kiera's body broken and destroyed, not to mention a few particularly cruel ones detailing acts so vicious that they destroyed her sanity, leaving her body intact but her mind wandering paths he couldn't reach.

He'd never wanted to actively kill a person before, but he did now, and it was all he could do to not demand the police fetch the bastard who had taken his fragile little gazelle, but pleading calls by his lawyer not to do anything foolish had, in the end, allowed him to regain control of his temper. He had Peter and Kiera to think of. If he was in jail for assaulting or killing the bastard Mikhail, care of them would fall to

Jake, and he'd never hear the end of that. No, he had to stay sane for their—

The words dried up in his mind when a policewoman escorted Kiera from the holding area. She had a resigned look, one that said she was past caring what happened to her. His heart broke at the sight of it, but a second later, he wanted to shout with joy. She caught sight of him and instantly, her shoulders straightened, her chin went up, and her eyes blazed with emotion.

She was furious, clearly angry with him at the ploy he'd used to get the police searching for her before the monster found her, and although he knew it would take some time for her to overcome the loss of trust such an act would cause, he was confident that with time, he would make her understand that he had done the only thing he could. He had needed as many eyes on the street looking for her as he could muster, and she'd just have to understand that this was the only way he could achieve that goal.

An almost overwhelming sense of happiness filled him at the sight of her. Happiness wasn't the right word, though. … Love, now that felt like a good word. What he felt when he thought of her was a warmth that seemed to glow inside of him, a connection with her whole being that went beyond mere sexual desire. He realized with surprise that even if he never had sex with her again, he would be content to simply have her in his life, to be saying delightfully unexpected things to him, to make him feel like a hero because he could protect her from the things that upset her, and to have her annoyed at him because she loved his chest so much.

He wanted to tell her about his day when they were apart, and what he was thinking, sharing with her everything from the amusing comment his assistant made, to the design for a new house he wanted to build for her. He wanted her to share herself with him without inhibition. He just wanted her in his life, and if that wasn't love, he didn't know what was.

"Hello, sweetheart." The woman of his dreams marched

up to him, her hair, normally a long, glossy auburn, poking out of a knot she'd evidently tied on the top of her head, making it look like she had a small auburn porcupine mounted up there. Dirt smudged her cheek. Her shirt was wrinkled and filthy, and pulled more out of shape than was normal. He braced himself for either a punch from her fisted hands or a slap. She could go either way. "You look like hell."

"Theo," she snarled; then to his amazement, to his complete stupefaction, she grabbed his hair with both hands and pulled his face down to hers, her body moving against him in a way that was probably illegal when performed in a police station. Her mouth was hot and demanding, and before he could take charge of the kiss, her tongue charged into his mouth, teasing his, twining around in it a way that instantly made him hard.

He fought a battle but managed to keep from grabbing her ass and pulling her up higher. Instead, he contented himself with holding her hips, trying to stop the dance they were making against his cock. When she allowed him to reciprocate the kiss, her mouth had softened, her body molding itself around his. It took an almost superhuman effort, but he managed to pull back out of the kiss.

He looked down at her, smugly pleased with himself at the heat that shimmered in her eyes. "Does that mean you've forgiven me?"

Genuine confusion filled her face. Her lovely, freckled face, the one with dirt everywhere. "Forgiven you for what?"

"For having you arrested."

The look she gave him was pure scorn. "I was frightened, Theo, not suddenly rendered stupid. I realized right away that you'd set the police to find me so Misha couldn't."

He smiled, his admiration of her rising to new levels. "I had hoped that would occur to you. Er … you knew that *right* away?"

"Of course." She took his hand, and gave a little lift of her chin to the officer manning the desk when Theo escorted her out of the station. "Well, almost immediately."

He raised one eyebrow.

"All right, it wasn't until I saw you standing there with your hair all angry that I knew you must have been up all night, too. Were you?"

"Up all night? Yes." He smoothed a hand over his hair. "I'm glad you realized that I would never, in any way, ever hurt you. Do you have any plans this morning?"

"Huh?" She blinked at him as she got into the back of a car that was waiting for them. "Plans? Other than shower and eat and drink a gallon of water, and maybe sleep for a day?"

"How about if we both do all of that in"—he consulted his watch—"an hour?"

"All right, but what do you intend on doing until then?"

"I believe we have a wedding to attend," he said, damning safety laws and pulling her up against his side as he gave the driver the order to go.

"Theo, you can't!" she said, giggling when he whispered into her ear what he wanted to do to her in the shower. "We can't! I didn't get a dress, and I haven't brushed my teeth, or my hair for that matter, and I think there was mouse poop in the shed I slept in, because I keep getting whiffs of something from my back."

"Nonetheless, we shall get the damned ceremony over so that we can get on with the wedding night." He kissed her temple, content for a moment to just hold her. He'd come so close to losing her, he didn't think he'd be able to survive that. Not now that he knew he loved her.

"But Anne wanted to be there. And we should have Peter. I assume he's with the Darts?"

"Yes. Anne and Melanie took him home after they saw a man chasing you down the street." He pulled back to give her a half smile. "Anne said you outran the bastard like he was standing still. You really are a gazelle, aren't you?"

"No, but I did have six years of track."

"Really," he drawled, thinking of his own time on the track team. He'd been a long-distance runner in high school, but had lost his edge midway through college, when he started staying up all night drinking. "We'll have to have a race sometime."

She slid him an odd look. "Why?"

"Just, you know, to see if my time is better than yours." He tried to look nonchalant, but knew she saw through it immediately.

"Uh-huh. Could it be that you, too, were on a track team?"

"Perhaps." He smiled, pleased he'd distracted her from fretting over the wedding. "We should make a wager. Something … fun."

She moved away from him so that she could better see him. "Like what?"

"Well …" He pretended to think about it. "Like if I win, you have to accept a piece of jewelry of my choice."

"I'm letting you give me a wedding ring. That's jewelry."

"That is functional, or at least symbolic. This would be something frivolous, purely for decoration."

"Hmm. And what do I get if I win?"

"The jewelry?" he asked, hopeful.

"No." Her eyes narrowed on him as she thought. "How about you have to go to work for a week solid without looking like a GQ businessman. You have to let me rumple your hair before you go, wear jeans or that ratty old pair of shorts that has a hole in the butt, and a shirt that has never seen an iron, no matter how many meetings you have, or other important businesspeople you have to see."

"Deal," he said. "Although my favorite lucky fishing shorts are not ratty. They work magic when I go out on the water. Their appearance is at the cost of all the times they have provided food for my table."

"Mm-hmm. I'll believe that when I see it."

"Kiera?" he said, pulling her hand to his mouth so he could kiss her fingers.

"What?"

"We're here. Shall we get married?"

She sighed, but scooted across the seat when he got out of the car, and let him help her out. "All right, but if Peter looks back on our wedding photos twenty years from now and asks when it was you married a bag lady, you get to explain to him that I was coerced."

He wanted to sing and dance and shout from the highest building, but instead, he took a firm grip on her hand to keep her from bolting in case nerves got the better of her, and entered the registry office.

It was over in ten minutes, and although they'd had to grab two strangers as witnesses, strangers who gave Kiera an odd look, he was pleased. She was his, truly his, and no one could take her from him.

"Did you give your lawyer the prenuptial agreement?" she asked on the way to the airport.

"Hmm?" He thought of the lovely ritual he'd had burning the agreement that she'd wanted him to sign. He'd almost set off the sprinkler in his office, but it was worth every moment of the lecture Annemarie gave him. "I don't initiate documents I don't intend to put into place," he said with dignity.

"OK." She relaxed, her hand on his leg in a proprietary move that left him damn near giddy with happiness. He had a feeling she hadn't been this comfortable with anyone in a very long time. "You made such a big stink about it, I worried you wouldn't turn it in, or whatever you do with them."

"Yes, sweetheart, by signing that agreement, I have made sure you won't get a single cent from me should we divorce." He prayed she never found out he didn't execute the agreement after all.

She nodded, adding, "Mind you, you won't get any of my parents' house money either, but I don't think you have designs on my fifty grand."

He did a little mental arithmetic, adding up his net worth. He wasn't yet on par with Iakovos's ten figures, but he was making good progress, and he had high hopes that with another eight years of hard work, he'd be there. "Your nest egg is safe from my poaching ways," he said. "Is it too early to buy Peter a pony, do you think?"

She burst into laughter, the sound of it easing the last dregs of fear that had clutched him so tight when Anne had called to tell him she was missing.

Any plans he had of a wedding night that commenced before noon were delayed by Kiera insisting that she needed serious baby time to make up for her absence, and then there were explanations to be made to the Darts, and food to be consumed.

By dinner, however, he put his foot down.

"We gratefully accept your wedding present," he said, handing over Peter's diaper bag, the small cradle he'd bought on a whim, a large mesh bag of toys, several jars of gourmet baby food, his bath toys, and the giant kiwi bird that he knew Peter couldn't sleep without.

"I don't know about this," Kiera said, standing next to him, almost wringing her hands with distress. "He's such a good baby at night. He hardly ever wakes up."

Anne smiled. "I have already promised three times that if he so much as sneezes, we will bring him right home."

"No matter what time of night," Kiera reminded her.

"No matter the time of night," Anne said solemnly. "I feel obligated to point out that we are literally just one hundred yards away. You could lean your head out of the window and yell, and we'd hear you."

"That reminds me," Theo said, giving Peter's head a kiss before making shooing motions to Melanie. She giggled as she wheeled the baby away. "You ... er ... aren't going to want to use the pool tonight. It'll be ... occupied."

Richard grinned broadly, and followed the women.

Kiera eyed him with an indescribable expression. "Is that so?"

"Yes," he said, taking her into his arms. He hadn't been able to have the joint shower that he'd planned on the flight over to the island, but he was determined to have the next best thing. "The minute you married me, I started a list of fantasies I wished to fulfill with you. Right now, licking water off your breasts, sliding my hands along your wet, slick flesh, and burying myself in your heat while floating in the pool is currently at the top of the list."

She looked from him to the pool, which, due to the layout of the garden, had a decent amount of privacy. "I don't have a swimsuit."

"Darling," he said in a voice made deep with desire. "What part of licking and tasting and burying myself in you makes you think the wearing of a swimsuit is necessary?"

"Right," she said, nodding, and to his amazement peeled off the clean T-shirt she'd put on. She eyed the distance across the long stretch of green grass, to the steps leading down to the pool area. "Race you there?"

"No," he said firmly, yelling the word as she took off. He sighed, pulling off his own shirt as he followed her at a walk. "It's not fair you trying to take advantage of me. I can't run with this."

She glanced down at the front of his jeans, shimmying out of her leggings so that she could do a seductive little wiggle against him. "Mercy, Theo. Not only are you slow, and clearly are going to lose our bet—"

"Tomorrow. We're going to run that damned race tomorrow," he growled, kicking off his shoes and ridding himself of both jeans and underwear.

She laughed, and waggled her ass at him when she peeled off her bra, her hair swinging across her naked back as she looked over her shoulder to him. "Not only are you slow—you appear to have trouble with your manly bits. It must be very uncomfortable to have your plumbing outside, instead of tucked away nicely, like women."

He lunged for her, growling deep in his chest, but she just laughed and did an enticing dance as she wriggled out of her underwear, throwing it to him.

He tossed it over onto the pile of clothes she'd shed, and stalked forward. "Right. You've impugned my speed—about which you know nothing, since you didn't go to school in England, as I did—but now you're telling me my cock is inferior? Prepare to defend yourself, woman. I'll show you why outdoor plumbing is to be desired!"

She stood at the side of the pool, laughing, and taunting him with her hips and breasts and those long legs, and looking like she might just run off into the gathering night, but he was on her before she could move.

"Now, wife, let me show you how we Papaioannou men celebrate their wedding nights."

"All right but I should tell you—" she started to say, but the words ended on a shriek when he tossed her into the water, diving after her, intending on touching all the various and sundry parts of her, but she didn't seem to be on board with that plan. She sank like a rock to the bottom of the pool, her arms and legs thrashing wildly.

And that's when he realized she couldn't swim.

"I'm sorry, sweet, I'm so sorry," he apologized a few minutes later while she knelt on the lawn beyond the pool, vomiting up water. "I just assumed that you knew how to swim. Everyone I know swims."

"You. Grew. Up. In. Greece," she said, raising her head and wiping a tendril of saliva from her lips, her eyes all but spitting anger at him. "On a damned island. Of course everyone you know swims."

"Do you feel better now?" he asked hopefully, his grandiose plans for a wild, steamy wedding night drifting away on the wind.

"I may just hate you," she said, getting to her feet and limping over to her clothes.

"Sorry about banging your knee on the railing, too."

She said a word that made him flinch.

"Why don't we take a nice shower together—"

She spun around to shoot lasers out of her eyes at him, or at least that's what it felt like to him. She lifted a hand and pointed a finger at him. "That's it. I'm divorcing you in the morning. And you'd better thank your lucky stars that you signed that prenup, because if you hadn't, I'd take you for everything you had."

With great dignity, she gathered up her clothes and started toward the house, still limping.

He would have to be dead for a good five months not to admire her ass as she did so. "If I told you that I'm in love with you, would that make things any better?" he yelled after her.

Her shoulder twitched, but she kept walking.

He smiled to himself. He couldn't think of a time when he'd loved anyone as much as he loved Kiera. She was the perfect woman, put on the earth solely so she could make his life worth living. He gathered his own clothing and followed her into the house, calling on all his persuasive powers to get her into a warm tub, where he convinced her he would make her knee feel better.

"First you almost drown me," she said, mollified enough that she allowed him into the tub with her. Since it was big enough to wash the pony he was even now planning on buying for Peter, she wasn't going to suffer unduly from his presence. "Then you break my kneecap. Is this how you famed Papaioannou men have wedding nights? Because if it is, I'm surprised any of you ever had wives long enough to reproduce."

"I assure you, that was just a horrible consequence of my own ineptitude." He sank into the water, pausing to narrow his eyes on her.

"What?" she asked, scooting a little closer to him.

"Would you say I'm clumsy?" he asked her.

"You? On the contrary, you're probably the most graceful man I've ever seen. You never seem to put a foot wrong. You don't trip over your own feet like me, and I never see you hitting your arm on doorways, which I always seem to do. Why?"

"Because it seems like whenever I'm with you, I'm always doing things wrong. I scared you that first night. I teased you, and damn near made you barf. I urge you to go to the mainland, and you spend a night on the run, with me worried out of my brain about you, and I want to make love to you in our pool on our wedding night, and just see how that ended. I think it's you," he said, not liking this feeling of incompetence. "Harry said I made that damned bachelor list. You don't make those if you are the sort of man who hits his wife's knee on a handrail coming out of a pool."

She stared at him for a moment, all but oozing disbelief; then her mouth twitched, and she was there, in his arms, sitting across his thighs, her mouth nibbling on his neck in that spot she liked. "You're absolutely right, Theo. The list people are right. I have been horribly cruel to you making you lose your mojo."

"That's it, exactly. I lose control around you." He allowed himself to be kissed, his hands filled with her delightful, silky breasts. "I don't like it."

"Well, I do. You're far too perfect. I like seeing this side of you."

He gave her a look that told her what he thought of that. "I'm anything but perfect. I can't be near booze. I smoked until I stopped drinking. I had a son I didn't know about because I didn't bother to stay in touch with Nastya. And I'm not as rich as my brother was when he was my age."

Her fingers trailed an intricate dance down his chest, touching and teasing and stroking. "But you don't drink or smoke now, and you embraced having Peter in your life. As for the last … is it a contest, this thing between you and your brother?"

"No," he said, sucking in his breath when her fingers found his penis. "All right, maybe it is, but only to me. Are you going to let me take the lead?"

She grasped his testicles, gently scraping her nails down them until his hips flexed, his breath stuck in his chest. "I suppose you've earned it, since it's clear that I am solely to blame for your loss of suavity. Theo?"

She was teasing him. His heart sang with the wonder of it; then she bent down and swirled her tongue around one of his nipples. He moaned, pulling her up so she straddled his thighs on the narrow seat that ran around the tub, his fingers flexing on her delectable ass, his mouth nuzzling one of her perfect breasts. He deliberately hadn't shaved that evening just so he had a bit of stubble. She *loved* his stubble. No woman had ever loved his stubble. It was just one more thing that made her the ideal woman for him. "Hmm?"

"Did you mean what you said?"

He stopped nibbling on the underside of one exquisitely perfect breast, looking up. One side of his mouth curled up. "Yes."

"But we've only known each other for, what, a week?"

"Sometimes, that's all it takes," he told her, and turned his attention to her other breast, allowing it to rub against his cheek. He wanted badly to know if she was falling in love with him, but couldn't ask. Not yet. Not while she was still recovering from their day from hell. "Now, what do you think of this?"

His fingers found her in the water, teasing and caressing. He wanted to taste her, but suspected he might drown if he tried.

"Oh, yes, Lord yes." She arched back, squirming on his fingers, the feel of her heat as he slipped one inside of her almost pushing him beyond his control. Her muscles gripped him as he slid a second finger in, and suddenly, it was too much.

"Please tell me you're ready for this, because try as I might, I can't think of anything but being deep inside you," he said, lifting her up.

"That sounds perfect to me," she said just as she positioned him, and sank down slowly, the cooling water lapping at her delightful belly as she moved on him. "This is ... hooo! This angle is *really* nice, isn't it! It's like you're touching all sorts of magical spots inside me."

He lurched upward, holding her hips where he wanted them, trying to slow his body's urges, wanting her to find her own pleasure, but his movements losing all rhythm until he simply thrust into her over and over again, her moans and wiggles and hands touching and tormenting him beyond bearing. He pulled down on her hips as he pushed up hard into her, his thighs tightening with the glory of it all, and just as he gave in to the climax that threatened to leave him senseless, her muscles spasmed around him, tightening to the point where he seriously thought he might just die right then and there.

He had no idea how they made it out of the bathroom and onto the bed, because Kiera claimed her legs had no bones, and he couldn't even think, let alone make his limbs answer his brain's demands, but as she drifted off to sleep, tucked into him, his body curled protectively around hers, he knew that this was what he'd been waiting for.

Now all he had to do was figure out a way to keep her safe.

TWELVE

"Theo, we have to talk."

"Mmm. With your mouth? I love your mouth. I love *you*."

The scent of him, a warm, sleepy man, *my* warm, sleepy man, made my toes curl. But a glance at the clock told me that we had just an hour before the Darts were due to bring Peter back. Theo's hands were wandering, and although his eyes were closed, one hand stroked along my back, down to my behind, his fingers curled around one thigh, pulling it forward over his hip so that his fingers slid down until they found sensitive flesh.

"I can't believe you are seriously thinking to do this when just two hours ago—are you taking some sort of male libido pill? Because if you are, I want to buy stock in the company."

His lips quirked. How I loved those lips. I spent another of the moments that had gripped me in the past twenty-four hours wherein I stared at the beautiful man who had somehow skipped all the gorgeous models of the Nastya ilk, and instead, chosen me to fall in love with.

Theo loved me. I cherished that nugget of knowledge, holding it tight to me. It seemed to me to be the most amazing thing, and yet, so perfectly reasonable. Of course he loved me. I was head over heels in love with him, so it was only right and fitting that he should return that love.

Only … the dark cloud of worry blotted out the joy that just being with Theo brought me. I stopped the hand where it was questing toward my fun zone, and pushed him over onto his back, parking myself on top of him so he couldn't distract me. "Theo, I'm serious. We have to talk."

"Wedding night," he murmured, refusing to open his eyes. "No serious talk."

"That was over once the sun came up, and we don't have long before Peter will be back. Dammit, Theo, I don't want to do this, but we have to."

He sighed, but opened his eyes, his hands, which had been drawing circles on my behind, stilled. "You, wife, have a very poor sense of timing."

"I know. You can add that to the other things I do to make you awkward and gauche, not that anyone but you thinks that. We have to make plans."

"About your ex?" He stretched, the muscles in his beautiful chest doing a dance that made me seriously rethink my need to have this discussion. "I've got my lawyer working on the charges hanging over you, and detectives looking around Auckland for him."

"What do you intend to do if you find him?" I asked, my heart turning to stone at the thought of Theo facing Mikhail's wrath.

"Press charges for assault to start with," he said, touching the faint bruising on my throat. "And whatever else we can drum up. While he's in jail for that, we'll work on putting him away for good."

"I would love nothing more, but you don't have any idea how ruthless he is. He never came out and admitted it to me, but I don't think he'd stop short of murder."

Theo just smiled at me and kissed my nose. "I will keep you safe, little gazelle."

That wasn't what I was worried about, and he knew it.

"I'll have to get a replacement driver's license," I said, thinking about all the things that I'd lost when my purse tangled around Misha. "Thank God my passport was here. And I'm sure he'll help himself to the cash—oh, no!"

Theo picked up his phone, checking his messages. "Hmm?"

A cold sweat rippled down my flesh. I pushed myself off Theo, my insides feeling like they were in the grip of an iron hand. "Theo, he has my bank card."

"So? My assistant canceled the card yesterday, after you told me your bag was gone."

"My name was on it," I said, wanting to run. "Marshmallows from the top down. Snail shells. Mandalas."

Theo looked at me with a little frown pulling his black brows together. "What are you round-therapy-ing about?"

"My name. My new name. Papaioannou. You had it put on the bank card because we were getting married."

His eyes narrowed as he thought about that; then he shrugged. "It doesn't matter. There are some benefits to being a rich man, sweetheart, and one of those is the ability to maintain privacy in otherwise public records. He won't be able to find us."

I had to leave. I had to get out of there. We all did. "Pizza. Cinnamon rolls. Pies."

"You are worrying unduly, but I know you can't help it. In time, you will see that I mean it when I say that I can keep you and Peter safe."

I watched him pad barefoot into the bathroom, my mind spinning around like a gerbil in a plastic ball.

He stuck his head out of the bathroom, seductive smile on his lips. "Shower?"

"I thought of leaving, you know."

The smile faded as he took a step toward me. "I thought you might."

"It seemed like the only thing I could do. The only way I could keep you and Peter from being used by Mikhail. I thought I would leave a note at your office and just disappear. I knew you'd be hurt and mad and …" I waved a hand in a vague gesture. "Annoyed, I guess. But I also knew you would get over it in time, and you'd eventually find someone else, and your life would be good. Without the threat of Misha looming over it to ruin everything."

He stood watching me, his lovely dark blue eyes unreadable. "You were incorrect in that. I would not have recovered. What made you change your mind?"

I stood up and wrapped my arms around him, kissing the tendon in his neck that always called to me. "I decided that I needed to trust you. To trust that you could do what you said you could do. I want to think we can get away from Misha, Theo, but I don't see how. And now he knows about my new name, and everything we planned is ruined."

His arms were tight around me, protecting me, comforting me. *Loving me.* He kissed my forehead. "I don't know when I've received a nicer compliment. I will work hard to make sure you don't regret putting your trust in me."

I bit the tendon as he nuzzled behind my ear. "You'd better not. Because I don't think I could survive a betrayal by you."

The shower was made twice as long because I had to keep dodging Theo's questing hands, but at last we were clean, dressed, and downstairs when Peter arrived home with his entourage.

I took one look at his happy face and immediately turned to Theo. "The little rotter didn't even miss us, and I woke up at least three times worrying about him."

"He had a lovely time, and was a very good young man," Anne said, smiling fondly as Theo swung Peter up in the air, making him shriek with delight. "He slept right through the night, and had himself some porridge for breakfast along with his formula. And a piece of garlic bread that I wasn't fast enough to get away from him."

I laughed, taking his hand and giving it a squeeze. He no-no-ed me, grabbing for my hair. "He has quite the reach, doesn't he?"

"I cleared the course earlier," Richard said, nodding toward the back of the house. "If you two are ready?"

"Course?" I asked, making faces at Peter that had him chuckling nonstop. "What—oh, the race."

"Ah, yes, I had momentarily forgotten about that." Theo stopped pretending to nibble on Peter's arm and leered at me. "I was distracted by a lusty wench in my bed. But now seems as good a time as any, eh, gazelle?"

I rolled my eyes, but smiled nonetheless. "I wasn't serious about the challenge, you know."

"Afraid I'll be that much faster than you?" Theo asked, looking smug. "I am a man, after all."

"Oh, it's on now," I said, marching into the bedroom to change out of my jeans and into a pair of leggings. I also put on my sports bra, and the only tight-fitting T-shirt I owned.

Richard explained as we left the house that there was a track that led from the beach up the hill and along the spine of the island. The sheep were fenced on either side of the track, which meant we wouldn't have to add hurdling sheep as part of the race. "There are no holes, no big stones, no obstacles," he said as we arrived at the far tip of the island, the northernmost end, which was soft sand. "Do you have a preference for the length? Melanie ran it this morning, while you were … er … sleeping … and it took her nine minutes to get to the top and back down to the bench."

He pointed to a spot halfway up the path from the beach, where a bench had been set so people could sit and admire the view.

"What distance was your best time?" Theo asked me, handing Peter to Melanie.

I eyed the path, noting the grade as it meandered up to the crest of the island. Assuming the part I couldn't see wasn't much steeper, it looked doable. "Fifteen hundred meters."

"Middle distance? I preferred two thousand, myself, but I'm willing to accommodate your preference," he said.

"You are graciousness personified. Do you mind if we have a quick jog along the course first, as sort of a warm-up and to get an idea of the terrain?"

"Not at all. It sounds like an excellent suggestion."

We spent five minutes warming up, then headed up the track, Theo in the lead. I watched his form, but didn't see anything obviously wrong with it. Damn.

It took us seven and a half minutes to jog along the track to the far end, stopping before the track veered downward to a flight of wooden stairs that led down to the beach.

"Stop here, I think," Theo said, and moved a rock to the middle of the path.

We got back to find the Darts all making bets with one another, a rock holding down a few bills next to Peter's stroller.

"Do I want to know who the odds are favoring?" I asked, as Anne, with a speculative look at Theo, *tsk*ed, and pulled another bill out of her wallet to add to the stack. "Thirty for me, Rich. Mind you make a note of it."

He duly wrote it down.

"I hate to let a fellow woman down," Melanie said, giving me a wry smile. "But Theo said his college track team won awards one year. And I really want to get a new mobile phone."

I turned to look at Theo. "Your team medaled?"

He grinned. "Did I not mention that?"

"No. No, you didn't."

"It must have slipped my mind."

"Uh-huh. Right, how much do I need to get in on this action?" I asked Richard.

He smiled, and wet his pencil. "I'm afraid that right now only Anne is backing you. If you wish to join forces with her, Melanie and I have eighty dollars on Theo."

"I'm so going to take that bet." I was incensed, and only in time remembered I didn't have any money since Misha had my purse. I looked at Theo. "Can you stake me?"

"I thought you didn't want my money?" he asked, his eyebrows raised in a show of innocence.

"As a loan. I'll pay you back when I get a new bank card. Can you match Anne's thirty dollars for me?"

He nodded, and Richard wrote down the bet.

"I am above such things," Theo said loftily, "but my son is not. Put him down for fifty. I'll make good the amount."

"On?" Richard asked, pencil poised.

"Me."

"Smug bastard," I murmured, smiling to myself.

"What was that?" Theo asked.

"Hmm? Nothing."

It took a couple of tries before we worked out a method of starting that was fair, and after deciding that three laps was a close approximation of fifteen hundred meters, we stood ready and poised.

"If you think you're going to let me win just because I'm a woman, I will never forgive you," I whispered to Theo as I took my starting position, butt in the air, hands dangling right above the ground.

"Would I do that?" he asked.

Richard held up his phone, and let the starter app countdown run. As soon as the whistle starting the race hit the air, I was off, not putting my full speed into the hill, since there was a nice flat stretch on the top where I planned to accelerate.

Theo passed me almost immediately, his long legs positively eating up the ground. I kept my eyes on the path, not wanting to stumble on any untoward rock, inhaling over the course of three steps, and exhaling for two, finding my rhythm almost automatically as I crested the top. He was about twenty feet ahead of me, and opening up ground between us. I let him, seeing his arms pumping harder than they needed to be. The rat was showing off, obviously wanting to impress me with his speed.

By the time he hit the turning point, I had closed the space until he was about fifteen feet ahead of me. He grinned as he passed me heading back toward the bench.

I put on a little speed on the way back to the bench since I was out of his view, and I caught a glimpse of surprise on his face when he turned and saw me on his heel. He powered past me up the hill, and I took the time to wave at the Darts, who were all yelling and cheering. I saw him glancing back as he hit the flat part of the spine. Thirty feet now stood between us, and I knew he was going to relax at the sight of it. He turned and headed back down the path, saying as he did so, "Getting tired, sweetheart?"

"Cocky, very cocky," I yelled at him, and decided enough was enough. I'd had my fun.

I let my pace pick up, my breath coming shorter, but still matching the stride, my arms relaxed and helping my feet push me forward. I caught Theo just as he was about to turn at the bench, touched it, and was three strides ahead of him before he could even turn. Anne cheered loudly. I kept my eyes on the path, feeling the familiar sense of euphoria that came from a run, hearing Theo behind me. I dug deep, pulling out memories of years of track meets, mentally shifting my legs into a higher gear. The sheep, the scrubby shrubs that dotted the spine of the island, and the black faces of angular rock that broke through the earth to reach to the sky all blurred past me. I touched the turning-point rock, and headed back on the last half of the lap. Theo touched the rock and turned, his breathing started to get ragged. I mentally shook my head at him and shifted gears one last time, wanting to throw my arms in the air and laugh with the sheer joy of it all.

Theo conceded when he crested the hill down to the bench, and saw me sitting there, waiting for him.

He slowly came down the path, his big chest heaving, sweat making his face shine. "Bloody … hell … what … are … you … bionic?" he asked between panting gasps for air.

I wasn't gasping, but my breath was definitely on the short side, and it took me a minute before I could answer. "Three-time collegiate champion in the mile."

"You … you …" He fell to his knees, laughing and mopping his face with his shirt.

The Darts swarmed us, helping Theo to his feet, holding out bottles of water, one of which I sipped gratefully. "I am so out of shape," I told Anne when she congratulated me for the third time. "Even given that this wasn't run on a track, my time is disgraceful."

"Later," Theo said, looking like he wanted to fall down again. "Later I will have cutting things to say to you about women who hide their status as college champion—"

"Three times, evidently," Anne said.

I grinned at her.

"Three times," Theo amended, glaring at me. "But now I'm going to allow Richard to assist my broken and aching body back to the house, while those of you who are superhuman monsters can bring my child."

I blew him a kiss, watching Anne divide up our winnings while Melanie wheeled Peter after the men.

I waited until they were out of sight before plopping myself down on the grass with less elegance than a drunk hippo. "Jesus, Mary, and Joseph, I thought he'd never leave." I lay back and stared up at the sky, finally giving in to the burn of my calves and thighs. "I never want to do that again. I thought I was going to die the last little bit down to the bench."

Anne laughed so hard she startled a pair of terns who were sunning themselves.

The following morning, I was so stiff I could hardly walk.

"You move like an elderly badger that's been run over a few times," Theo commented when I hobbled to the bathroom.

He had just emerged from the shower and stood upright, one extremely gorgeous naked man, with his sleek skin, and rippling muscles. I hated his body at that moment, all strong and supple and evidently not in the least bit affected by the race.

I snarled something rude at him and headed for the toilet. Theo stood before the mirror shaving, something that fascinated me, but I tried not to stare while brushing my teeth. He finished and dropped his towel, striding out of the bathroom like the Greek god he was. I glared at his tempting butt, picking up his towel and hanging it before returning to the bedroom to pick out something to wear. He must have thought I was still in the bathroom, because he limped over to one of the closets containing his suits, making soft little moaning noises while trying to flex first his feet and calves, then his back.

"If the elderly badger fits… " I said from the door, and grinned when he frowned at me.

"My next wife isn't going to be a bloody gazelle," he called after me as I slipped on a pair of leggings and a tee and went to get Peter up. "She's going to be a sloth. Do you hear me? A sloth!"

I was engaged in convincing the baby to try a little minced pear with his yogurt when Theo emerged from the bedroom clad in the pair of shorts he referred to as being lucky.

"I thought you were going to your office today?" I asked, confused.

"I am." He waved a hand down his torso. "I lost the bet. Would you like to tousle my hair yourself, or would sticking my head out of the window of the helicopter be enough to mess it up?"

I looked at the knee-length, stained, faded shorts, and walked around behind him. A hole the size of an orange gaped, revealing his black underwear and exposing the sweet curve of one of his magnificent butt cheeks. I returned to face him, my eyes narrowing on the formfitting tank top that clung to every muscle of his chest and belly. Dammit, I could see his six-pack through it.

"I changed my mind," I said, my eyes on his chest and bare arms. "Wear your suit. Maybe two. Can you fit three on at the same time?"

He laughed, kissing me hard and fast, a promise in his eyes when he returned to the bedroom to change. He no longer walked like a badger.

"I hate to say this to you, because the man is your father, but there are times when he's just a big ole poopy-head. No more pear? Would you like to try this bit of banana? I'll put a tiny bit of peanut butter on it since you didn't have an adverse reaction to it yesterday."

Peter accepted the quartered slice of banana, spreading it between his fingers before eventually conveying it to his mouth.

"I'm having new bank cards for you couriered out today." Theo emerged from the bedroom clad in a black suit with a thin gray stripe running through it. "In case you want to do any shopping."

I raised my eyebrows.

"Online shopping," he said, cocking his head when the sound of the helicopter could be heard over the surf.

"We don't have Internet," I pointed out.

"Which is why I've provided you with a limitless data plan. You know how to use a tablet, don't you?" he asked, nodding to the table where the tablet computer sat.

"Of course."

"Good. I'll get another mobile phone for you, as well—"

His phone rang as he spoke. He glanced at it, a little frown on his brow as he answered it with a curt, "Yes?"

"I believe a little shopping for you is in order today, sir," I told Peter while I wiped up his face before setting him down. "Some sort of a waterproof swimsuit to go over your diaper would do nicely."

I glanced at Theo, going to ask him what he would think of the ladybug outfit, but the words dried up on my lips as I caught sight of his body language. He'd turned so his back was to me, his shoulders hunched up, the one hand holding his laptop case white with strain.

I gave Peter a toy and silently moved over to Theo.

"—will warn you that I will not tolerate you harassing my wife in any way," he said in a low voice, ugly with threat.

Fear washed over me, leaching all the pleasure out of the morning. I moved around to Theo's side, holding his arm.

He tried to turn away from me, the fury on his face almost as frightening as the thoughts that were twisting and tumbling through my head.

"I've said all that I'm going to say," he spat out, and hung up on the caller.

"Oh, God, my phone," I said, the image of Mikhail's face red with anger fresh in my mind. "I forgot to cancel it yesterday."

"I didn't." Theo's jaw was so tight, I was amazed he could talk. "I left it on hoping he'd call. I wanted to tell him what I'd do to him if he even thought about contacting you again."

Part of my brain, the part that still remembered the bad times, urged me to run from Theo. He was angrier than I'd ever seen him, and angry men were dangerous. I felt sick to my stomach as I put my hand on his arm again. "I'm sorry," was all I could say.

His furious blue eyes turned to me. A muscle twitched in his jaw. "Three men will be arriving today. Richard will meet them at the helipad. If they do not show him the proper documents, he will ensure they get back on the copter and return to Auckland."

"What three men?" I asked, shrinking back from the look in his eyes.

He blinked and looked down at his arm where I'd withdrawn my hand. Carefully setting down his laptop bag, he took me by the arms, and looked into my eyes. "I'm not mad at you, wife. I will never be mad at you." He made a face. "Well, when you beat me so easily at a race I was fatheaded enough to think I could win, then I might be a tiny bit irritated, but ninety-nine percent of that was directed at myself, not you."

I tried to summon a smile, but couldn't. "I should have told you, so that you could have given it your best shot."

He gave a short bark of laughter, his expression returning to one I knew and loved. He pulled me into his arms for a kiss so hot, it just about made my toenails steam. "My love, I *was* giving it my best shot. More than that. I was trying with every aching atom of my body when you loped past me like I was standing still."

"What three men?" I asked again.

"Security team," he said, releasing me and picking up his laptop bag. "Richard will see them first. Don't go up to the helipad until he tells you it's all right."

"Do we need security men on the island?" I asked, worry gripping me again with its icy fingers.

"No, but it will mean I can work in Auckland without giving myself an ulcer." He patted my cheek, kissed Peter, and was out the door before I could catch my breath.

"I have to do something," I told Peter when I took him out on the patio to watch Theo's copter disappear to the west. "I refuse to let him get hurt. I refuse to let you get hurt. Maybe if I find whatever it is that Mikhail wants, he'll leave us be."

"No no no no no." Peter pointed to a bird.

"A flash drive," I said, shaking my head. I certainly didn't have anything like that, but with nothing else I could do, I took Peter in to play in the bedroom while I pulled out my duffel bag, laying out all my clothing. Peter happily disregarded his toys in favor of crawling into the bag, talking to himself as he pulled several T-shirts in with him.

"I've worn all of these in the nine months since I left Misha," I told him, examining each shirt carefully. I didn't know how small a flash drive could be made, and had no idea how one could get into my seams, but I felt each one, then turned my attention to my jeans and leggings, socks, underwear, even the underwire on my bra. The soles of my shoes were intact, and once I wrestled Peter out of the bag, I went over it inch by inch, but it, too, was clean of any USB devices.

"And why would he hide it in my stuff, then get mad at me for having it?" I knee-walked over to the nightstand where I'd placed the four books I'd taken away with me, all paperbacks, none of them looking like anything but a book. "Hmm."

I eyed the narrow rectangular wooden tray that sat on Theo's dresser, getting up to look at it. I'd collected sand for it the previous night, filling the Zen garden tray before placing my five rocks on it and using the tiny wooden rake to make a pleasing swirly pattern. "It's just a Zen garden. How can you hide anything in rocks? Oh, this is hopeless."

"Hello? Kiera? Richard wanted me to tell you that some men will be arriving in fifteen minutes, and that you should stay in the house until he checks them out. Hello, Peter. Are you hiding? Are we going to play peekaboo?" Anne knelt down as she entered the bedroom, tickling Peter's stomach when he poked his head out of the duffel bag. He chuckled and offered her a couple of slobbery fingers. She told him he was too charming for his own good, and looked over to where I sat on my heels. "What do you have there? Oh, one of those meditation gardens."

"Yes. Swami Betelbaum recommended it. He said it's good for us to see what patterns have meaning to us each day, but to be honest …" I looked down to where I was holding the tray, and carefully set it back on the dresser, next to a picture of a woman who Theo said was his sister, and another of his brother and sister-in-law. "My mind is so confused, I don't think there's a meaning at all."

"I know things seem bleak now, but I think you'll find that Theo is immovable about some things, and keeping you and Peter safe is definitely one of those things."

"Yes, but who's going to keep him safe?" I wanted to cry, but knew that was an irrational action.

She patted my arm, but had nothing else to offer other than I had to have faith in Theo.

Faith in him wasn't my problem, but I decided I'd gone around that particular circuitous thought pattern enough already. "Are the three security men going to stay on the island?"

"Yes, in the guesthouse. Richard said that we can take two of them with us when we go to the mainland."

I made a face.

She laughed. "I know you don't want to go there now, but when you're ready to do a little shopping, we'll take the bodyguards, and I promise we won't let you be kidnapped again."

"I could use some new clothes, but I think I'll wait for a time when Theo can take me himself."

Richard brought the three men down to meet me a half hour later, introducing them as George, Paul, and John.

"I'm sorry," I told the three men, giving them all apologetic smiles. "I don't want to do this, but I kind of have to. No Ringo?"

They made the polite sort of smiles that said they'd heard the quip many times before. George, who was a tall Maori man with lovely tribal tattoos on his neck and an even lovelier Australian accent, said, "I'm afraid we had to leave him behind. I understand from Mr. Papaioannou and Mr. Dart here that you've been having a bit of trouble with an unwelcome ex-suitor."

"That's one way of putting it." I had Peter on my hip, rubbing his back, since he was getting sleepy, and I wanted to put him down for a nap before it got too late.

"You don't have anything to worry about with us here," Paul said. He was almost as big as George, but blond with a crew cut and a thick New York accent.

"You just let us know when you want to go to the mainland, and we'll detail an escort for you," George added.

"Did Mr. Papaioannou talk to you about your bugout bag?" George asked.

"My what, now?"

He explained that I needed to make a small bag with those items necessary to a stay of a few days away from home, as well as one for Peter.

"OK, but …" I glanced at Anne. "I don't really have any clothes I can spare to put in it."

George raised an eyebrow at me. I decided he didn't need to hear about my weird quirks. "I advise you to get your bag together as soon as you can."

I promised him I would, thanked them all, and let Richard and Anne escort them off to the guesthouse, which sat higher on the cliff. Peter and I settled down for a nap together on Theo's big bed, my mind alternating between worrying about Theo, wondering where the flash drive was that had Misha so worked up, and thinking about going to the mainland to get some much needed clothing.

I didn't hear the noise until Richard shouted my name.

"Huh?" I sat up, pushing my hair out of my face. Next to me, Peter was still sleeping, his warm body smooshed up against me. "What's wrong?"

"Kiera where are you—oh, thank God. Get the baby. Anne, grab the things he'll need. Where's your bag?"

"What's going on?" I asked, panic filling me at the sight of Anne's tight expression. She dashed for the baby's room. I picked up Peter, my flight instinct riding me high, turning as I tried to figure out where I should run.

"Melanie!"

She ran into the room and took Peter from me, murmuring something about getting his favorite blanket.

"Someone please tell me what's happening!" I almost screamed, desperate, frightened, and confused.

"Is this yours?" Richard asked, throwing my duffel bag on the bed.

"Yes. Why am I packing? Is it the bugout bag thing—" I paused, listening to an unfamiliar noise overhead. "Is that a plane?"

"Yes." His face was grim as he ran to the window to try to peer up.

"Are they ready?" John appeared at the bedroom door, a phone in his hand.

"A plane." It took me a minute before I realized the significance of that. A normal plane wouldn't put everyone into a panic, but a plane that was clearly buzzing the island … it had to be Misha. I didn't bother wasting time talking; I jerked open the drawers where I'd just put my things away an hour before, and threw them all into the bag, dumping the sand of my Zen garden into the trash, and flinging the tray and rocks, along with my paperbacks, into the bag before running to the bathroom. In two minutes, all my worldly possessions were in the bag in the living room, while Anne,

Melanie, and I tried to pick the most vital of Peter's items. George just about had a hissy fit at the giant kiwi bird, but grabbed it with one hand, and the giant wheeled suitcase that we'd filled with as much of Peter's clothing, toys, and care items as we could fit.

Richard emerged with an identical bag containing some of Theo's things.

"Where are we going?" I asked, flinching when the whine of the plane Dopplered, the sound increasing as it returned for another pass of the island. "One of the boats?"

"It's not safe enough. If he has firearms …" George glanced at Peter, held in my arms.

I fought the nausea that rose with that unfinished sentence. "Then what are we doing?"

"Theo's on his way, Kiera," Anne said, an arm around me. "And he's bringing the police. They'll scare off that bastard, and he'll take you to the airport."

"He's sending me away?" I asked, my heart feeling like it was going to break. Was Theo moving himself and Peter to the mainland while I went elsewhere? I didn't want to leave him and the baby, but that was just selfishness. I had to go. I couldn't blame Theo for getting rid of me, but it hurt nonetheless.

"You're all leaving. Did you get their passports, Rich?" Anne asked.

"Right here," he answered, giving them to George.

"We're all going? Theo, too?"

"Yes," Anne said, patting me on the arm. "It'll be all right, Kiera. Just you see. Theo is very resourceful."

The whine of the plane grew louder and louder as it approached, leaving me with a ridiculous need to duck. Paul entered the house, gesturing everyone away from the windows.

"Just in case," he said.

Just in case of what? I wanted to ask, but simply clutched a half-asleep Peter, taking comfort in the baby smell of him.

He was warm, sleepily draped on me, sucking slowly on a clump of my hair.

It was a hellish nightmare of a half hour before Paul and John—who had been skulking around outside watching the plane, which was clearly trying to both intimidate us and look for a place to safely land—called George. He returned a minute later. "Two choppers are coming in now," he told us. "One is the police. Everyone stay here. No one leave the house. Do you understand?"

He looked at me as he spoke.

"There is nothing I want less than to risk this baby's life," I told him.

"Good. Keep that as your goal, and you'll be fine."

He disappeared while the Darts talked quietly to themselves. I listened hard for the sound of the rotors, but when the wind was blowing to the south, it carried the sound away. I wondered what was going on up there. Would Misha try to enact some sort of air battle? Or would the presence of the police cause him to slip away? Normally, he gave the police a wide berth, but if he was feeling safe because of any police buddies he had, who knew what he would do?

I paced back and forth with Peter, now fully awake and fussing to be let down, but I couldn't seem to let go of him. A gust of wind whirled into the room, and Theo was there, holding us both, murmuring words of love and comfort, his arms hard around us.

I wanted to sob at the joy of seeing him hale and hearty, and clutched his sleeve with one hand. "Did the police—"

"Scared him off." He turned to George, nodding at him. "We'll be off. Did you get everything gathered?"

"Yes, sir. Your man there accessed your safe and pulled the things you wanted."

"Good." He turned me, his hand on my back. "We'll leave before he thinks it's safe to come back."

"Go where?" I asked once we were seated in the copter, George riding shotgun, and Theo back with Peter and me. I didn't know how John and Paul were to get off the island, since there were only four seats, but I decided they were more than able to take care of the Darts should Mikhail return.

He looked like he didn't want to answer for a minute, then said, "Greece. We're going home."

THIRTEEN

The last thing Theo wanted to do was to go crawling to Iakovos admitting that he couldn't take care of his own family, but his pride was easily sacrificed in order to keep Kiera and Peter safe.

"What do you mean you're in Greece?" Jake's voice all but snapped at him from his mobile phone. "It's five o'clock in the morning!"

"We had a hell of a flight. The baby and Kiera ate something in Australia that didn't agree with them, and puked all over the jet I booked. The baby, not Kiera, although she puked, too—she just kept hers confined to the toilet. I think Peter's teething again, because he barely slept and didn't seem to like the flights, which is odd because he doesn't mind the copter rides at all, and Kiera's knee flared up again despite her running like the gazelle she is, and she swore it was fine until that bastard started buzzing the house, and she tripped and fell going to the copter, and it made the knee bad. Kneeling at the toilet repeatedly to vomit didn't help either. We've had ice on it."

There was a moment's silence. "On the toilet?" Iakovos asked.

"What? No, I'm talking to him now. You still look green, sweet. It'll be just one more short flight; then you can die in peace. Hello, Iakovos? You there? Kiera is still feeling poorly, and I think the baby just shat himself again. We'll be there in an hour, God willing." Theo hung up in order to take Peter from Kiera after seeing her face, ignoring the foul smell that emerged from the diaper, hauling the baby into the bathroom to clean him up.

Theo mused on the short flight from Athens that he always had an image of how he wanted to return to his brother—triumphant at his ability to make his own fortune rather than working as Iakovos's flunky, with a gorgeous woman on his arm, one dripping in diamonds and gold, enough to choke a horse … and, more important, impress Jake with his ability to survive just fine on his own, thank you very much.

Iakovos was at the dock on the island he owned, ostensibly to greet him, but Theo knew the real reason he was there was to see just what a mess Theo had made of his life.

And there his brother was, waiting for them, a tall, imposing man who had a few inches on Theo, his arms crossed over his chest while he watched impassively as the boat that had picked them up on the mainland tied up. Theo smiled wanly at his brother, all the fantasies of arriving on a yacht of his own, an elegant, jewel-clad woman at his side, dissolving into the wind. He held Peter with one arm, all too aware that his attempts to clean the baby in the men's room at the small airport a half hour's drive away were more than a little lacking. Peter was red-faced and snotty, puke stains down his front, his no-nos coming with indignant wails, punctuated with little snot bubbles that Theo desperately wiped on the tail of his own shirt, since he had quickly run through all the wipes they'd packed.

"Sorry about the early morning arrival," Theo said, feeling like he was a good hundred years older than his thirty-four years. "It just seemed best, given the situation. This is my son."

Iakovos stared in horror as Peter, with a wet, angry hiccup, opened his mouth and vomited, the stream narrowly missing Iakovos's shoes. "Oh God, he's at it again. Kiera, he didn't keep the apple juice down. This is my wife," he added when Kiera lurched forward from where she'd been hunched over a bucket that had obviously once contained chum, her face pale, wan, and with a faint green cast that exquisitely highlighted the black circles under her eyes. Her hair, normally a long curtain of shiny silk, was now hanging in lank clumps, and as he put out a hand to help her from the boat, he noticed with alarm that a section of her hair on the side was matted together with what looked like dried baby vomit.

"Hi. Nice to meet you. Theo has told me absolutely nothing about you. Do you have a quiet room where I might die in peace?" Kiera asked, clutching the bucket.

Theo would say one thing about his brother: when faced with an emergency, Iakovos didn't waste time. "I am delighted to meet you and Peter," he told Kiera. "I am sorry to see you are feeling unwell. I have an exceptionally nice room for you to rest in peace, although I hope not permanently so. Theo—" Jake's eyes raked him over. "You look like hell. Come along, let's get you all sorted."

Harry bustled out just as they reached the house, her eyes alight with pleasure until she got a good look at his face. Or it might have been Kiera's. Perhaps it was the fact that they had to stop and let the baby retch up the last of the apple juice they'd tried to give him to keep him from being dehydrated. Regardless, she took one look at Kiera, and after merely kissing Theo's cheek, she took the baby, not even once wincing at the smell coming from him.

"Kiera, is it? Iakovos said something about you and Peter having food poisoning. It's absolutely the worst thing, isn't it? Come along this way. We've kept Theo's rooms, and I'm sure you'll be very comfortable in there. And don't worry about your baby—we have four children of our own, and the things Matilda—she's our nanny—has had to put up with would boggle your mind. She's a godsend, and worth her weight in gold."

Theo wanted to droop with relief when Harry rallied the staff into caring for Kiera and Peter. Kiera opted to forgo a shower in favor of lying on his bed and moaning softly to herself. It was only with an effort that he managed to get the chum bucket away from her, giving her instead a small, clean trash basket.

"I've called the doctor," Iakovos told him when he left Kiera after having peeled her clothes off her and poured her into his bed. "I'm surprised you didn't do that yourself."

Theo held up a hand. "Could you save the judgments until later? I've been awake over thirty hours taking care of Kiera and Peter, and trying to get us all out of Australia without anyone knowing where we're going. Oh, would you send the boat back in an hour or so? Our security detail was following, but they had to catch a later flight."

"Security detail?" Iakovos asked, stopping Theo en route to the set of rooms now known as the nursery. To his surprise, Iakovos enveloped him in a bear hug, thumping him on the back before releasing him as he said, "Christ, you smell rank."

"It was Peter. He shit all the way up his back, and there was nothing to clean him with. Remind me to send an apology to the airport later."

"You have had a time of it," Jake said, the two of them entering one of the nursery rooms. A middle-aged woman stood with Harry, Peter now naked and being carried over to a bath.

"The baby has not eaten anything solid?" the woman asked him in Greek.

"No. We tried juices, and he kept some down, but the latest came up as soon as we got here." Theo felt so tired, he wondered if his limbs had turned to lead. It was almost too much of an effort to speak.

The nanny nodded, and quickly washed Peter, getting him dried and into a onesie that Theo didn't recognize. "We will give him ice chips first, then a little juice if he keeps that down. The doctor will tell us if he needs medicine."

Theo was so grateful to have Peter in the hands of an expert, someone who knew what she was doing and didn't feel utterly and completely helpless, that he just nodded, feeling tears form in his eyes.

"Don't worry, Theo, Matilda is a miracle worker," Harry said, giving him a squeeze on the arm. "Why don't you lay down for a bit? We'll take good care of Peter."

"Thank you," was all he could say. He didn't like the way his voice sounded, thick and awkward. It was all so unlike the impression he wanted to make for his brother, but he simply had no energy left to care.

"Satisfied?" Jake asked him, gesturing toward Peter.

He nodded again, and let his brother escort him out of the nursery and back to his bedroom.

"I should explain—" he started to say once he reached his door.

"Later," Jake said, giving him a little push into the room. "You look almost as bad as your wife. When did you get married, by the way?"

Theo rubbed his face and tried to count the days. His brain refused to budge. "Don't remember. Days ago."

Iakovos gave him a long look. "Get some rest."

Theo summoned up the last few remaining wits, saying, "Don't let anyone on the island who you don't know."

Iakovos shot him a piercing look. "Why?" he asked.

"I'll tell you later." Theo stumbled into his room, barely having the strength to close the door and kick off his shoes before he collapsed down onto the bed next to Kiera. She had fallen asleep with the trash can clutched in her arms.

He sank into the bed, rolling over until he was spooned up behind her, and immediately fell asleep.

He woke up briefly to find a young woman giving Kiera a shot for her nausea, assuring them both that the baby was doing much better, and had taken some liquids and was holding it down. She told them that sleep would do much that medicine couldn't, and he let himself drift back into the exhausted sleep filled with hellish images of the last thirty-six hours.

When he woke again, it was evening, and the bed next to him was empty. He used the toilet, and flinched when he got a glimpse of himself in the mirror, wondering where the man who Kiera thought was too handsome for his own good had gone. He showered, managed to scrape a razor across the grisly visage that was his face, and pulled on clean clothes before going in search of his wife and child.

He found them together, sitting in the nursery, Kiera on the floor with Peter, who sat between her legs, no-no-ing loudly while banging a plastic cup on Kiera's leg.

"You look a hundred times better," Harry said, getting up from where she was sitting with Jake on a couch with one of their girls, watching Kiera and Peter. She hugged him, giving him another kiss on the cheek just before she whispered, "I like your wife a lot, but I'm going to give you holy hell later for getting married without letting us know."

He kissed her back, nodded to Jake, who sat with a girl of about four on his lap, and knelt next to where Kiera sat. He eyed her. "You're not green anymore."

"No, thank God. Whatever was in that shot the doctor gave me was a miracle. Peter's feeling much better, too, aren't you?"

Peter babbled his agreement and climbed over her leg to bang the cup on Theo.

"I don't think you've met our youngest, Theo. This is Rose," Harry said, brushing a hand through the girl's dark hair. She went a little shy at the attention, turning in her father's lap and hiding her face against his chest. "Yacky insisted she be named for me."

Kiera's eyebrows rose as she glanced at Theo.

"When Harry met Iakovos, she couldn't say his name. She called him Yacky," he explained.

Iakovos rolled his eyes. "She could say it perfectly well. She just chose not to."

Harry giggled.

"But Rose ..." Kiera still looked confused.

"Her name is really Eglantine," Iakovos said. "Which is French for Rose. Since she threatened to geld me if I insisted our daughter have that name, we settled on Rose."

"Tell me," Harry said, getting on the floor to take Peter

from Theo, holding him up so he could bounce. "How long did it take you to spell Papamoomoo? Please tell me it was months, because otherwise, Yacky and the girls will give me hell."

The twins and the boy Theo remembered last as a baby burst into the room, their arms full of toys that they said they had rounded up to donate to Peter.

"He has a mega crap-ton of toys," Kiera told them, "but I'm sure he'll like to play with these while we're here."

"And with that opening," Iakovos said, prying his daughter off his chest, placing a kiss on her head before giving her a little shove toward where the other children were trying to get Peter to crawl over to them, "I believe we adults should have a little talk. And food, if you can stomach it."

Kiera looked pained. "I think I'm going to pass on that offer, although the doctor said I should push fluids, so if I could get a pitcher of ice water, that'll do me just fine."

Theo hesitated for a few seconds, then got to his feet and held out a hand for Kiera. "If you don't want to leave him, we won't," he said softly in her ear.

She gave him a wide-eyed look, then tipped her head toward where Peter was happily no-no-ing his cousins as they took turns showing him the toys. "He's having fun, Theo. I don't know if he's been around other children, but socialization is very important for babies. It teaches him how to interact, and to learn about social mores and values, and how to deal with expectations that do not fit in with his personal view of the world."

He laughed and kissed her soundly. "I'd just like to know what social mores and values he'll learn from Jake's kids."

"I heard that," Iakovos said as he left the room with Harry, his arm around her.

Theo followed suit, feeling remarkably relaxed for the first time in what seemed like eons.

"We've put your security detail up in the guest cottages," Harry told them as they went out onto the patio, the soft evening air filling Theo with a sense of happiness that was almost indefinable. It was something about the smell and sound of the sea, of the wind that ruffled Kiera's hair—now once again back to its silky-curtain state—that made him simultaneously insanely happy and horny as hell.

"Do you want to eat first, and then tell us what's going on?" Iakovos asked when they sat down at a white metal table, solar lanterns dotted around the patio giving the space a soft glow. "Or tell us and then eat?"

"Eat," Theo said, aware that, along with his sudden arousal, he was also starving. "What we have to tell you is going to take a long time."

Kiera confined herself to several glasses of lemon water, juice, and tonic water while Theo consumed a goodly part of a roast dinner, letting the polite conversation that Harry and Kiera kept up wash over him.

"Oh, I meant to ask you if you needed something for your knee. I gather you hurt it falling down?" Harry asked Kiera while Theo was finishing up a second helping of lemon herb potatoes.

"That just kind of aggravated it. Well, so did the race. It was originally injured when Theo bashed my leg on the steps of the swimming pool after he tried to drown me."

Harry stared at her, a fork loaded with salad held immobile in front of her mouth. "He tried to …" She looked at him and blinked, then set her fork down. "I think I need to hear this from the start. Wait, a race?" She glanced at Iakovos before turning back to Kiera. "Do you swim, too?"

Theo laughed, suddenly remembering Jake's tale of how Harry had handed him his ass in the lap pool. "I'd forgotten about that. I wish now that I hadn't, because it would have reminded me not to be so sure of my superior male abilities."

"You're not slow," Kiera told him, a teasing light in her eyes that he loved to see. "You're just not as fast as me."

"You told me that beating me almost killed you."

"Eh," she said, waggling her hand. "I just said that because your superior male ego was wounded."

By unspoken consensus, the discussion about why they

had descended upon Iakovos was held until dinner was over, and they were seated in the living room, Harry and Iakovos on one couch, while Theo pulled Kiera down next to him on another.

"Right," Iakovos said, glancing from Harry to Theo. "We have about half an hour before we have to put the kids to bed. Perhaps you'd like to tell us now why you're here."

"Not that you aren't welcome," Harry said, digging an elbow into Iakovos. "Naturally, we're delighted to see you again, Theo, and I'm so happy to know Kiera and little Peter, who looks just like Nicky did at that age."

"Go ahead," Iakovos said, draping an arm around Harry's shoulders. "Tell us everything."

Theo looked at Kiera. Her eyes were watchful, her lips pressed tight together. He knew that if he explained everything, she wouldn't protest.

"I don't think I will, actually," he answered his brother, brushing Kiera's hair back from her cheek. "Tell you everything, that is. Not all of it is anyone's business but ours."

Her eyes widened, and flickered to Iakovos before she leaned into him. "That's not very polite, Theo. We're guests."

"Fair enough," Iakovos said, giving him a little nod.

Harry raised her eyebrows and considered her husband. "You're not going to object to that?"

"For what reason?" Iakovos asked her. "He's protecting his family. I'd do the same."

"I swear that one day I will understand you, and then you're going to be sorry," Harry told him.

Iakovos smiled. "I live in fear, my wild one. Go on, Theo. Tell us the important points."

Theo quickly detailed the pertinent facts, leaving out the method of his meeting Kiera, and giving the explanation that her ex-boyfriend was unbalanced and sought vengeance against her.

As soon as Theo described the escape from his island, and subsequent journey to Greece, Iakovos leaped up, his face furious. "And you came here? To my home? Where my children live? Christ, Theo, did you even think about the danger you were dragging after you?"

Theo was on his feet the second Iakovos started yelling. Kiera made a distressed noised and rose, as well, her eyes worried. "Of course I wouldn't deliberately endanger your children. Do you think I'm a monster? There's no reason the bastard should follow us here; thus, no one is in danger."

"You don't know that!" Iakovos snarled, getting into Theo's face. "You have no idea what this maniac is capable of."

"Theo." Kiera's voice was reed thin. He felt her grab the back of his shirt.

"I have a good idea of the lengths he'll go to, yes. I've had two detectives looking into his past, and he's only once left New Zealand, and that was to go to California for four months. That was almost five years ago. Christ, Jake, do you think I'm so heartless that I'd risk Harry and the kids?"

"What the hell has Kiera done that this man is determined to get his hands on her?" Iakovos demanded.

"Golf balls," he heard Kiera whisper behind him. "Baseballs. Billiard balls."

He turned and saw the fear making her lovely eyes dark. "Basketballs. Love, don't do this." He brushed his thumb across her cheek.

She glanced beyond him to where Iakovos was pacing back and forth in front of them. "He's angry, and he has every right to be. This is my fault."

He pulled her into his arms, hating the way she struggled to keep from shaking with fear. "Jake isn't angry, not really, not at you or even me. This is all bluster."

"The hell it is," Iakovos snapped.

"Stop scaring my wife," he told his brother in Greek. "The man she's running from abused her horribly, both physically and mentally. I don't want to tell you to stop yelling in your own house, but dammit, stop yelling. She doesn't like it."

Iakovos glared first at him, then at Kiera; then to Theo's amazement, he apologized. "I'm sorry for losing my temper,

Kiera. I don't hold you to blame for the actions of what must surely be a madman."

Kiera separated herself from him, but kept one hand firmly on the back of his shirt. "I feel awful about this, I really do, although I'm starting to believe that what you said is true, and Misha has gone mad. I don't know why he insists I have a flash drive. Maybe it doesn't really exist, and he's just gone off the deep end, and has decided I'm the one who is causing him all the problems in his life. I just don't know."

Iakovos frowned, but Theo knew it was not directed at either Kiera or him. "Tell me again what you had when you left him."

She described her possessions. "There's nothing there. Not only have I worn the clothes and washed them repeatedly in the nine months since I escaped, but I've searched the duffel bag numerous times. Even assuming either Misha hid something in it, or I inadvertently got the flash drive snagged on it, or tossed into it without my knowing, there's nothing there."

"We'll examine your things in the morning," Iakovos decided. Theo wanted to bristle at the implication that they were so inept they could miss something as big as a flash drive, but at the same time he had wanted to go through Kiera's bag himself. "Sweetheart?" he asked her, leaving the permission up to her.

She made a helpless gesture. "You're welcome to look at everything, but there's nothing there. There's just nothing there."

"If you don't have this flash drive that your ex wants so badly, then it has to be some other reason he's making such an effort to terrorize you," Harry told Kiera. She slid her gaze over to Theo. "I wonder if it could be as simple as jealousy. Maybe he's so bent out of shape that you and Theo found each other that he's being vindictive in hopes that it will drive you apart."

A little blush rode Kiera's cheeks, but to his surprise, she answered the question despite her obvious embarrassment. "I don't think so. Theo and I only met a couple of weeks ago."

Harry looked from her to Theo, and then to Iakovos, laughing as she squeezed his arm. "Well, he's definitely your brother."

Kiera looked confused.

"I told you that Papaioannou men make up their minds quickly," he told her with a cocky smile.

"It only took Yacky and me a few days to know we were meant to be together," Harry told Kiera.

"Speak for yourself, woman," Iakovos said, trailing his fingers along the back of Harry's neck. "I knew I wasn't going to give you up after you spent one night in my bed."

"Which is why it took you almost a year to tell me you loved me," she said, grinning at him.

"You knew full well I was madly in love with you," he answered, and leaned forward like he was going to kiss her, evidently remembering in time that they weren't alone.

"See?" Theo told Kiera. "This is the sort of role model I had growing up."

"If so, then I need to thank your brother for teaching you well, because you didn't wait a year to tell me how you feel." The look she shot him was so heated that he had to remind himself that if Iakovos could restrain himself from kissing his wife, then Theo could do the same.

"Oh, to hell with it," he said, throwing manners to the wind, pulling Kiera onto his lap, and kissing her with a thoroughness that she deserved. She'd been sick, he told himself, and he hadn't been able to worship her as was her due while she had been unwell. He owed it to her to remind her just how much he loved her.

"And this, I think, is where we leave," Iakovos said, Harry laughing openly. "Come along, sweetheart. Let us put those four hellions you gave me to bed, so that we might retire and engage in those acts that Theo is quite likely to perform right here in the living room unless he remembers just how public a place it is."

"I'm so glad we got you snipped," he heard Harry say as they left the room. "Because if we hadn't, and we do all the things that Theo clearly wants to do with Kiera, we'd be likely to end up with another half-dozen children."

"Bed?" Theo asked, pulling his tongue from where she'd been sucking on it.

"Oh, please," she said, her breathing ragged, and her eyes molten with desire. "We should probably check on Peter first, though."

He touched her lower lip, the soft curve of it captivating him. He loved her lips. He loved her mouth, especially the way she moaned into his when he kissed her. He loved everything about her, not the least of which was the fact that she had so completely embraced the son he hadn't known existed. "Would you be happier if we moved him to our room to sleep?"

She thought about that for a few seconds, obviously reluctant to hand over the care of Peter to someone else, even someone trusted by his brother and Harry. "No," she said, shaking her head. "It's not like he's a newborn who needs to be fed during the night. He sleeps pretty well, and so long as we tuck him in, and get him up in the morning, I'm perfectly happy to have him sleep with the others."

"We can consider this a second wedding night," he said as they stood up, and, suddenly possessed of a wild urge, swept her up in his arms. "I shall ravish you appropriately, or as appropriately as I can given that my hamstrings and calf muscles are still recovering from that damned race."

She giggled when he feigned a limp. "Serves you right. Theo …"

"Hmm?" He stopped outside the nursery door, letting her slide down his body until her feet were on the floor.

"Your brother …" She bit her lip.

"Is many things, but no, he's not really angry with us. We yell a lot in my family when we're excited. It's when he goes cold and quiet that you know he's truly angry." Theo thought back to a night nine years in the past. "Trust me, I've seen it firsthand."

She cast a curious glance up at him but said nothing when they went to tuck Peter in. Harry and Jake's twins had their own room, while the two youngest shared a bedroom off the nursery playroom. Peter was parked in a crib in that same bedroom, where even now Iakovos and Harry sat with all four children huddled together on one bed while Iakovos read *Alice's Adventures in Wonderland* to them.

Kiera shot them a glance when they went over to the crib where Peter was sitting chewing on the beak of the giant kiwi. "Do you think we should do that?" she whispered to Theo.

"Read to him?" he asked.

She nodded.

He thought about it. "I don't see how it could hurt, although I don't know how much he'd understand. We'll start doing that when we're in our own home."

Her eyes were shadowed. "Will we be going back to New Zealand?"

"Yes." He held Peter, and leaned down to kiss the tip of her nose. "Unless you preferred to live here? In Greece, not specifically in Jake's house."

She looked thoughtful. "Oh. That would be … it's pretty here. I like the sheep island, though."

"No reason we can't spend time in both places. I have my eye on an estate that I've heard will be going up for sale soon. It's no private island, but it's a nice property a few miles down the coast, right on the water, with a private access road to keep all your deranged ex-boyfriends from the house."

She pinched him, but he could see she wasn't averse to the idea.

They took turns holding Peter, Kiera singing softly to him so that she didn't disturb the bedtime reading, and then when he started sucking his fingers, they tucked him in, and turned off the light nearest the crib.

They returned to Theo's room, where he did indeed fulfill his promise to ravish Kiera.

"I thought your calves and hamstrings were out of action," she said in a breathy voice when he stripped her naked and gently pushed her on the bed before all but tearing off his clothes and following her down. "Ooh, Theo! Really? You're going all masterful tonight?"

"Absolutely, my lovely wife." He eyed her long legs, dipping his head down to kiss a hot path up one of them. "Tonight is all about making you writhe and moan out my name. Shall we start here?"

Suddenly, her legs tensed, her thighs closing around his hand. "You're not ... you're not planning on doing oral sex, are you?"

Worry was evident in her mind. "I was, as a matter of fact." He studied her face. An interesting parade of emotions passed over her face, fear, distaste, and curiosity. "I take it you don't wish to?"

She made a vague gesture with one hand. "I knew this was going to have to come out sooner or later. I ... I'm not comfortable ..." She cleared her throat and looked at his shoulders rather than his face. "Misha used it as a way to punish me. Not what you were going to do, but the reciprocal."

He mentally swore, and added a few more tortures to the list of things he wanted to do to that bastard when he found him.

"I told you that I would never ask you to do anything you weren't comfortable doing," he told her, stroking her inner thigh. "That will always be true, Kiera. I would like very much to taste you, taste the true essence of you, but if that makes you uncomfortable, then I simply won't."

"If you did ..." She made another vague gesture. "Would you want me to do the same? To you?"

"No," he said, gently spreading her legs. "Someday perhaps you'll feel like it, but even if that never happens, I'll be more than satisfied with you, my swift, adorable gazelle. You didn't mind me touching you there before; shall we start with that and see if you are comfortable with more?"

"That sounds wonderful. And I like touching you, Theo. I don't mind touching your penis. The other is just ..."

"Then we won't do that, although I will admit that the thought of your fingernails scraping up my scrotum like you did the first time we made love has me almost wild with the need to lie back and let you do just that. But first, let's try a few things here."

He loved how responsive she was to him. A few days before, she'd admitted in an embarrassed whisper that she had never been as quick off the mark as she was with him, and he delighted in watching her body's response to his hands and mouth. He nibbled on her belly and hips while allowing his fingers to caress all the sensitive inner parts of her, and when he sank a finger into her heat, he thought he might just have to throw his good intentions to the wind and take her right then and there. She writhed beneath him, her hands clutching the sheet as her chest heaved.

"Tell me if you want me to stop," he murmured into her pubic bone, kissing a path down the crease of her thigh. He waited a few seconds, letting his whiskers tickle the insides of her thighs. She didn't protest, so he gently touched the delicate folds of her secrets, the taste of her reminding him of the salty tang of the Aegean. She tasted hot, and wild, and he was infinitely grateful that she'd trusted him enough to allow him this pleasure.

When her hips started jerking convulsively, he moved up her body, taking her legs with him while he paused to kiss each of her breasts, but he couldn't stop himself. He slid into her warmth, the drawing feeling in his thighs and balls telling him that he didn't have much time. He nipped her on her shoulder when she bit his neck, her hands running up his back, her nails scraping in a gentle but arousing manner. He breathed on her lips. "Do you want to taste?" he asked.

She looked away for a moment, then shyly turned back, her lips parted. He savored her mouth even as he pumped into her, allowing her to taste herself on him, the combined heat of her mouth and body too much for him.

"Tell me—"

"Theo!" She screamed his name loud enough to make his ears ring, bucking beneath him, her inner muscles gripping him with a strength that never failed to amaze him.

He gave in to his own release, plunging and thrusting and pushing himself into her with wild, uncontrolled strokes until they ceased to be two separate people, their souls joined in a way that Theo knew would last the length of his lifetime.

It took a long time for him to come down off the post-orgasmic high, but when he did, it was to find himself on his back, with Kiera looming over him.

"Next time," she said, her eyes downright smoky with satiation. "Next time it's my turn."

His eyes opened wide. "You mean—"

"Screw Misha." She made a face. "Not literally. I'm not going to let him ruin something that clearly needs to be a part of our lovemaking regime. OK?"

"OK," he said, smiling as she snuggled into his side. He was filled with a sense of quiet elation. He had shown Kiera that she had nothing to fear from him, and been rewarded with her trust. Nothing could stop him from making sure she was insanely happy with him. Nothing, and no one.

FOURTEEN

When I came out of the bathroom the following morning, I found Peter once again in my duffel bag. Theo sat on the floor next to him, my things spread out before them in a semicircle.

"I thought I'd take a quick look before we let Jake at your belongings," he explained. He gestured toward the small stack of things. "This is all of it, yes?"

"Yes." I looked at my pathetic collection of clothing. "I wish now I'd let you give me those things you bought for me. I feel like the poor relation compared to Harry."

"They're in my suitcase," Theo said, picking up my paperbacks, shaking them in case something was stuck in them.

I stared at him in surprise. "What? I thought you sent them back?"

"No, you told me you didn't want them and to send them back, but I thought that every now and again I could sneak one into the dresser, and you wouldn't notice it."

I cocked an eyebrow at him.

He grinned. "All right, I knew you'd notice. But I hoped to soften you up over time. I still have the bracelet, too, and plan on working on you to accept that, just as soon as life settles down for us."

"I don't need jewelry, Theo," I said, fully cognizant that I was being more obstinate than was necessary. I went over to the suitcase that Richard had packed for him. "Are you sure it's here and not back in New Zealand? Oh." Underneath a couple of pairs of pants and underwear, two familiar carrier bags lay somewhat squashed.

"I thought you might want them." He ran his hands over the Zen garden tray, pressing the edges like he suspected it might have a secret compartment. "I just told Richard to grab the clothes, though, and not the shoes."

I pulled out the items, sticking all the teddies back in the bag, thought for a moment, then pulled out the one in champagne-rose lace, and added it to the stack of clothing. Theo waggled his eyebrows at me.

"You only get this if you are very, very good," I told him, taking the clothing with me into the bathroom.

"Oh, I am. I really am. Ask anyone. Except my brother," he called after me. "He's clearly jealous of me."

When I returned to model a blue-and-white-striped knit off-the-shoulder shirt, and a navy blue midthigh skirt, he whistled. "Look at your mama," he told Peter, who was sitting between Theo's legs, banging my Zen rocks together. "She's got a pair of legs on her, doesn't she?"

I gave in to a little eye roll. "Like you couldn't see that in the leggings?"

"Oh, I could, and I did. It's just different when your legs are bare." He leered at my legs, making a lovely wave of warmth wash up from my chest.

I knelt down next to my two menfolk, eyeing my meager possessions. "I take it you didn't find a secret compartment in the tray?"

"No," he said, making a face as he stared at the now neatly stacked clothing. "I made a thorough search of the bag, as well. I don't suppose there is anything buried in your deodorant stick?"

I shook my head. "I bought everything in my cosmetics bag after I left Misha."

"Then I just don't know where it could be, assuming the drive is real, and he's not insane."

"No no no," Peter agreed, grabbing for another rock, smacking it on the other two he had.

I picked up the last one, running my fingers around its pleasing smoothness. "There's just nothing, Theo. How are we going to make Misha understand that?"

"We're going to have to rely on the detectives to dig up something on him," he answered, rubbing his jaw, instantly making my fingers itch to do the same. I loved the line of his jaw, loved the angle it made from the long planes of his face, and the way it smoothed into his chin. Just the thought of that jaw rubbing on my inner thighs right before his mouth possessed me had me shifting restlessly. "If we can get a charge to stick to him, we can—"

The thought of tasting Theo the way he'd tasted me hung tantalizingly large in my mind. A little part of my mind rejected such an idea, the memories of Misha forcing me to do such things all too fresh in the nightmare part of my brain, but I told myself that being made to do something and wanting to do it were two entirely unconnected things.

I slid a glance down at the fly of Theo's jeans, and wondered if we could let Peter visit his cousins just long enough for me to prove to myself that I could enjoy giving him pleasure.

"Kiera."

"Hmm?" Perhaps when Peter went down for his nap? That was usually a good solid hour, and if we had the nanny to help if he woke up early, then I could spirit Theo away and have at him.

"Do you see what I see?"

"Your crotch?"

He turned his head slowly, his eyes simmering with sapphire heat. "No, although now I want to know why you answered that. But it'll have to wait. My question was regarding this."

I glanced down to where he gestured. Peter was still pounding my Zen stones together, but one of them had broken.

"Oh, he broke it. There must have been a stress fracture—" I stopped when I realized that the stone wasn't broken. The two halves had separated cleanly, and beyond them, sitting between Peter's naked little feet, was a small rectangular metal object.

Theo picked it up with the tips of his fingers, holding it up for us to see. "That looks like a tiny flash drive," I said in a voice that sounded strangled even to my ears.

"It sure as hell does." He took the broken stone away from Peter, slipping the flash drive into a space inside it. "Where did you get this rock?"

"The same place I got the others—from Swami Betelbaum's shop … oh." I examined the other half of the stone. "This one is different. It's not really rock."

"No." His gaze was speculative. "I believe it's one of those security devices used to hide valuables. This looks like it's made of some form of stone polymer mix."

"Holy crap," I said, the full implications hitting me. "I really did have his flash drive."

"Yes." Theo's eyes met mine. "And I'd very much like to see what's on it."

"You and me both," I said, getting to my feet and picking up Peter when Theo got out his laptop. We sat on the bed while he plugged in the flash drive, and quickly looked through the folders contained on it.

"That looks like spreadsheets," I said, frowning at the familiar Excel symbol. "But I don't know what those are."

"Financial statements," he said, clicking quickly through the folders. "Those are bank records that have been exported. And this …" He stopped and gave me a long, speculative look.

"What?" I asked.

He clicked a couple of times, then turned the laptop so the screen fully faced me.

"Borland House, South Church Street, George Town, Grand Cayman, CJ," I read aloud. *"Dear sir/madam, enclosed is your log-in information including secure password for account num-*

*ber 433/pre/19iJ2FFM. Per your request, the account has been
set up for GIRBAC, Mikhail, Chebet Imports, 222 Old Treasury
Building, Mauland Court, Wellington, New Zealand.* Is this
one of those offshore bank accounts? The kind people who
do hedge funds and such use?"

"Yes." He smiled a long, slow smile. "And we have his
account number and password."

"Holy shit," I said, feeling the moment called for a little
profanity. "No wonder he was so frantic to find me."

Theo reclaimed the laptop and tapped on the keyboard.
"I'll just turn on a VPN and go check the account."

"What's a VPN?"

"It allows me to mask my IP and location," he said, giving a wry twist to his lips. "Jake would skin me alive if I let
anyone trace me back to him. Ah, there we go. Now let's see
what dirty little secrets your ex has…"

He stopped talking, his eyes narrowing on the screen.

"Is it that bad?" I asked, feeling my blood run cold with
fear. I clutched Peter so hard he squawked and banged one
of the Zen stones on my hand. I set him down and gave him
his chew toy, trying to see the screen, but Theo closed the
lid and pulled out the flash drive, tucking it into his pocket.

His face was grim.

"Don't you even think of leaving this room," I told him
when he stood up and turned like he was going out the door.
"Not without telling me what has you looking like you've
turned to a very handsome Greek marble statue."

His lovely dark blue eyes were guarded when he faced
me. "Do you have any issue at all leaving Peter here with
Harry and Jake?"

"No," I said. "You mean to go into Athens? Do we have
to see someone at a bank? I'm sure he'd be fine if we had to
leave him overnight, although we'd have to ask your sister-
in-law first."

He took my hand, his thumb rubbing over my fingers
while he obviously picked his words with care. It was that
fact that scared the crap out of me, making me grip his hand

with fingers that shook. "I think we're going to be gone a bit longer than overnight. We have to go back to New Zealand, Kiera."

"Why?" I didn't want to say the word, didn't want to know the answer, but at the same time, I knew I couldn't hide away any longer. I had Theo and Peter now, and if that meant confronting Misha, then so be it. "So we can give Misha back the flash drive? We could just mail it or courier it to him, couldn't we?"

He shook his head. "We're going to have to talk to the police there. No, not police—the Financial Action Task Force."

"Who are they?" I desperately fought the urge to run, to drag Theo and Peter to somewhere safe, where we could hide.

"They handle money laundering and terrorism financing. Jake had to deal with them on an investment in Australia about ten years ago, when the man trying to broker a deal turned out to be laundering money." His thumb swept a path across my hand again. "You can stay here, sweetheart. I won't make you go back if you would rather not."

"This isn't something we could do from here?" I asked, knowing the answer even before the words left my mouth. If this was something Theo could do without traveling all the way back to New Zealand, he would.

"We will need to meet with them in person. They'll have to take statements. Fingerprints. And I want to make sure that they don't let any potential dirty cop allow your ex to get away."

"You are the bravest person I know," I told him, so overwhelmed with love that the words just came out. His eyes widened in surprise at the words of praise. I tipped my head back and kissed him, letting my lips savor his mouth.

He was sweet and hot, and just the taste of him on my lips started tingles in my private parts. He filled my heart with joy and lit my soul with love. He was the man I had waited my whole life for, and I was so profoundly grateful for him that I was willing to do anything to have a future together. "I love you, Theo. I love you so much that even though I want to drag you and Peter to the nearest cave and hide there, I'm going to do what you want. Because I trust you with every bit of my being. So, husband, let's go to New Zealand and nail that bastard."

"I'm going to fulfill every last erotic thing you're thinking right now," he promised, chucking Peter under the chin. "And then I'm going to tell you just how proud I am of you, and how I can't imagine living my life without you. But first, I need to convince Jake to let me use his private jet so we don't have to wait around at airports."

He left before I could make a pointed comment about his brother owning his own jet. It hadn't seemed as bad when Theo hired one to get us out of Australia, because he felt a need to get us safely out of Misha's reach. Besides, I told myself, hiring wasn't the same as owning.

"Welcome to Wonderland, Alice," I told Peter. He burbled and no-no-ed, which I took to mean he wanted to find his cousins for a little playtime.

I found Harry outside on a lush green lawn, with the younger children splashing in a wading pool, while the older girls, Melina and Thea, raced around in swimsuits, chasing each other and throwing themselves into a full-sized pool. Both girls seemed like they were born to the water, and Harry, who sat under a shaded table, called a reminder to them not to roughhouse in the water before she turned and greeted me.

"There's the youngest Mr. Papamaumau. Does he like to play in the water? I brought out an old pair of Nicky's swimmers," she said, smiling where the five-year-old Nicky was playing with a bunch of dolphin toys in the wading pool. Rose, a year younger, was carefully and delicately picking out each blade of grass that floated on top of the water.

"I think he'd like that," I said, and peeled off Peter's clothes in order to wrestle the waterproof pants over his diaper.

Peter was no-no-ing happily when I put him in the water, although he didn't want to sit still for me to put sunblock on him.

Once he'd been suitably protected, I sat on my heels next to the wading pool, ready to rescue him if the older children played too rough, or if he tipped over into the water. "Harry, if Theo and I had to go away for … for a couple of days, would you be open to watching Peter?"

"Of course," Harry replied immediately. "I'd be delighted to have him, even if he wasn't such an easy baby. Nicky, he's not hurting the dolphin by chewing on it. His gums hurt and it makes them feel better to chew on things."

"I should have brought out his chew toy," I mused, watching absently as Peter gnawed on the fin of one of the herd of plastic dolphins that floated in the pool.

"His what, now?"

"Chew toy. He likes chewing on it. I hate to leave Peter, but Theo thinks we're going to have to go to New Zealand."

"Really? Why?"

She leaned forward, her hands on her knees, while I told her about finding the flash drive in my Zen rock. "What did it say that had Theo so upset?" she asked when I was done.

"I don't know." I shaded my eyes to watch two tall men stride across the lawn toward us. Theo was clad in his favorite pair of shorts, which I sourly noted Richard had managed to pack, and a tank top that let me admire the ease with which all his muscles worked in unison. Iakovos likewise wore a pair of knee-length shorts and a short-sleeved shirt, and I had to admit that he wasn't hard on the eyes at all, but I couldn't see why he made number three on the bachelor list while Theo was shoved down to number ten. Theo might not be as tall or imposing as Iakovos, but those blue eyes set with very black lashes could make my knees melt. And the line of his jaw … and chin. And that spot on his neck that I was forever wanting to bite.

"Hoo, it's a little hot in here, isn't it?" Harry said, fanning herself as she watched the men approach.

"Very," I said, swallowing a couple of times.

"Do you ever look at them—well, in your case, Theo—and wonder just what the hell you did to deserve such gorgeousness all rolled up in fabulous man-ness?" Harry asked, her eyes on her husband.

"Every. Single. Day," I said.

"Have you seen other women give Theo the eye yet? The first time someone clearly made a play for Yacky, I just wanted to mess up his hair so he wasn't so damned gorgeous."

"It doesn't work," I said, my eyes narrowing as I thought of some woman trying to get her clutches on Theo. "It just makes them look like they've had a vigorous night of lovemaking."

She was silent for a moment, then cleared her throat. "Yes, I can see where that might backfire."

I gave her a quick smile. "I'm going to rely on you to give me pointers on how to pick off the chickies who think they can touch Theo."

"I have an entire list of things I say at parties. Also, spilling things on the interlopers works wonderfully. So does stepping on their tiny elfin-like toes."

"That sounds very specific."

"It is." She made a face. "Not anymore, because the woman in question is dating a man, or so Dmitri told me."

"Dmitri?"

"Yacky and Theo's cousin. He's in the US right now, but he should be coming home next week. You'll see him then."

"No, she won't," Iakovos said as he and Theo stopped in front of us. He bent to kiss Harry before duly admiring one of the toy dolphins that his son showed him. Peter got very excited and no-no-ed Theo, splashing the water with a dolphin.

"Why won't she?" Harry asked.

"We're leaving in an hour, just as soon as the jet is ready to take off." Theo glanced down at me. "Can you be ready?"

"Yes, but we want to know what you saw in the Cayman bank that made you want to go right now," I said.

"The amount of money that was held in the bank was not that of a small-time crook," he answered. "Your ex is clearly involved in a very big money-laundering scheme, the sort of big that is beyond individuals and is used by terrorists, extremist groups, or countries."

I shook my head, unable to process the idea of Misha having that much power. "You're kidding. Misha?"

"I wish I was joking," Theo answered.

"But ... he's never been a big-time player."

"Unfortunately, he is now." Theo's eyes were dark with concern.

I shook my head again. "I never knew. I mean, I had an idea that his import business wasn't as kosher as he said, but money laundering? That never occurred to me."

"Did you ask Harry?" Theo squatted next to me, holding out his hands for Peter when the baby tried to climb over the edge of the wading pool to get to him.

Harry replied before I could. "We're happy to have Peter for as long as you need. Matilda loves babies, and was trying to convince Iakovos that just because I'm forty and he's been snipped doesn't mean we can't have more babies."

Iakovos gave his wife a glare. "Do you have to tell everyone about that?"

She giggled, and nodded at Theo. "Hey, they have to worry about birth control. We don't. We win."

"Point taken," Iakovos said.

Theo gave me a speculative look. I held up my arm and flexed my bicep. "Implant. It's good for another three years, so don't even think about it."

He laughed, and grimaced when Peter banged the toy dolphin down directly on Theo's crotch. "The point may be moot if you keep doing that, Peter. I need to make a few calls to make sure everything is ready for us, but if you're ready to go in about half an hour, that'll give us time to get to the airport."

I stayed with Peter as long as I could, feeling torn about leaving him, but knowing that if a few days away could ensure peace from Misha for the rest of our lives, then the separation was well worth it.

I won't say there weren't a few tears I sniffled back when we took the boat to the mainland, and Harry held Peter in her arms, waving his little fist good-bye. I clutched Theo's hand, watching until they were too small to make out anymore, swallowing back the big lump of tears.

Theo sniffled.

I looked at him in surprise.

"What?" he said, pulling me down onto a seat next to him.

"You sniffled."

"Don't be ridiculous. I'm a man, and thus I do not tear up at saying good-bye to my ten-month-old son who I just found out about two weeks ago."

I leaned into him, wrapping my arms around him, amazed that such a wonderful man was mine. "I'd tell you that I was sorry we have to do this, but I know you'll tell me it's not my fault, so instead, I'll just hug you and rub your back in a comforting manner, all right?"

"Deal," he said, and hugged me tight, his chin resting on my head for the duration of the trip to the mainland. One of Iakovos's staff was driving the boat, and normally I would have enjoyed looking at the lovely green-blue water, the amazing village that seemed to cling to the side of the cliff as it spilled down to the sea, and just the whole wonderful ambience of Greece, but I was too upset to appreciate any of it.

The trip back to New Zealand was much less horrible than the one out, but with the frequent refueling stops, it took over a day. Theo spent most of the time working, dealing with not only the situation with Misha but his own businesses, which he'd had to push aside while he got us to safety.

"I hope we get some sort of private-jet frequent-flier miles," I told him when we stepped out into the heat of Wellington almost twenty-six hours later. "I feel downright rummy."

"It's better than flying to the States," he pointed out. "I always feel out of it for a couple of days after one of those flights."

The following two days were spent closeted in various government buildings making statements, telling our story over and over again until I thought I'd go mad if I had to tell just one more time how it was that we found the flash drive. Statements were taken in person, on video, and in writing that neither Theo nor I had had knowledge of the drive, or what it contained, until we found it.

As annoying as that was, it was relatively smooth sailing until the officials who were working with us suggested that the best way to make sure Misha was convicted was to catch him red-handed. And that meant I had to give him back the flash drive.

"No," Theo said before I could even respond to the suggestion. "It's too dangerous. He almost killed her last week, and that was on a public street."

I thought about what the official—whose name was Dermot—said when he explained that given the circumstances, they needed a watertight case against Misha to ensure he was convicted, which was what Theo demanded.

"You'll be wired and have a GPS tracking unit on you," Dermot told me, ignoring Theo, who stood next to me, his legs braced wide and his arms crossed over his chest. "We'll pick the meeting place carefully, and will have undercover officers seeded throughout the area. If, at any time, you feel threatened, you will have a panic button that will send the extraction team in."

I looked behind Dermot to where George, Paul, and John stood. They wore their usual impassive expressions, which, oddly, I found reassuring.

"Absolutely not," Theo said, looking downright belligerent. "It's out of the question. What if he shoots her? We'll find another way."

Dermot gestured away the question. "We will naturally protect her—"

"No!" Theo thundered. "There's nothing to stop him from shooting her."

Dermot shook his head. "On the contrary, there are a great many things we can do to prevent that."

"Such as?" I asked, torn between fear and a strange calm determination to see this through. I wanted a life with Theo. Misha had to be stopped in order for that to happen.

"This is New Zealand, not the US." Dermot's eyes were steady on mine. "We have a relatively low rate of gun-related violence. And naturally, we will make sure there are a number of security cameras monitoring whatever location is chosen."

Theo snorted, and muttered something under his breath.

"What would you do if you were me?" I asked George.

He raised his eyebrows. "If I wanted the perpetrator put away for good, I'd do as these gentlemen suggest."

"Kiera, leave the room," Theo demanded, and tried to shoo me out the door. "I will deal with this from here on out."

I resisted being shooed and stood firm. "Do you trust them?" I asked George.

"Yes," he said without even the slightest hesitation.

"All right." I turned to Theo, my thumbs stroking the line of his jaw, which I loved so much. "I know you are trying to protect me, my love. I know you don't want me to be traumatized anymore by Misha. I know you don't ever want me to feel frightened or terrorized by him again, but you have to think about something important."

"What's that?" he asked, his curiosity getting the better of his animosity toward the government men.

"The bone-deep satisfaction I'm going to have when they haul Misha away in handcuffs, knowing that there is no way his dirty-cop buddies can save him. It'll be the best therapy I could ever have."

He thought about that, pulling me close to say softly in my ear, "I don't want you to do this. I won't be able to protect you from him."

"You already have, you adorably wonderful, yet silly, man," I said, biting his neck. "Let me do this, Theo. It won't be fun, but oh, how I want to see him go to prison."

It took another half hour of persuasion, pleading, and bribery before Theo finally agreed to let the plan go forward.

"But only if we take a few of our own precautions," he muttered darkly when we, accompanied by George, Paul, and John, climbed into a car to go back to the hotel where we were staying.

"What precautions?" I asked.

He just smiled and cracked his knuckles.

I made a mental note to have a private chat with George so I could warn him to keep Theo from attacking Misha on his own. I had no doubt that Theo could hold his own in a fight, but Misha had no honor or sense of fair play. And I was not going to risk the man who made my life complete. Not when, for the first time in five years, I had a future worth preserving.

FIFTEEN

Theo made the call two days later.

"We have the flash drive," he said, his voice emotionless, but I knew he was holding back the desire to threaten Misha with any number of dire actions.

I could hear the rash of Russian spilling out from the earpiece of the phone before Misha said, "Where is it? What do you do to it?"

"Let me make this absolutely clear: Kiera didn't know you'd hidden it in her Zen garden rocks. If you think about trying to hurt her or otherwise harm her in any way, the drive goes to the police immediately."

Misha, predictably, snarled obscenities at Theo, who waited until he finished before he added, "Do you understand? If you so much as lift a finger toward her, we'll turn the drive over to the police."

"I understand," Misha said, his voice silky smooth, a sound that sent goose bumps down my arms. I knew that voice; he was at his most dangerous when he spoke like that. "Where is Kiera? I will talk with her."

Theo raised his eyebrows at me. I nodded and took the phone, holding it angled so he could listen. "Theo doesn't want me handing over the drive to you," I told Misha. "He wants to give it to the cops, but I told him that since it was yours, I didn't feel right in doing that."

"Good, you good girl," he said, laughter in his voice. I quelled the warning bells screaming in my head and willed myself to ignore the note of fat satisfaction in his voice. "You don't listen to this man. He doesn't treat you like I do."

That was the understatement of the year.

"Where do you want to meet?" I asked, my eyes on Dermot. He nodded.

"You come to warehouse in Wellington."

"How about we find somewhere neutral, where I won't be walking into a group of your buddies?" I tried to remember all of Dermot's instructions for successful negotiating, and which areas they were prepared to set up in advance.

"Warehouse," Misha insisted.

"Theo would never allow that, and you know it as well as I do."

Misha spat out what I knew was a derogatory Russian word. "The Dominion."

"The park?" I asked.

"Yes. Simmington Point, by the pool. Is neutral enough?"

I ignored the mocking tone in his voice, my eyes on Dermot. He gave me a thumbs-up. "All right. What time?"

We settled on a time that evening. Misha had wanted me to go out there immediately, but Dermot said they needed time to secure whatever area we had chosen, and also, night was better in terms of hiding Specialist Response Team members.

Two hours before the time I was to be at Dominion Park, a glorious stretch of land that sat right on the bay, Theo pulled me into our hotel bedroom.

"You remember everything I told you?" he asked.

"Yes. Are you sure about the name?"

"The detectives came up with three names, but only one is active right now."

"OK. I wouldn't want to get an innocent person in trouble."

"We will only precipitate an investigation," he told me, his hands on my shoulders. "Nothing more."

"Just remember I'm counting on you," I said, giving in to temptation and biting his chin.

He looked surprised for a moment, then cocked his head, offering me his neck. I laughed and gently bit that, as well.

"I should call you vampire instead of gazelle," he murmured, his hands getting busy with my ass.

"Theo, stop. You'll mess up all my equipment," I protested, squirming when he slid one hand down into my leggings.

"Oh, your equipment will be very messy by the time I'm done with it," he said with a sexy growl, wiggling his fingers against sensitive flesh.

"Fine, but you get to explain to Dermot why they spent an hour fitting me up with everything, and you took it all off me in two minutes."

He sighed, but pulled his hands back after giving my behind a little pinch. "Just remember my restraint later. I will expect much reward for it."

"You better believe I will."

His smile faded. "Are you sure about this, Kiera? It's not too late to have me deliver it."

"He won't gloat to you like he will me," I said, giving him a smile that had a lot more wattage than I felt. "There's little Misha loves more than to tell me how brilliant he is. We can't risk losing that admission."

"All right." He took a deep breath. "Just remember what I told you to do."

I saluted him. "Roger Wilco and all that jazz."

We left shortly after that. Dermot had a handful of agents planted around the park, watching the traffic, but no one had seen anything suspicious thus far. We sat in the groundskeeper's building nearby, waiting, watching the video feeds, each second dragging by.

An hour before I was due to meet Misha, word came into the building that he and four of his buddies had been spotted in the park heading toward the pool area. There was also an increase in the usual number of police in the area.

I leaned against Theo, saying nothing. My fate, I believed, was at that point set.

Security cameras showed the movement of Misha and his men moving casually through the park until one by one, the men disappeared from the video feeds.

Theo's arm tightened around me when Misha moved out of range of a trail camera.

"Not long now," Dermot said, giving me a smile.

I tried to smile in return, but suspect it came out more of a grimace since he looked vaguely horrified.

"Are you ready, love?" Theo murmured in my ear.

"Yes." I turned to kiss him. "I'm trusting you, Theo."

"I look forward to when this is over, so that you can tell me in a very tangible way how sorry you are that you ever doubted me," he said lightly, but I saw the shadows in his eyes. He was just as afraid as I was.

He slipped away, leaving me with Dermot, George, and one of Dermot's men.

"You'll be fine," George said, giving my shoulder a pat before he, too, left the building to take up the position Theo and he had agreed upon.

My stomach turned on itself while the last few minutes crawled by.

"I wish I knew what he was doing," I said softly. "I hate being blind like this."

"His men have hidden themselves," Dermot replied, listening for a moment to his headset. "The police are gathering on that side of the park, although only one of them has approached the pool building. Are you ready?"

"Is it time?" I said, suddenly nervous. I wiped my hands on my leggings, my heart quickening.

"A little early, but he will be expecting that. Let's give him what he wants, hmm?"

"Chocolate doughnuts," I told him. "Mothballs. The great big planet earth."

Dermot said nothing when I opened the door and made my way out of the building, slipping through a clutch of trees that stood near the building, before appearing on a paved path. I looked around nervously, knowing Misha would expect that, not that I was in the least bit pretending to be worried.

It was about half a mile to the pool, and the crowds started to thin as the sun went down. I followed the paved walkway down to where the glistening eight lanes of water turned inky before the blue-white lights that ran the length of the pool came on one by one with a soft buzzing noise. A few people were in the pool, swimming laps, but all the families had left once the open swim time ended. I strolled by the tall white fence that kept park-goers from entering the pool area, nervous enough that I felt like I'd never again be able to eat.

"You come."

Misha's voice sounded behind me, so unexpectedly that it made me shriek and whirl around. He stood almost close enough to touch me, having come from God knew where. In his hand he held a gun. At the sight of it, something inside me snapped. He was so predictable, so trite. I wanted to yell at him that he needed to get a new routine.

"Yes, I came." I allowed my expression to slip into fear. Misha loved to make people afraid. "I just want you to leave me alone."

"Why? So you can screw this man, this Theo who threatens me?" Misha's lips peeled back in a smirk as he gestured toward me with the gun. "I told you he lies to you. You are *my* woman. You always are my woman."

"I was with you for five long years, Misha. I did my time," I said, going a bit off script, but I felt like I needed to keep the conversation real so he wouldn't be suspicious.

"Is not over," he said, stepping closer to me, his eyes traveling over me in the possessive manner I was used to seeing. This time, however, it made me physically ill. "Give me flash, then I take you back to hotel and we fuck."

"Not so fast," I said, crossing my arms over my chest. "Let's talk about what's on the flash drive for a minute. I looked at it, Misha. Theo doesn't know I did, but I loaded it up and saw everything."

He snarled, his hands flexing convulsively.

"Looks to me like you are dealing with a lot of money that isn't yours." I tried my damnedest to mimic Theo at his most urbane. "I know you, and I know that you're not one to let that much money slip out of your grip. So, what say we make a little deal?"

A slow, ugly smile spread over his face. "I knew you want something. Is too good you saying you give me flash. How much?"

"How about three million?"

His smile grew, and I knew that, like me, he was wired. "You want me to give you three million for flash?"

I shrugged. "If you want it back, yes, I want three million. That's pocket change compared to the amounts listed in the documents."

He took a step closer, and knowing that the old me, the me he scared the peewadding out of, would have backed up, I did so. Right through the gate that led into the pool area. Dermot might not approve of my apparent improvisation, but I trusted Theo and George to have my back.

"Don't think you can scare me, Misha. I hold all the cards here. Your name is all over the documents on this drive."

"Is my property. You take it from me, and now you want moneys to give it back. Is blackmail, Kiera."

"Is money laundering, Misha," I answered in a faux Russian accent.

His smile twitched, but he held on to it. "Is no concern of yours."

"I just have one question," I said, taking another step back. I was about six feet away from the edge of the pool, where a couple of people unconcernedly swam laps. "You never had this sort of money when we were together. What happened?"

He glanced to the side, and for a minute, I thought he wasn't going to answer. "I tell you because you cannot hurt me. I have protection, you understand? I can snap you like piece of branch, and there is nothing you can do to stop me."

I made a horrified face. "I just want you to leave me alone."

"You will be alone," he laughed, completely at his ease. "You will be very alone. Your rich man, he won't be able to help you. Give me flash."

"Not until you tell me how you got this much money."

He rolled his eyes. "I have big deal. I told you I was important man, big-time man, but you never believe me. You always try to keep me down. But now I am on top, and your rich man is nothing compared to me." He jerked his thumb toward himself. "I have the power now, and it will crush you, because you cannot stop me."

"The police—"

"Police work for me," he snapped, suddenly lunging forward until he had me in a painful grip on one arm, the other hand reaching into my shirt to pull out a thin wire that was taped to my chest. He jerked it out, causing me to gasp when the small recording device came up, as well.

I stammered something inane.

"You think this will trap me?" He tossed the wire into the pool behind me, laughing again when he saw the look on my face. "I know about your plan. You want me to admit that I help terrorist group to wash moneys so you can go to police and say, here, here Misha admit to crime. But I tell you that police work for me. They will not listen to you. Give me flash now, and maybe I let you stay alive so you can tell your rich man that he will never be as good as me."

"And if I refuse?" I asked, bracing myself for a blow.

"Then I take." Misha shoved his hand in my front pocket, pulling out the stone with the flash drive nestled inside it. He opened it, taking it out before plugging it into a device that hooked into his phone. He looked at it for a few seconds, then nodded. "You stole my flash. You try to blackmail me. You try to kill me."

The startled look on my face was all too genuine. "I *what*? I've never threatened you, not even when you tried many times to kill me."

"You try now. I have witness. Police see you pull gun on me and try to shoot me."

Before I could protest, he pulled me up against his body, shoving the gun into my hand, pressing my fingers all over it before taking it back and tucking it away.

I snarled a rude word and shoved him back, worry filling my mind. I had a horrible feeling he'd just used my body to shield his actions from the cameras. "No one would believe anything so insane, Misha."

"You will see. Now is all over. Good-bye, Kiera."

"What?" I asked, backing up a couple of more steps. Behind me, I could hear the ripple of the water as someone swam past.

"Is too bad you try to kill me," he said, raising his hands as if I was holding a gun on him, looking over my shoulder to where one of the security cameras filmed us. "Too bad you are not smarter."

The man in a police uniform who appeared behind him yelled at me to stop and put down my weapon, his gun pointing straight at my chest. "Wait—Misha—"

"Stop! Drop the gun or I will shoot!" the policeman called, glancing at the camera behind me.

"She says she will kill me!" Misha yelled dramatically, backing up, his hands still in the air to show he was unarmed. "Shoot her now!"

I fell backward just as the policeman's gun spat three times, the sound of it echoing off the walls of the pool building, startling birds into loud protests. I was thrown backward by the impact, feeling as if three freight trains had hit me right in the gut, the collision with the cold water when I struck the surface shocking me into oblivion. I felt myself falling downward, my eyes wide and staring while I watched the glow of the lights getting dimmer and dimmer as I sank to the bottom of the pool.

And then Theo was there, his arms around me, pulling me upward with strong kicks of his legs, until we both broke the surface. I gasped, dragging air painfully into my lungs before sinking again, and getting a mouthful of water. Theo hoisted me up again, one arm under my breasts while swimming to the ladder. I was dimly aware of lights and voices, a lot of voices, and strong hands that pulled me up from the pool. I collapsed on my belly, vomiting up water when I gasped more rasping lungsful of air.

Theo was at my side, his hands on my back, calling for a doctor in between murmuring things into my ears about how proud he was of me.

"I'm all right," I said, getting to my knees, flinching at the pain in my belly as soon as I was done heaving. "I don't need a doctor."

Theo pulled off my oversized tee, his fingers jerking at the straps that held the concealed body armor on my torso. Three bullets were flattened into it, I absently noted when Theo, his hands on my breastbone, reached for my bra clasp.

"No, Theo," I said, grabbing his arms to stop him. "Really, I'd like to do this without baring my breasts to everyone."

"You're bruised," he said, touching the marks on my chest with a featherlight touch. "You might be injured elsewhere."

"I'm not," I said with a little laugh that made my chest and belly hurt. I accepted the dry shirt that George handed me. Like Theo, he was dressed in swim trunks and was wet. "But you can take off the other wires."

Together they peeled off the two other recording devices that Dermot had set to catch Misha's admission. I pulled on my tee and let Theo help me to my feet, while George toweled himself off.

"Did you get it?" I asked Dermot as he came over to see how I was. "Was it enough?"

"We did, and it was. We have footage from all three of the cameras we set up this afternoon that clearly show the policeman shoot you without provocation upon Mr. Girbac's instructions."

"And the recording? Is it enough to put him away for life?"

"Not on its own, but along with the records we copied from the drive, yes, that should just about do the job."

Theo hugged me carefully, his body wet and cool against me. His breath was as harsh as mine, causing me to cock an eyebrow at him. "Why are you out of breath?" I asked him, nuzzling his neck, nibbling on his earlobe before kissing along one side of his jaw. "I'm the one who got shot."

"You try swimming laps for twenty minutes solid, and see how slow your breathing is," he said, one arm around me while we moved toward the pool building, where the bulk of the action was. I could see Misha sitting on the ground, his arms bound behind him, as well as the policeman who shot me. Beyond them, Armen was being patted down before also being handcuffed. A group of three other police were being interviewed by Dermot's people and a man whom Theo identified as the police commissioner.

Misha turned his head when Theo and I approached, intending on walking past him to the park outside the gate. The expression of anger he wore turned to fury when he saw me, his face turning red, obscenities in English and Russian falling from his lips.

"I can't help myself," I told Theo, pausing a few feet away from Misha. "Do you mind? It will make me feel better."

"Not at all. May I help?" Theo asked politely.

"Of course." We strolled over to Misha, Theo's arm around my shoulders, my arm around his waist.

"I don't think you've met my husband," I said to Misha. "His name is Theo, and he's the man who thought up the plan to get you to admit your ties with corrupt police."

A look of surprise flashed in Misha's narrowed eyes.

"That's right," Theo said, giving me a swift kiss. "While you were convinced Kiera was trying to get you to name your connection with the terrorist group, she was really getting your admission of complicity."

"See, we didn't need you to admit you were laundering money," I told him, enjoying myself greatly. I knew I should be ashamed of taking pleasure in his downfall, but all those years of abuse were finally being soothed from my soul. They would never be obliterated, but seeing Misha caught in his own web of deceit went a long way to easing the pain. "The government agent—that's him over there, watching Armen being taken away—says there was more than enough proof on the flash drive to convict you. We just wanted to send your dirty friends to prison with you. And thanks to Theo, we know the names of three of them. I don't suppose it will be long before the other two join you."

Dermot signaled to a couple of men, who yanked Misha to his feet. "You die," he snarled, almost frothing at the mouth as his gaze locked on mine. "You die."

"Someday, yes." I leaned into Theo, feeling about as good as a woman who'd taken three bullets to the body armor could. "But until then, I'll have the man of my dreams making me incredibly happy."

Misha was dragged off sputtering and spewing vile threats toward both of us.

"You didn't tell him I was fabulously rich and successful," Theo complained, giving me a little frown. "Not to mention incredible in bed. I thought you were going to wound his ego? How can you do that if you don't drive home the rich, successful, and a sex god parts?"

I laughed and pinched him on his entirely too attractive butt. "How about if I send him a copy of the most eligible bachelor list, so he can gnash his teeth over just how inferior he is compared to you?"

"Not a bad idea," he said, steering me toward the car that George and Paul had waiting. "Although I wonder if we shouldn't get a divorce."

I stopped and gawked at him, not sure if I'd heard him correctly.

"I can't be on the list if I'm married, sweet. If we got divorced, I might be able to go up a few levels. I'd like to get to Jake's number three. I think number three might just break Misha."

"Argh!" I said, punching him in his six-pack. "That's it. I'm going to go live in one of the cottages on your brother's island with Peter, and look for a man who isn't handsome, and sexy, and caring, and loving, and perfect in every way except for his unbearable ego."

"Ah," he said, kissing the tip of my nose. "But will he be able to outrun you?"

"You can't," I pointed out, getting into the car.

"Wife, I let you win."

"You did not! I won fair and square."

"Because I wanted you to win. You needed it to make you feel good about yourself."

"I heard the way you breathed behind me. You know, when I beat you to the bench. You were running your balls off."

"I breathed heavily on purpose, so you didn't know I was letting you win."

"Oh! That's it. We're having a rematch. On a proper track this time. We'll see who needs to feel good about herself."

"A rematch will simply prove to you that I let you win, but I'm happy to oblige if you think your ego can take the beating," Theo said with a laugh, the sound making my heart happy.

SIXTEEN

"I'm only letting you do this because I love you, husband," I told Theo.

"You are graciousness personified, wife," he said gravely, and held up a scanty bit of lace and a couple of strategically placed ribbons. "What about this one?"

I considered it for a minute. "I don't know that pink is your color. Plus, won't your bits fall out of that crotch? It looks awfully skimpy."

"We'll take this one, too." He tossed the lingerie to the salesclerk, who stood with her arms full of clothing, a look of great happiness on her face as she no doubt calculated her commission on my shopping spree. "Now, how about a dress suitable for a party?"

"A party? We're going to a party? When? Where? Here in Athens, or at your brother's house?" I pulled Theo away from where he wanted to linger in the lingerie section of the trendy shop. The salesclerk followed, staggering slightly under the growing stack of clothes.

"I don't have a particular party in mind, but I'm bound to be invited to one sooner or later."

I slid him a fast glance, but he merely looked interested when a second salesclerk pulled out dresses for his approval, just like I wasn't standing right there with a brain and a knowledge of what looked good on me. "I suppose I should have one nice dress. Harry said something about having a family party once your sister gets back from visiting your English relatives."

"No, not that one. Blue or green," Theo told the second clerk who all but tossed the offered dresses aside and snatched a couple more from a third clerk.

"I can't help but notice that there are several other shoppers here," I told Theo.

He stood back and eyed the dress that the second clerk held up. "That has merit. I don't care for the fussy bit at the neckline, but the line of it is good."

"And yet," I said to no one in particular, since I was evidently not important in the whole "buy Kiera new clothing" scenario. "And yet, all three of the salespeople are right here, waiting on you like you're a Greek god come to earth."

"Madame would like blush, yes?" the third clerk asked, her gaze firmly affixed to Theo when she rushed up with a very pretty floor-length rose-and-silver dress. The material moved like it was made of water, sliding effortlessly over her hand.

"Too long," he said, shaking his head. "I want something to show off her legs."

"And that's the point where I stop this disgusting little show," I said, taking the water dress from the clerk, and shooing her and the other one away. "He's taken, ladies. Very taken. And probably will be taken again just as soon as we get to his brother's house, because I have a lot of unbridled joy to work out of my system."

"Kiera," he said, frowning, but a little quirk of his lips let me know he was about to say something I was going to find outrageous. "I have let you get away with your aggressive ways in private because I felt you needed an outlet, but I draw the line at you announcing to these kind women—yes, thank you, we will find anything else on our own, as my wife says—I draw the line at you informing them that we will be having incredibly arousing sex so intense that you are left a damp, panting blob of sated woman by the end of it."

"Aggressive! Me?" I gasped in faux outrage, plucking a pretty bluish-green dress from the rack and adding it to the stack that I would try on. I knew Theo favored the color, and decided since he'd worked so hard to make sure the New Zealand officials had information about Misha's dirty cop friends, he deserved a little reward. "I have no idea what you're talking about. Thank you, I'll try these on now. No, you don't have to wait. My very much married and taken husband will stand outside the dressing room and hold the ones I want to keep."

The salesclerk shot Theo a look, sighed, and went to stand by the counter.

I entered the small dressing room, pulling closed the garish paisley curtain that served as a door.

Before I had my shirt off, Theo stuck his head in, saying softly, "I sincerely enjoyed the way you were aggressive all over me last night, sweetheart."

My cheeks warmed when I remembered how clumsy I was trying to give Theo pleasure with my mouth. "You're just being kind. It was a disaster, and we both know it."

He gave me a crooked grin. "I will admit that having my delicious wife attempt to give me a blow job, only to end up in a fit of giggles so intense that she triggered an asthma attack, was a bit daunting to my ego, but I have high hopes that one day you'll be able to face my cock without bursting into untoward laughter."

I kissed him on the corner of the crooked smile. "It just struck me at the wrong moment how silly penises look when you're face to … er … head with it, and I solemnly promise that I will make every effort to attend to it properly tonight."

"Oh no. Tonight is my turn. Try on the green dress first," he said, removing himself from the dressing room.

Four hours later, Harry and Iakovos were at the dock on their island to greet us, Peter in Iakovos's arms.

"Look how big he is!" I said, running forward to take him, laughing when he no-no-ed happily, pointing at Theo even as he grabbed a bit of my hair and stuck the end in his mouth. "I can't believe how much he's grown in just five days. Did you miss us, Peter? Yes, that's your papa. Isn't he handsome? One day, I'll explain to you how he's like a black hole, attracting women to him with a sort of gravitational pull, but until then, just remember that it's what's inside you that matters."

Theo, clutching three massive stuffed giraffes by one hand, and two boxes containing kids' versions of digital video cameras in the other, set everything down to hold Peter out at arm's length. "You've definitely grown. Did you have fun while we were off buying you an entire case of baby wipes?"

"I hope those are not for our brood," Iakovos said, nodding toward the toys. "We can barely house the things they already have, and that's with Harry insisting they donate toys they no longer play with."

"We couldn't bring Peter a giraffe without getting Rose and Nicky one, as well," Theo said, booping Peter on his nose with that of the stuffed giraffe. He screamed with happiness, his little fists beating on the giraffe's head before he pulled its nose into his mouth.

"Kiera finally decided to break down and buy some things she needed," Theo announced when Iakovos's eyes widened at the sight of the bags being hauled up toward the house. "I thought hell might freeze over when she suggested a shopping trip, but we all survived."

"Just barely," I said, holding Peter's little hand while we all headed for the house. "My bank account will never be the same."

Iakovos shot me a look, but didn't say anything.

A few hours later, Peter went down for a nap, and Theo and Iakovos went off to do a little of what I assumed was male bonding, but which Theo assured me was important business.

I sat with Harry, watching her four children play, feeling more content than I ever could have imagined.

"They didn't know you were there?" Harry asked, looking as happy as I felt.

"I'm pretty sure they didn't. I was coming out of the bedroom, and the door blocked me from them."

"What did Iakovos say, exactly?"

I glanced at her. "Does his exact wording matter?"

She grinned. "No, but I'm curious nonetheless."

"All I heard was Theo saying he didn't know what else he could do, and he didn't want to make me seriously angry."

She nodded.

"And then Iakovos said that you were just the same way."

"They just don't get it," she agreed.

"No, they don't."

"It's a matter of pride," she added.

"I'm not going to say that Theo having ample income to keep us in private-jet rides, and his own island, isn't nice, but it's not why I fell in love with him."

"Yacky knows I don't give a hoot about his money," Harry said complacently. "I have more than enough for myself."

"I have money I inherited," I told her. "It's not a lot, but it's enough to let me get whatever I want. Within reason."

"So what did Theo say?"

I reviewed the conversation I had overheard. "He asked Iakovos how he coped with it, and he—your husband—said that he simply made sure that whenever you insisted on spending your personal money on things like dresses and getting your hair done, he put money into your account to compensate."

Harry pursed her lips.

"And then he told Theo that's what he should do for me: make a note of how much money I have in my account, and then keep topping it up so that it stayed at that amount. He said that it was the only way to deal with our sort of obstinacy."

"Obstinacy," Harry said on a snort.

We exchanged glances, and both burst out laughing. "Do you think they will ever realize that we know exactly what they are doing?" she asked me.

"I wouldn't dream of letting Theo know," I said, sitting

up straighter when the man who made me ecstatically happy just by the sight of him emerged from the house, wearing his horrible ratty shorts, Iakovos at his side. "It would hurt his feelings. Besides, there's nothing to stop us from putting the money back in their accounts."

"I take whatever Iakovos slips in my account and send it to local animal charities," Harry said. "To be honest, I think he knows, because he gets the charity receipts, but he hasn't said anything yet." She smiled as Iakovos peeled off his shirt and dove into the pool, and quickly shed the cover-up she'd worn over her swimsuit. "If you'll excuse me, I need to go show him again what he's doing wrong with that crawl."

Theo's eyebrows rose when he stopped in front of me. "Did you want me to start teaching you how to swim?" he asked, nodding toward where Iakovos and Harry were in the middle of the pool, pausing when he saw Harry fling herself on Iakovos, his hands on her butt as he hoisted her higher, kissing her with an oblivion to everything else. "Er ... maybe we'll use the lap pool for your lessons."

"I think that can wait." I stood up and reached behind him, finding the hole on the backside of his shorts. "We have an hour before Peter gets up, husband. Can't you think of anything else you'd rather do with that hour than teach me how to swim?"

His eyes lit as he scooped me up in his arms and started toward the house. "Yes, indeed I can. I'm going to take you to my bedroom ..."

"Ooh," I said, nibbling on his ear.

"Where I will set you down on the bed ..."

"I like how you think," I murmured, moving over to his jaw, gently nipping it.

"At which point I will rub my hands down your long, long bare legs to your slightly ticklish feet."

I shivered at the thought of his hands on me.

"I'll slip off the charming espadrilles you are now wearing ..."

I bit his neck. "And?"

His smile was made up of pure wickedness. "And then I'll get your running shoes, and we'll go have that race."

I pinched his arm, so happy I couldn't believe that less than a month before, my life was nothing but terror and the conviction that I was a hairsbreadth away from death.

"Ovaries," I told him.

He raised his eyebrows.

"The head of a penis, at a certain angle, if you squint."

His mouth quirked. "Testicles when they're sucked tight after fingernails have been dragged gently over them. I love you, wife."

"I love you, too, husband." He carried me up the curved flight of stairs toward his bedroom. "Did you really let me win? Because I just don't see how that could be—"

His laughter filled the hall, the whole house, and my soul.

EPILOGUE

"Hello, sweet. How was the library?"

I jumped a little at the unexpected voice, spinning around to say, "What are you doing here?"

Theo leaped back, his eyes on the roller I held in my hand. "Almost getting my new suit splattered with Midday Bliss Yellow, evidently. I thought I'd come home early to see how playtime went."

"Those who startle people who are painting a room deserve what they get." I eyed the suit, but it was paint-free. Theo held his hands behind his back, though, and that immediately had me curious. "Baby and Me time at the library was good. Peter enjoyed playing with the other children, although a little girl with sharing issues sneezed on him, so we can all expect to get sick, according to George. He's with Anne and Melanie now so I can finish painting. Peter, that is, not George. What do you have behind your back?"

Theo smiled, and set down three packages onto Peter's sheet-covered crib, then carefully removed the roller from my hands before kissing me soundly. "I have no doubt we'll get the plague from the child who didn't want to share with Peter, and presents."

I gave him a long look, and accepted a rag to wipe my painty-hands on. "Theo—"

"Birthday presents," he said quickly, his eyes positively filled with laughter.

"My birthday isn't for another three weeks," I pointed out.

"These are early presents." He handed me a small black box.

"You rotter. You know full well I can't refuse a birthday present without being a jerk." I frowned at the box. "If this is a ring—"

"It's not a ring," he said quickly.

"I don't like rings," I reminded him, twisting my wedding ring with my thumb. "This one excluded."

He just smiled smugly at me, the generous bastard. "Open it."

I sighed the sigh of the martyred. "Fine, but if it's jewelry, you know what I will have to say." I opened the box to find a pair of stud earrings, the only kind I wore. They were the same blue-green stones as the bracelet he periodically tried to give me. "Damn," I told him, looking up to glare at the love of my life.

"Don't like them?" A little doubt flashed in his eyes, instantly making me feel like the biggest heel in the world.

Mindful of his suit, I leaned forward to kiss him, relishing the heat of his mouth on mine. "No, just the opposite. They're lovely. Simple, with no diamonds or flashy bits, just two little stones. I love them. I will accept them as a birthday present." I held out my hand.

He beamed at me, pulling a small business-card-sized paper from his pocket and handing it to me.

THIS GIVES THE BEARER THE ABILITY TO GIVE ME ONE PRESENT VALUED LESS THAN ONE THOU-SAND NEW ZEALAND DOLLARS, the card read. I'd given it and a few others of its ilk to Theo the month before for his birthday.

"Thank you," I said, tearing up the card and tossing it into the trash.

"Birthday present number two," he said, giving me a familiar long white leather jeweler's box.

"Really?" I asked, pursing my lips at the box. "You're going to blow your big card now? I told you I wasn't going to give you another one."

"I like to live dangerously," he said with the cocky grin that made my knees melt.

I told my body we had serious present-receiving business to attend to, and that we could romp all over his body later, reluctantly taking the box. "If it's that bracelet again, I've told you, I don't really wear jewelry, so thank you, but I don't need it."

"Open it," he said, nudging the box.

I opened it. Inside it sat a set of keys, and a slip of paper with a number written on it. The number was my birth date. "Keys?" I asked, looking up in confusion.

"To our new home."

I gasped, pleasure filling me. "You closed on the Greek property?"

"I did. They accepted my offer last week." He peeled off his suit jacket, carefully setting it out of range of the paint things I was using to brighten up Peter's room. Then after a moment's thought, he removed his shirt, and pants, as well.

"Theo!" I said, mildly scandalized as I glanced around the room. "You want to make love here? On the drop cloth?"

"No." He hesitated, then added, "Well, yes, but mostly, I want to hold you, and you, wife, are covered in paint. Now you may thank me properly for buying you a house that is only a few miles away from my brother's island, so that you and Harry can see each other frequently, and Peter can play with his cousins."

I flung myself into Theo's arms, kissing him all over his adorable face before letting myself have a quick nibble on that tendon in his neck. "You are the most wonderful of all husbands," I told him once he released my tongue. "But what's my birth date doing with the keys?"

"It's the security code to get through the front gate. Hmm. How long did Anne say she'd keep Peter?" He eyed the drop cloths spread around the floor with a speculative glance that I didn't have any problem interpreting.

"Just an hour." I gently bit his chin. "But that was forty minutes ago."

He looked thoughtful, but sighed and released me. "I'd go for it, but I have one last present to give you."

"You owe me a card first," I said, holding out my hand.

He frowned. "But the house is for all of us."

"It's a present," I said, shaking the box with the keys in it. "You know the rules."

"Did I mention that my next wife is going to be a gold digger who wants me only for what she can get out of me?" he asked in a decidedly disgruntled voice as he pulled out a stack of cards, quickly shuffling through them.

"Yes, every time you try to force me to take extravagant presents from you. And I'd like to point out that I *do* let you support me in this lavish lifestyle, so you have no reason to be so crabby about me not wanting to have jewels or cars or that sort of thing."

"Here, you unnatural woman, you," he said, giving me one of the cards.

I checked it. *THIS GIVES THE BEARER THE ABILITY TO GIVE ME AN ITEM COSTING MORE THAN FIVE THOUSAND NEW ZEALAND DOLLARS, BUT LESS THAN THE PRICE OF AN ISLAND.*

"Boy, you are really going through these," I said, tearing it up. "You only have the big one and a bunch of minor ones left."

He grinned. "Ah, but I'll have a birthday next year, and I know exactly what I will be asking for."

"Mmm-hmm."

"And now your third and final present. The best one of all," he said, presenting me with another bracelet-sized jeweler's box. "And you'll want this."

He made an absurdly dashing bow when he handed me a card.

THIS GIVES THE BEARER THE ABILITY TO GIVE ME SOMETHING PRICELESS.

"I hope this is worth blowing your big card on," I told him, tearing up the card and opening the box. "Because after six months of marriage, I'd think you would know when I'm serious about something—oh."

Inside the box was a folded piece of paper, not the pretty teal sapphire bracelet I expected.

I glanced up at him, startled for a moment by the look of love in his eyes. "If this is the deed to the Greek house—"

He just smiled, standing there all gorgeous and male and tempting. I had to drag my eyes off his chest to unfold the piece of paper, my eyes moving over the words, unable to take them in for a second.

Goose bumps rippled down my arms and legs as I worked my way through the legalese, looking up to stare in openmouthed wonder at Theo. "She said yes?"

"She did."

"Did you have to pay her?"

He was silent, and I knew that he did. I decided that was not something I wanted to dwell on. Whatever choices Nastya had made in her life, she'd done the right thing by giving custody of Peter to us. I shook my head, trying to process the surge of joy inside me. "He's really mine?"

"He always was. Just as I am."

"For which I'm truly thankful. But now … I can adopt him?"

Theo held his arms open. I flung myself onto him a second time, allowing him to pull me down onto the floor, my hands busy on his chest and arms even as he divested me of my clothing. "Yes, my delectable one, you can adopt him. Now you will never get away from me."

I giggled when I stroked a hand down that magnificent chest to his belly, and lower. "Why would I want to get away from the man who makes my soul sing?"

He nuzzled my neck, his hands busy on my breasts before he paused, looking at a slight bruise on my arm where my birth control implant had been removed the day before. "Are you sure about this?"

"Yes." I slid my hands lower, cupping his genitals, gently using my fingernails on his testicles. "Are you?"

He growled at me, his eyes hot with passion. "We have a lot of catching up to do if we expect to give Jake and Harry a run for their title of most kids."

I laughed, nipping his shoulder. "I'm not saying I want to have four children, but I think Peter would like a sibling. You're going to have to be fast, though. Anne should be here in less than twenty minutes."

"Oh, I'm fast," he murmured, sliding his hands up my thighs, parting them as he did so. His body was hot and hard when he moved into me, filling me with so much love, I wanted to shout. "And speaking of that, we really need to have that rematch race. … Oh, dear God, wife, don't Kegel on me like that or it will all be over before it starts!"

TO: HARRY

Apologies for text, no time for a call. We're on our way to Wellington to see Peter's grandma before we fly to Greece. Should be at your place Sunday evening. Race over. Sorry you couldn't be here. Hope the morning sickness passes soon. Will Iakovos get re-snipped? Please inform him his brother is a slowpoke, and I beat him by over seven seconds. He's demanded a re-rematch just as soon as he can walk without groaning. Love to you all.

A NOTE FROM KATIE

My lovely one! I hope you enjoyed reading this book, which I handcrafted from the finest artisanal words just for you. If you are one of the folks who likes to review books, I'd love it if you posted a review for it on your favorite book spot. If you aren't a reviewing type, fear not, I will cherish you regardless.

I'd also like to encourage you to sign up for the exclusive readers' group newsletter wherein I share behind-the-scenes info about my books (and dogs, and love of dishy guys, and pretty much anything else that I think people would enjoy), sneak peeks of upcoming books, news of readers'-group-only contests, etc. You can join the fun by clicking on the SUBSCRIBE TO KATIE'S NEWSLETTER link on my website at www.katiemacalister.com

ABOUT THE AUTHOR

For as long as she can remember, Katie MacAlister has loved reading. Growing up in a family where a weekly visit to the library was a given, Katie spent much of her time with her nose buried in a book.

Two years after she started writing novels, Katie sold her first romance, *Noble Intentions*. More than fifty books later, her novels have been translated into numerous languages, been recorded as audiobooks, received several awards, and have been regulars on the *New York Times, USA Today*, and *Publishers Weekly* bestseller lists. Katie lives in the Pacific Northwest with two dogs, and can often be found lurking around online.

You are welcome to join Katie's official discussion group on Facebook, as well as connect with her via Twitter, Goodreads, and Instagram. For more information, visit her website at www.katiemacalister.com

CPSIA information can be obtained
at www.ICGtesting.com
Printed in the USA
LVHW041008190523
747483LV00012B/94

9 781945 961403